THE REPLACEMENT

JACQUELINE WARD

First published in 2023 by Bloodhound Books.

www.bloodhoundbooks.com

Print ISBN: 978-1-5040-8555-7

For anyone who ever felt replaced.

CHAPTER ONE

You always remember where you were when something like that happens. When you should have done something but didn't.

I was standing on the driveway when my phone beeped again. Another reminder to look at it. I'd ignored it, as I had for most of the weekend, and lifted my face into the morning sunshine as Tim drove away from my home. After the past twelve months of my separation and impending divorce from Daniel, every tiny wave of calmness that washes over me is a gift. So, after spending a lovely weekend away, I felt perfectly still.

Until Daniel's car pulled into the driveway. He must have passed Tim on the main road. Of course, neither would be any the wiser. Tim hasn't met Ben and Angel yet. I only see him when Daniel takes our children for his half of the shared parenting. My hand went to my new smart watch as it began synchronised buzzing with my phone. It would be Tim, I thought, telling me how much he'd enjoyed the beautiful time we'd had.

Before I could look, Angel and Ben spilled out of the car

and ran into the house. My heart almost burst with love. It's the same every time they come back. I miss them every moment they are away from me. Even so, as I saw Daniel I felt the serenity of the past three days ebb slightly. I'm thankful it gets less and less with time. I also know full well why this happens. Yet I remained calm as a familiar feeling bubbled inside me.

Every time he brings the children back, I promise myself I will not scan the car for her. I will not torture myself with her sitting in the back seat with Angel while Ben rides up front, even though he is too young. A huge investment in my well-being over the past six months has left me with a good understanding of what I need to do to move on from this.

Yet, in that moment, the feelings I had when I found out about her were momentarily just as strong. The sadness and the desperation. The utter anger at what they did. And the shame of what I did back then. I have learnt to stay calm now. I no longer lose it or shout or scream. In fact, most of the time, I hardly care. But I know now that the second Daniel appeared on my driveway marked the first moment I became involved. As I scanned the car, I told myself I would do a twenty-minute yoga workout later to rid myself of the negativity.

But she wasn't there. I blinked into the sunlight. I shaded my eyes to see further inside the car. No. She definitely wasn't there. Daniel stared back at me. Then he got out.

'Angel told me she had an extra tuition.'

He stated it rather than asked a question. I nodded.

'Yeah. She needed some reading help.'

I almost added that it was no wonder, was it, with everything that had happened? No wonder our children felt unsettled. But instead, I looked past him into the car at Jem's cardigan on the front seat.

'It costs thirty pounds an hour. I wondered if you could pay for it. Or half?'

The silent implication that this was his mess and not mine hung over the words. But he just laughed and walked away. His trademark swagger that always belies the cool, calm exterior. I know Daniel Wade back to front. I know where he came from, where his roots are. He's no different from the rest of us council-estate kids, but he likes to think he is. He moved from selling used death-trap cars into the luxury motor business and made his money there. Lots of it. He wears his hair longer and, since he met her, he's adopted her faux hippy style. Smart-casual and guru-like.

He got into his car, and he was gone. My heart twinged after him. I know with every fibre of my being that it is just a sentimental hangover. He cheated on me with her, and it changed my life. It changed me. Yet I still watched him every time he drove away from me. Even though Tim is my happiness now, I watched him. I went inside and pressed the boost button on the heating. It can get cold in early October. I heard the boiler fire and thought about my bank account emptying as the large house became warmer.

We'd bought it as a doer-upper and half-finished it. I am forever grateful that we did the sprawling downstairs first. Reception room, lounge, and a beautiful stone kitchen. I pulled out a pizza and some frozen chips from the freezer and put them in the oven. I'm back working full time now, but my salary only stretches so far. Tomato sauce and mayonnaise on a tray and some fizzy drinks. I could hear Angel talking to someone on the phone and, as I leaned over, I saw Ben was watching a box set that was a little too old for him.

'Hey. Turn that off. Ben. Turn it off.'

He frowned at me, the same crease as I'd seen on Daniel's brow earlier. 'But Dad said...'

'Never mind what Dad said. You're home now.'

Free from her phone call, Angel chirped in.

'We've got two homes. That's the modern way.'

I'd heard it all before. And I knew whose words Angel was repeating. Of course, it hurt the first time, but I had agreed to co-parenting. I didn't want to, because those two were joined at the bloody hip from the day he bought that house and she moved in, but what choice did I have? The kids come first and that's what they want.

For me, I hadn't really known what to expect of my newly single status. I'd imagined wild weekends. Parties and men and lots and lots of sex, but it didn't work out like that, thank goodness. I'd been dreading the dating circuit. Almost immediately, my best friend Lisa met some guy at work, and I was left at a loose end. I don't like going to bars alone, so I found a local coffee shop. Just so I could get out of the house more over the three days the kids were gone.

'Yes, love, I know. But you're here now and it's my rules. Okay?'

I was gentle. I love my children above everything, and I would never compromise that. But I have come close. What happened to me was enough to drive anyone to the brink. I shudder at the thought of it. But I stepped away just in time, and only a few fragments of that remain to puncture the peace I have woven around us three.

They both nodded at me as I appeared with pizza and chips. I watched their looks of approval and how they sat on the sofa close to each other, trays on laps. My rules aren't so stringent. I want them to love being here so much that they miss me when they are gone. That the time they spend with her is boring in comparison. I don't have much money, but the little I have is spent on the best for my children.

It was worth the lonely occasional weekend sitting here in the cold and dark. I'd worked out that I could still have the internet on as it costs the same whatever I use. Same with the

TV. But everything else is kept to a minimum. My luxury is my contract phone and my smart watch. I need to carry a sense of affluence over to my job and they serve the dual purpose of tracking my return to peak happiness. I'd learnt to do my own French manicures, but a phone was a necessity of my work, so it stays. Parts of weekends are spent with Tim now in beautiful hotels and cosy restaurants. Dancing and laughing. But once I get home, the phone goes off, as it had been since Daniel dropped my children on the driveway. Home time is for Ben and Angel. Tim completely understands. He's happy for us to take it slowly. No pressure.

I left it until the pizza was nearly finished to bring up the burning question. I hadn't even looked at the message because I thought it was from lovely Tim. Or Lisa, finding out how it had gone with him.

'So, how was the weekend?'

Angel's eyes never left the screen. 'Dad bought us Chinese. In cartons. And dandelion and burdock.'

I glanced at the pizza carton on the distant kitchen side, and the almost charred pizza crust on the tray.

'That's nice, love. What did you all have?'

I felt a stab of guilt at my curated question. Ben paused his viewing to think.

'Well, it was a banquet.' Of course it was. Of course. He continued. 'But I only ate the noodles. And some prawn crackers. Angel had sweet and sour chicken and Dad had this chilli beef thing and seaweed.' They pulled a face at each other, and I laughed my relief that at least we were united in our hatred of fried cabbage.

I waited. Angel was nodding.

'Yes. I had to ask Dad to help me with the chopsicks.' My heart warmed. I love them so much. They are perfect and funny and everything I ever wanted in life. They say the funniest things and I miss them so much when they are with Daniel. And her. Chopsicks. She looked very serious. 'We had ribs. And chicken wings.' A long pause. 'Dad gave the delivery boy a very big tip.'

I'd opened my mouth to speak, but Ben jumped in. 'I might be a delivery boy. When I'm old enough. They get to keep the tips.'

I smiled, but my tone betrayed me. 'Not everyone tips as well as your dad. Or has takeaways. Not everyone can afford them.'

I'd ruined the mood. They fell silent and went back to the TV and dunking cardboard chips in unbranded ketchup. I watched them blinking at the screen and wished again it could be different.

'Where was Jem, then?'

It spilled out. She wasn't in the car. I suppose half of me hoped they had split up. That she had packed her bags. They continued blinking at the TV. Ben became spokesperson.

'She's gone away for a few days. Dad said she'll be back soon.'

Angel looked at me, her eyes brimming over with tears. I thought for one awful minute she was going to tell me she missed her. Her bottom lip trembled. 'She'd better be back soon because Pepe misses her. He was crying.'

Pepe. Jem loves that dog more than my kids. That was one of the reasons I could tolerate this awful situation. She wasn't really mum material. It was all an act. But she did love that dog. Where had she gone without him? My mind raced through hospital to abortion clinic to all-inclusive beach holiday.

'She left Pepe? What did Dad say?'

Ben shrugged. 'Nothing. He just put him in the kitchen. He tried to take a chicken wing, but Dad wouldn't let us get the chicken off the bone like Jemi does.'

Jemi. She'd insisted that they call her Jemi. *Like mummy, but not because we've already got one of those,* Angel had helpfully explained. I made my breath deep and even. I've come so far. She is the only thing that can ruin my sense of peace.

'Oh. Right. So, when is she back?'

They just shrugged and carried on with what they were doing.

So now I am in the kitchen. I'd taken a holiday today to bathe in the luxury of my happiness with Tim. It was our six-month anniversary. Six months since he sat down opposite me in that coffee shop and made me feel like a woman again. We'd taken a walk in the countryside and then gone for a meal. I knew it would be beautiful, and I wasn't disappointed. He'd given me a gift box tied with a yellow ribbon and pursed his lips in anticipation.

'Open it. It's so special.' He'd taken my hand. 'You're so special to me, Lauren.'

It was a diamond and sapphire bracelet that took my breath away. I'd only just begun to know him. He was the opposite of me and Daniel. We're both outgoing people who like to get ahead. I'm all over social media, especially these days in my self-proclaimed recovery period and my new business – I even have a page where I track my progress. Daniel is just vain and preoccupied with himself. He tries to pass it off as part of his job, but Facebook could not have happened a moment too soon for him. Lots of curated pictures of him with the flashy cars he deals.

But Tim is not on social media. He told me he is a very private person and doesn't need his life splashing all over the internet. He is absolutely fine with my openness as long as he plays only a tiny role. Curiously, Jem also shies away from all but Instagram, where she posts infrequently. I find it fascinating that both me and Daniel have chosen shrinking violets. Lisa is suspicious of anyone who is not posting on social media every twenty minutes, but Tim's calmness and poise is infectious. I'd go as far as to say that being with him is giving me something much better to do than nosey into other people's lives online.

When we said goodbye this morning, I was left with a feeling of almost-love. If it wasn't for this lingering itch about Jem and what happened last year, this would be perfect. We didn't need to show everyone how happy we were. When we were together, the world just disappeared. But now he's gone, it's back. Ten minutes ago, I remembered my phone had buzzed that morning. I'd tidied the scatter cushions and switched off the TV.

The kids are in bed. It's ten o'clock. I hear the boiler click off and I pull a crocheted shawl around me.

I take out my phone and switch it back on. I see it's a message from her. Jem. Sent on Monday afternoon. I'm confused. She's never messaged me before. She only has my number for school emergencies on Daniel's insistence. Whatever the message is, it's bound to annoy me to the limit of my sanity. Yet, somehow, I have to see. I can't tear myself away from this. From her. Not yet. The glow lights up the table and I press the message icon.

Her face appears, tanned and smiling. Perfect white teeth and a string of daisies around her neck, probably threaded by my husband. Ex-husband, I correct myself. My teeth involuntarily clench, and I read.

Lauren. You've got to help me. Please.

CHAPTER TWO

I wake early, running over various scenarios in my head. I wish I'd read the message when it arrived. I went over everything the kids said and Daniel's expression when I saw him earlier. He would have mentioned it if something was wrong, so there was no confusion when the kids told me. Daniel is one of those men who is very straightforward about what he wants. That way, when I wanted something different, he presented a fully evidenced case that you had earlier agreed to something, therefore if there was a change, there had to be a reason.

He was very clear about what he wanted at the start of our relationship. Not in a bad way. No demands. I agreed initially that we would go out together. When we were in the throes of hectic romance, I readily agreed that there would be no more girls' nights out or hen parties. I couldn't imagine life without him. Further down the line, when I wanted to go to a baby shower or even to the gym, he objected. He was perfectly calm about it. No bullying or nastiness. He didn't even try to stop me when I insisted. He'd just gradually put me into a wife-shaped box called Sturgeon Hall.

He treated others the same way. He climbed the promotion ladder at work rapidly and pushed people into little compartments. Anyone who didn't follow his exact lead was calmly pushed away from him. He wouldn't cause a drama or a scene. Daniel just knew what he wanted.

As I lay there, I knew what it looked like. Jem asking for help, then not being there when the kids were dropped off implied that it might be something to do with Daniel. It also looked like I had an overactive imagination. I should have rung her straight away and demanded to know what she wanted. Why she had messaged me, of all people? Why me, after everything that has happened?

I'd seen it all. I'd worked on missing persons cases and murder cases in my previous job with Lisa, before I left to work at the doctors' surgery. She works as a counsellor at the police station. I used to work alongside her, helping victims of violence and abuse. I knew what horrors life held. Surely, if anything was wrong, Jem's first call would be to the police? Or a close friend or relative. I was neither. It doesn't make sense that I would be the person she came to. And I just couldn't imagine Daniel being responsible for her needing help so badly that she'd contact me.

She was so full of confidence and had her shit together at the very point in my life when I was scrambling to stop everything crumbling around me. What help could she possibly want from me?

I went down to the kitchen in the early hours and read the message over and over. At three thirty, I typed a message to her.

Are you okay? What kind of help do you need? L x

I dithered about the kiss. We are not friends. Oh no. Not at all. But I need her to trust me if I am going to find out what is going on. My finger hovered over the send button a million times, but I didn't press it. My mind raced over the possibility that this was a trick. A set-up. Another way to hurt me. I didn't reply and I was proud of myself for not engaging this time. But none of it made sense.

I hardly slept all night. Which is why I find myself driving up the A6 towards Daniel's place. I dropped the kids off at school on autopilot, and put my foot down so I would make it there and back in time to start work in at the surgery at ten. It's a push, but I need to know. I call Lisa, my voice of reason. If anyone could make sense of this, it was Lisa. Two rings and she answers.

'Hello?' She sounds sleepy. Like me, she's seen and heard it all.

'It's me. Guess what happened yesterday?'

She laughs. 'Oh, please tell me you won the bloody lottery, and we're running away. I had far too much wine last night, and this is the Tuesday morning from hell.'

I laugh but hurry on. 'Get a bacon butty. Anyway, I got a message from her.'

Silence. She is as incredulous as me.

'Jem? From Jem? She messaged you? You're kidding me? Good God.'

'Yeah, I know. She wasn't with him when he dropped them off. Kids said she'd gone away for a few days. But she left Pepe.'

More silence as Lisa processes this.

'Wow. Just shows you never know a person. What was the message? Does she want you to cover the meditation class?'

She laughs loudly at her own joke. Jem is a life coach. She reinvented herself when she met Daniel and now gets a lot of business from his wealthy clients. Lisa is particularly scathing as it took her six years to qualify as a counsellor and Jem printed some business cards and letterheads and morphed into a female version of Russell Brand overnight. I laugh too.

'No. She said: *Lauren. You've got to help me. Please.*'

'Oh. That sounds–'

I pre-empt. 'Serious? Yeah, I thought so too. She's not there, but her dog is. And the message...'

Lisa sighs. 'You're on your way over, aren't you?'

I snort. 'Yeah. I'll just show him the message. And, you know...'

Her voice raises several octaves. 'We talked about this. Loads. Don't do it. Just turn around. Phone him. Seriously. There'll be some yogurt-weaving explanation. Or she's just throwing a tantrum cos she's not getting attention. Or interfering with parenting. They might have even had their first row.'

Her summary is concise, and I have to admit she is right. I pull into a layby.

'But what if something is wrong?'

We both fall silent. Lisa breaks it.

'Is it really any of your business now? Look, I know you worry about the kids when they're not there, but you have to let him get on with it. It could be bloody anything. If you really are concerned, tell the police, then leave it. Or just send the message to Daniel and say you're concerned. You've got enough on your plate. And what would Mr Mystery think?' Lisa is super-suspicious of Tim. She cannot understand him wanting to take things slowly. Or his rigid stance on social media. She is quiet for a long moment. I hear the cars whiz by and my heart beat. 'You need to move on, mate.'

I know she's right. I have tried a thousand times to prise myself out of the very end of this relationship. In my rational mind, when I am working, raking through the ashes of other people's personal lives in counselling sessions, I know this. I realise some parts of my need to know are irrational – but I am not the only one. I see cases every day of one partner or another who has hired a private eye or alerted the press; their story is my side of this marriage. I'm not even angry any more. I just need to let go.

But this is not a marriage. The marriage is over. Yet I *can't* let go. That I am alone for half the week doesn't help. I want my children to know their father and they seem to like her. But those days they are not there seem longer and emptier than the days they are. More than once, I have thought my driving past her home when they are there and phoning to make sure they are okay is really something else entirely. I tell myself I am over it, not jealous. But Lisa hit the nail on the head over wine and nibbles.

'Over it, are you? You know what the litmus test is, don't you? If she left, would you go back if he wanted you to?'

I had pulled a face and laughed, but sometimes, late at night, I question it. I still feel his touch – his particular way of kissing that place behind my ear that makes everything tingle. But most of all, I feel like he is mine. Not that he belongs to me, but that I have a claim on him. I don't want to feel this way. I don't. It's a weight and it stops me from moving on. That and what I did. I pull out of the layby and, while Lisa tells me about her weekend of lust with another new man, I get it absolutely straight in my mind that this is not me homing in on Daniel while Jem is away. Is it?

No. I am genuinely concerned about her welfare. I have good reason to be. She hates me. So why would she ask me for help? I am simply finding out what she wants. Lisa finishes her account of rampant sex, and we laugh.

'...so, after that he asked to see me again, and I just laughed.' She pauses. 'So, all in all, it's a combination of tiredness and wine and I'll be at work later on. You got anything on today?'

I hurriedly compare my weekend with hers. No comparison, I think, as I tingle about the weekend Tim and I spent gazing at each other.

'Oh God, yes. I just hope my client today doesn't do the silence thing or I'll just go home.'

I've been developing a clinic of my own over the past year. A wellness clinic. Not Jem's kind of wellness, more of a place where people can come along and really open their hearts about their hopes and fears. Then we draw up a plan for the future. Positive psychology. And it's all come together perfectly to keep me on an even keel. I even feel lucky for a second until I remember the message and where I am going. We laugh, then I become sombre.

'Look, I know what you are saying about Daniel. I'll just go over there and make sure he knows about the message and then I'll leave it.'

She tuts. 'I still don't see why you have to go over. But it's your call. Look, I'm going to get some coffee. Let me know what happens.'

I end the call and I'm turning the corner into his drive. His car is there, and I can hear Pepe's squeaky bark. Her car is gone. As I pull up, I peer around the side of the house. Pepe is outside in the garden. Alone. I get out of the vehicle and go around the side. He jumps up at the makeshift enclosure and I lean over and pat his soft head. The chicken wire is rough and held together with cable ties. I'd know Daniel's DIY skills anywhere. I peer up at the house.

He bought it immediately after we split up. He spent a few weeks in rooms arranging the sale, but no cooling-off period to see if we got back together. No, Daniel knew what he wanted. Her. She moved in straight away. I have to admit it is a beautiful place, and she has made this garden lovely. It's not as roomy as our house, but the vintage copper sign on the gate reads 'The Rosarium'. She has themed it. Roses everywhere. In every room. Very pink. Very Jem. Daniel appears from the back door.

'Oh, Daniel. I wanted to...'

He looks mildly irritated. 'Not this again. Please. Not again...'

I hold my hands up. There had been a time, just after we split up, where I would come here and sit outside. I'd sneak around the back and torture myself by peering through the back window. I wanted to reassure myself that she wasn't replacing me. That she wasn't playing mum.

It had the opposite effect. It looked for all the world that they had fallen into an easy family pattern with little effort. Doing their own thing, then eating her vegetarian home-cooking and freshly baked bread around a big oak table. Then perfect pictures on her Instagram feed. I feel embarrassed as he stares me down, waiting for a response.

'No, no... it's...' I fumble in my pocket for my phone. 'It's this.'

I find the message and hold it up in front of him. He takes my phone and reads it. I read him. He just looks confused. He hands the phone back to me.

'Okay. Look, I hope this isn't more drama?'

I shake my head. 'She sent it to me.'

'Did she? Really? Look. She's gone to see a friend for a couple of days. She'll be back soon.' We both look at the dog. 'We're a couple. I don't mind looking after Pepe.'

I blink at him. My eyes drift to the chicken wire and the ties. The small space and no water. I speak quietly. 'At least get him some water. You are feeding him, aren't you?'

Daniel's dog-sitting skills are about the same as his parenting skills. He shakes his head and rolls his eyes.

'Okay. You win.' He heads back into the house and appears with a piece of paper and an overflowing dog dish. He reaches over the wire and sets the dish down. I see his tanned skin as his shirt rides up and the hairs on my arms stand on end.

'See. She left this pinned on the fridge. Not that it's any of your business.'

I read it. *Hey Dan-Dan. Jemi's just gone to see Tracey – back in a couple of days. Love and love x* It certainly has her hallmark on it. He takes it back.

'Just before you go, I hope you aren't suggesting that I'm putting Jem in danger. Because I can tell you we have never been happier. Or more in love.'

Standard Daniel. Painfully straightforward. He looks me right in the eyes and I feel my heart drop through my soul. This man told me forever. He told me he loved *me.* In this moment I doubt my motives. I feel the same depth of pain I felt on the day I discovered them together. But I just nod. He continues.

'So, you'd better not be at your games again. Because I'll just phone the police.'

At one time I would have got angry and started to shout. But I am either used to it, or I no longer care as much. This realisation rallies me.

'Or I might. Over this.' I hold the phone up. 'Aren't you even a bit concerned?'

He smiles. 'No because I know you are just trying to discredit Jem. If I thought it was real, I'd call the police myself. But sadly, I know what you are capable of. So, I won't.'

I turn and walk away. I know full well I can't call the police. I also know that he really does not know what I am capable of, or what I have done.

CHAPTER THREE

I never meant to take it so far. I am a good person but somewhere it all went wrong. I'd been very happy working with the police. And especially with Lisa. We were great friends and we spent breaks and lunchtimes together giggling like schoolgirls. Training was my first role after my psychology degree, then writing copy manuals for the counselling and advice services. As I moved upwards, passing Lisa and into management, I missed the hands-on sessions. The face-to-face honesty that this particular line of work brings. But there was no way back through the ranks and, after one particularly difficult abuse case, I decided to go freelance.

It gave me more freedom to work both with Lisa on contract work at the station and start my own practice. I was, and still am, dedicated to my clients and, like a pro-bono lawyer, I often double up sessions giving free hours to those who most need it. It's been years since we last worked together, but we have remained firm friends. Daniel was on the up and paid all the bills. And when we bought Sturgeon Hall, which is less a 'hall' and more a four-bedroomed Victorian town house, it gave me time to work on planning and making a start on the renovations.

Daniel was out a lot, and he would come home to a scene of domestic bliss and talk of what we would do to our new home.

I'm good at my job. I really care about people, and although I had a little time off around the split, I kept going because I didn't want to let anyone down. But it also makes what I did all the worse.

It feels worthwhile and it just about pays the bills. It's a constant balance between affording luxuries and doing a job I love – and getting over things. He was paying the mortgage and all the bills at first, but she convinced him he didn't need to do that. No. He just needed to pay what the state told him to. I knew the income he declared was not his real profit – I had seen his accounts. But I couldn't prove it. I couldn't prove he dealt in cash. So, I took it. And worked at my business. Working with people who were depending on me was, at one time, the only thing that kept me getting out of bed on the days the kids weren't there.

I told myself at the time I was doing it because those people deserved to tell their stories. I saw myself as a warrior for social justice. What I didn't realise was that I would soon join the ranks of the hard done to. The spurned. A shiver of bitterness runs through me when I remember those days. I tell myself I didn't see it coming, but from the early days I had sensed that Daniel was not entirely focused on me.

It made me even keener. I wanted him and I would keep him. We were social animals before we had children and would spend nights in city bars and clubs entertaining his clients. The luxury lifestyle had to match the luxury cars. Daniel knew how to cast a spell of affluence. How to capture them in his web of expensive gifts. Names on guest lists. Vintage champagne.

I saw how he looked at the women, scanning the club. He would chat to them, and I told myself that it was okay. *It's okay, Lauren. He's going home with you.* But I learnt to know his type.

Long blonde straight hair. Thin. Always thin. Tanned. I dyed my auburn hair blonde and invested in hair straighteners. I spent time at the beauticians and on the tanning beds. But I couldn't do anything about my weight. I wasn't heavy. I was normal.

When the kids came along, I worried about those women in the clubs. About what he was doing when he took clients out and I couldn't go. I focused on the children and on becoming a stay-at-home parent extraordinaire while I went part time at the station. But I needn't have worried because Daniel was never late. He always came home, and he was always in the same immaculate state he left the house. He would eat a late dinner and finish some business in his office. Then we would go to bed and make love. Every night. It was tender and gentle. Just the memory of it makes me upset and, as I sit down at my desk, I feel a lump in my throat. Then I remember Tim and the memory dissolves into the past where it belongs.

I call him. I dial his number. I've been waiting to speak to him since the moment he left yesterday, but I don't want to appear too keen. While I wait for him to answer, I scroll through Instagram. Every decent detail of Lisa's dirty weekend adorns her profile. I smile. She looks very happy. I'd taken a selfie outside the hotel where Tim and I stayed and posted it. I scrutinise myself for a grain of negativity and there is none. When I told Lisa about the hotel over coffee last week, she blinked at me.

'A hotel? Again? Bloody hell. He must be made of money. Couldn't you have stayed at yours? Or his?' It hadn't escaped Lisa's attention that I had never been to Tim's house. She's an experienced online dater and can spot a snag early. She flagged Tim's online anonymity and dubbed him International Man of Mystery. She also noted his reluctance to 'take me home'.

But we aren't young people. We've both had long-term

relationships. He told me he'd split from his partner four years ago. They'd been together ten years and he wanted to make sure his next relationship was the real deal. He told me he lived in an apartment he rented when his relationship broke up. Compact, he said. He's never invited me there, but he did tell me he wanted to treat me right. And he has. I know she is only concerned, and I'd smiled my response.

'All in good time. We don't need to rush it. And I spend a lot of time indoors so I'm enjoying this. Nice hotels. Good food and, well, Tim.'

But I did wonder. I scanned the profiles of all the places I knew he went socially. And his work website. He works in window design and fitting. He's got a qualification in planning, and he designs the more complex jobs. There is a tiny picture of him on the site where he is in the middle of a group of colleagues. I snipped it and now it's the cover photo on my phone.

He finally answers. 'Hello. How you doing?'

I laugh and tut. 'Well, Mr Darcy, I'm very well, thank you.'

The hotel we'd stayed in at the weekend had resembled the stately home with the lake that Colin Firth had emerged from in the *Pride and Prejudice* film. He laughs.

'So, what can I do for you?'

I pause. I don't know, really. Except our relationship represents my moving on, but I can't say that. Too deep. I go for light and airy.

'Oh, I don't know. Just checking in.'

And there it is. The spark inside me. The twinkle of love that I had doubted I was capable of anymore just six months ago. He laughs again.

'Nicely timed. I was going to message you. Next time you're free, I've got a nice little excursion I think you will like. A bit farther afield, this time.'

A text message pings onto my phone. I open it while he tells me where it is and how he found it. It's an old country pile down south. It looks beautiful but I feel a niggle of irritation.

'Looks lovely. But... I don't know. I'd rather stay local.' Silence. He knows what is coming. 'Maybe we could stay at yours for a change?'

'Yeah. Of course. I just didn't want to... rush you. Your house is so spacious and my apartment... well... it's... smaller...'

Oh my goodness. He's nervous about me seeing his man cave. Of course he is. And then there are the trust issues. He mentioned he had been badly hurt by his ex. He never said she had cheated, but that's how it seemed. Lisa hadn't factored that into her three-point critique.

'It's fine. We're together, Tim, and it will be fun.'

He laughs. 'Okay, okay. Next time, then. But give me time to tidy up.'

The bubble of suspicion pops and I almost laugh out loud. This is exactly what I need. This. Tim and his bashful don't-mind-my pants-on-the-floor casual attitude. I feel myself relax.

'I will. Thanks. It'll be a change. Something new. Look, I'd better go.'

He tuts. 'So soon? I was hoping for an in-depth review on the weekend. But I guess I can cook you dinner and we can have a repeat performance.'

I'm thrilled. It's flirty and gorgeous. Cook me dinner. I have no idea what I was worried about. I end the call and message Lisa.

> National emergency over. I'm going round to his for dinner.

She replies with a smiley and all is well in the world again.

My first client of the morning is a woman on her final

appointment with me. She has made leaps and bounds and I am proud of her. She came to me after a split with her boyfriend where it meant she had to start again from scratch. It's this kind of outcome that makes my job so satisfying. As she closes the door to the room I rent from my local GP, I wonder if she has any lingering thoughts about her past. She seems happy, but does she hold a kernel of bitterness in her heart?

I know many people do and that it takes a while to get over a relationship. I know that in most cases the sourness of the break-up grows smaller and smaller until it is subsumed by new joy, and this is where I am now. Just waiting for that joy to swallow up the whole sad affair and have done with it.

I also know that joy is an almost insurmountable hurdle to climb over. Because while most people beat a path through any bitterness, jealousy and revenge in their own minds, and emerge stronger, I took it further. Most people don't act on it. Most people have one episode of acting out and then learn that the consequences are not worth it. That the momentary rush revenge gives is temporary and soon replaced with guilt.

Not me. Oh no. Not me.

I drive to Angel and Ben's school and, once they are home and fed and in their respective rooms doing whatever nine- and eleven-year-olds do, I sit at the kitchen table with my laptop. I don't want to do this again. I don't know what happened between my joy at speaking to Tim and now but I do know it has something to do with her message – it's been on my mind, making the worry resurface. I never meant to do this in the first place, and I deeply regret it. But if something really has happened to her and the police find the remnants of my heartbroken actions, all paths lead to me.

I open the laptop and try to think about the message. I glance at my phone, wishing again I had rung her. I always seem to be covering my tracks. I click on an icon on the desktop and quickly type in a username and password. My heart is in my mouth as a screen appears. A beautifully decorated lounge with a feature wall of pink roses. A huge burgundy chesterfield and a wall-sized TV. I click on Screen 2 and a glo-white kitchen appears. Screen 3 is the upstairs landing. I hover the cursor over Screen 4. I am a good person. I hated myself then and I hate myself now. But it was *her*. She drove me mad. She drove me to this.

I stop for a moment. The kids. I could lose them if I am ever found out.

Yet I click. I click and a country bedroom appears. A stylish, modern four poster with cream and pink roses on the lush duvet cover. And on the far wall, a new addition since I last looked a long time ago. A picture of Daniel, Ben, and Angel. And *her*.

CHAPTER FOUR

I didn't look for long. The house was still and empty. Like a prop waiting for my kids. I switched it off and slammed down the laptop lid. Where is she?

I sat until the early hours, swinging between telling myself I am imagining something is wrong and this is just Jem being Jem and worrying that Daniel isn't taking it seriously enough. All tinged with a dread of being found out and a strong suspicion that this is nothing to do with me.

I turned my phone off at 3am and slept fitfully, and now I am dog tired with a day of client records to complete. Ben is reading his homework over his Coco Pops and Angel is eating toast and jam. She talks into the cheap orange juice she is about to drink.

'Can I have a phone? I want to do TikTok.'

I shake my head. 'Nope. Not yet. You know the rules. No phones. Family time.'

She stares at me. She is so beautiful. All red hair and attitude, she reminds me a lot of me when I was her age but much prettier. But she has Daniel's thinner face and shaped chin. It makes her look elfin. Ben is like my dad. Dad lives in

Spain now with his new wife. After Mum died, he decided to live each day like it was his last. I miss him, but we Zoom as much as we can. Ben has his eyes and nose, but again, Daniel's face shape and chin. He chews, then laughs.

'No way, Angel. You're not having TikTok. You're too young.'

A battle ensues and I exit to the lounge. The early morning sun streams through the windows and in this moment, I hope I can hold on to the house. It seems doubtful – I won't take any work that compromises my already limited time with the kids. Even at weekends I work as hard as I play, maximising the time I am without them and Tim is busy to write up my continuing professional development and do research to develop my business.

But ends barely meet and I don't know how long I can stretch this out. The awful reality is that even if I agree to sell, there is little or no equity. The house isn't finished. Some rooms are barely a shell and there is no chance of me continuing the work.

Many, many thoughts raced in my head after the break-up, and one of the clear front-runners was how Daniel managed to buy The Rosarium. He still owns half our home; I couldn't afford to buy him out. Then, all of a sudden, the kids were telling me that Daddy had a new house.

It all happened so fast. Just over a year ago, I was blissfully unaware that he had been sleeping with Jem for six months. I'd been over to Spain to see Dad with the kids. Ben had been sick, and I got a flight home a couple of days early. I'd tried to call Daniel, but he hadn't picked up. I'd imagined him up a ladder, decorating a room to surprise me. Which illustrates just how deluded I was.

Daniel is not the DIY type. He is, it turns out, the type who sleeps with his mistress while his wife is away – in their bed. His car was there when I arrived home. I'd left my car in the airport car park when we left for Spain. I'd collected it and driven two very tired children home. As I pulled up outside, I saw a Mini with a Union Jack on the roof parked snugly beside Daniel's convertible.

A client, chimed my stupidity without even a suspicion. The kids hurried wearily inside and slumped on the sofa. Ben's hand was on the remote before I could even suggest an early night. I was undecided between finding my husband and bringing in my bags. I decided on the former, and halfway upstairs I knew something was wrong. I could hear music. Daniel is not a music person. Even then, my mind jumped to him hiring a decorator. I had spoiled the surprise.

I walked along the corridor to our lovely room with the curved terrace at the end and an en suite. Our beautiful oak bed and a plush green carpet. The music got louder, and I caught what it was. 'Sweet Home Alabama'. Old, cool music that reminded me of my mum.

I caught sight of bare skin through the slightly open door. I thought I had caught him unawares, dressing or washing. Not that it mattered. I had seen him naked every day of our marriage. We had no secrets. Or so I thought. A flash of blonde hair. A high-pitched laugh. Buttocks. My husband's hands. His wedding ring. Me in the room.

They froze. I stared for a long moment, then left. A minute later, he was downstairs in the kitchen. He shut the door that led to the lounge.

'Look, Lauren, I...'

'Who is she?'

He sucked in his lips and pulled his T-shirt down. 'She's... I've...'

I wanted to go for him, tear at him. Push him. But I am a good person and I know that is not the right thing to do. That violence is never the answer. Even when you want to kill someone. In a way it was worse. I had been through a lot with Mum dying, then Dad going away, but that moment tainted me. I was never the same again.

She was suddenly behind him. I don't remember her smiling. But she touched him. Her hand glanced his arm. Her long blonde hair, curled at the ends, bounced around her shoulders. She was wearing skinny jeans and a blue shirt. Sandals. She could have been shopping in Lidl rather than just caught in our bed.

'Out.' I didn't shout. I just said it. 'Both of you. Out.'

They stood looking at me.

'It's over, Dan. I told you. It's a deal breaker.' It was like someone else was saying it. Someone who knew they could be a working single parent. Someone who wouldn't descend into some kind of torturous madness. They just stood there. Her hand went to his shoulder. He looked at her and she nodded.

'I know. I was going to tell you. We're together. I'm leaving you.'

I almost laughed. He had to have the last word. I'd already thrown him out, but he ignored that and rejected me. 'Out. Just get out. Now. The pair of you.'

He stared at me, mesmerised by my hardly ever seen anger. I rarely raised my voice. But he stood his ground. 'We need to tell the kids.'

I made an incredulous gasp. 'We. Meaning me and you, Dan. Their parents. Not her.'

It had already set in. The hate. The irrational scorn. Even then. He just nodded.

'Okay, have it your way. I'm going. But I'll be back tomorrow, and we'll need to come to some arrangement.'

She was already out of the door. Into her car and smiling

through the open window at him. He raced after her, down the drive and out of our lives.

I opened the door to the lounge. Ben and Angel were oblivious. They were both asleep on the oversized sofa, Angel's leg over Ben's. I shut the door.

I went upstairs and walked back along the corridor to our bedroom. I opened the door and stepped inside. I could smell her. Rose Peonia. Expensive. The bed was crumpled and there was a bottle of champagne on the dresser. Two glasses on the bedside table.

I took the glasses – they were from my mum's set – and the bottle, and quietly shut the door. Following that, I have only been in that room once. Some of my clothes are still in there, but most of them were still in a smaller room at the front of the house. I ordered a bed for that room and have slept in there ever since.

I bundle Ben and Angel into the car. I will go straight into town after dropping them at school. I collect my laptop bag and do my 'keys, money, phone' routine. I break my own rule and check my phone before we set off. Thinking about her that day, the look on her face when she knew Daniel was leaving. The smugness of her ever since. Holding my daughter's hand. Smiling at Ben. She wouldn't ask me for help unless she was desperate.

I know Lisa has a coffee and muffin every day before work at the Blue Bear Café. I need to talk to her. Lisa doesn't know the full story, but she knows some of it. When I arrive, I breathe a sigh of relief as I see her in her usual spot, alone. As I open the door and walk towards her, she nods. She stands and hugs me to her.

'I know, love, I know. I could hear it in your voice the other day.'

I order coffee and hot buttered toast. Lisa is lovely. She is pragmatic and her truth hits you between the eyes – a by-product of years of working with survivors – but her words are pricked through with love and care. She chooses the next ones carefully.

'So has it triggered something?'

I nod. She saw me broken and she watched me mend. 'I don't know. I feel the same about Tim and I don't feel angry. But I can't stop thinking about that message.' I almost add that my gut feeling is hardly ever wrong.

She pulls in her lips. 'What did he say?'

She means Daniel. She never liked him, even before Jem.

'He said she's gone away. He showed me the note she left. Pepe was there and... I don't know, Lees, it all seemed above board. He wasn't upset or anything. Kids said she'd gone away for a few days. But that message.'

I pull it up on my phone. Past the picture of the hotel Tim sent me. Past his lovely text. I hand my phone to Lisa. She reads it. She is silent for a moment. I hear Adele's 'Hello' play in the background of the café chat. Then she gives me her analysis.

'It is strange. And asking for help. But have you thought it might be her trying to cosy up to you? If she's in this for the long haul, she might be trying to get you on side.'

I almost spit out my tea. 'What? Jem?'

She laughs. 'Just playing Devil's advocate, mate. There could be loads of bloody reasons, but on the face of it... I don't bloody know. But you have to close this off one way or another.' She leans forward. 'Because if you don't, you'll be parked outside his house at midnight in night vision goggles before you know it.'

I blink at her. Classic Lisa. Say it how it is. Although I don't have the night vision goggles. I open my mouth to tell her I am past that and it will never happen again. Then I remember the glow of the screen last night and me checking her Instagram account.

'I know. I need a plan.'

A plan is our go-to. Our lifeblood. Lisa and I always have a plan. And that's what I've built my business on. Structure and planning. Lisa smiles again.

'It seems to me you've got two choices. Ignore it. You definitely don't owe Jem anything. You aren't obliged to help her. Or, if you really think she is in danger, ring it in. Tell someone friendly at the station. Either way, make a decision to put it behind you. Delete the message.'

I sip my coffee and think.

'Yeah, I know you're right. And I guess if she had left from a friend's place and she was in trouble and hadn't arrived, they would have phoned Daniel or the police?'

She nods enthusiastically. 'Yes! That's better. It's not your problem anymore.'

We chat about a woman we both used to work with and then it's time for her to leave. She kisses my cheek.

'Don't go back there, love. You've come so far.'

I nod and smile and watch her pass the coffee shop window. Lovely Lisa. I know what I need to do. I tell my clients to forgive if they can, but at least forget. Move forward. This is what Lisa urges me to do like any friend would. And she would be completely right if she knew the full story. But she doesn't.

CHAPTER FIVE

I open my case files and order another coffee. I could do them at home as usual, but Lisa is right. I need to move forward. I need a new plan. I tell my clients to set mini goals and this can be mine. A side goal.

In the past, my goals have been simple. My children. My family. I know I am competitive. When Angel and Ben were in infant school, I would spend hours making the best fancy dress costumes for non-uniform day and stand in front of them at Christmas concerts mouthing the words. I was proud of everything in my life. My home, my children. And my relationship.

But that competitive nature shifted up a notch to having to win when she appeared. I can't remember the exact moment. I didn't want Daniel back. Oh no. She could have him. It was my children. Almost overnight she became their 'other mum'. I'd watched her smiling at them and touching Angel's hair. My rational self told me she was just trying to be kind, but some primal feeling deep, deep inside stirred. And anyway, who knows what she was capable of. After all, she had stolen my husband. This was my tack at the time; blaming Jem and absolving Daniel. She had stolen my husband and she was stealing my children.

At first, I thought I would be able to stand it. I knew other families went through this. Several of my friends had split with their partner and were now in shared parenting arrangements. I talked to them, found out what happened and then realised I really had no choice. If I tried to argue, the family court would rule, and I didn't want to drag the kids through that particular brand of acrimony. Besides, Ben and Angel wanted it. They wanted to spend time with Daddy, and they never complained about Jemi. They took the whole thing a lot better than I did.

But something took over. Something unexpected. It was more than my competitive nature. It was something dark that I didn't understand. When it became clear that I couldn't win by giving my children the treats Daniel and Jem did, that Daniel and Jem had a disposable income and I didn't, that my children would regularly bring back expensive clothes and games, the rules somehow changed.

I didn't notice it. I'd been harbouring resentment but told myself that I was going through the seven stages of grief for my relationship, and I was at the anger and bargaining stage. Looking back now, and in comparison to the reconstructive stage I am at now, it was obvious. But that anger pushed into the frustration at not being able to be the "best parent" and into having to win some other way.

In the warm café, I suddenly go cold. Just the thought of those months shakes me. I tearfully told Lisa some of what I did and she was kind. She told me that lots of people lose the plot when their relationship fails. I told her I didn't expect it to happen to me and she assured me it would pass. She told me she knew people, men and women, who had done much worse in the wake of a dead relationship.

I can't go back there. I can't relive that awful feeling of not being good enough. I cannot sink to those depths. It became a habit, the checking and sadness and desperation, a hole that I could hardly climb out of. But I did. And here I am. I know Daniel and Jem are in my life forever unless I cut ties and keep away from anything to do with them.

I brighten. Perhaps Jem's message is an attempt to get pally after all. But Lisa is right, I have no responsibility to them. To her and especially to Daniel. I need a boundary. Yes. A boundary. That's what I need. I open my notebook and draw a stick woman. Me. Then a line. Then a stick man and another stick woman. I write Dan and Jem above them. Then I simply cross through each one with a line. Out of my life. For good.

It feels great. I sip my almost cold coffee and look through the coffee shop window out into the world. I'll move forward with Tim. A bolt of excitement surprises me and I smile to myself. Yes. I'll introduce him to the kids, and he can come over when he likes. I'll tell him what has happened with Daniel, and he'll understand me better.

But I need to be responsible. I need to make sure that before I draw this line in the sand, I do the right thing.

I'm only triggered by the message because of my guilt. I know that. It's a straight choice – I either go backwards or forwards. I have no other evidence at all that anything is wrong. This is another lesson learnt. I need to forgive myself for something I did at a different time. I had been in a different place, teetering between pain and guilt and wondering if I was enough of a woman, and had resorted to anger and bargaining with them. Yes, it got out of control, but now I can move on.

I focus on updating my client records and, just before twelve, my phone pings. My heart leaps as I automatically assume it's a text from Jem and check myself with my new plan. But it isn't. It's an alert. It's telling me that one of the cameras at

Daniel's has picked up movement. I must have activated that notification last night.

I open the app with a view to turning it off and catch a glimpse of Daniel walking across the landing. My eyes linger on him longer than they should. He stops and is talking to someone. Laughing. I can't see who it is because of the weird camera angle. Maybe she is back. He leans forward, then throws his head back in laughter.

I switch quickly to the lounge, then the kitchen. There is a tan Mulberry Bayswater bag on the white worktop. Jem doesn't use Mulberry. I move to the bedroom, but it is empty. Back to the landing and they are gone. I do another quick circuit around the cameras, then check myself. What the hell am I doing?

I've got the opportunity to be with Tim and develop my practice. Work to keep the house and have nice holidays with the kids. Which is more important, the opportunity to be happy and earn money, or my obsessions with *her*?

This needs to stop now. I can't do anything about the cameras, and I am going to have to live with that. But I promise myself I will remove the app from my phone and laptop as soon as possible, and never look again. I feel a sense of mourning but stop myself.

Mulling over my broken marriage forever isn't going to do any good at all. It's clear they are in this for the long haul – Daniel even told me so himself. Yes, it hurts, but I need to get over it. I've resisted a relationship with Tim even though I like him. I told myself I just wanted fun, but I know deep down I wanted someone I can just throw away if Daniel decides he wants me back.

The moment of clarity jolts me. It isn't going to happen. I need to move on.

I tap out a message to Tim.

> Hey. Are you free tonight for a chat? About what you asked me at weekend?

He could come to mine. Once the kids are in bed. It's give and take, isn't it? He's let his guard down and he's going to cook me dinner at his. So, I can see him on the nights I have the kids.

I don't want to be alone to pore over every detail of my broken relationship. To think of new ways to punish myself and them. To "win" at entertaining the children. It had turned into a competition and that too had to stop. I am horrified as I suddenly wonder if Tim was a distraction for the times it all got too painful. No. I like him. A lot. And we're good together.

I press send and I am proud of myself. I scroll through my contact list and settle on Dave Pilcher. He's Desk Dave, my contact at Central Park Police HQ. Dave does the press chats and fends reporters off. He answers in two rings.

'Lauren. How's the new job? What can I do you for?'

He's a good guy. He's also a solid wall of silence at the right times. His face gives away nothing and we all knew that if we didn't do what he said, we were off his contact list.

'It's more of a personal matter really, Dave. Have you got time for this?'

He laughs. 'Not really, but go on.'

I laugh too. And wonder if I am doing the right thing. 'Okay. You know my ex?'

He cuts in. 'Dodgy Daniel. "Don't buy a car from me" Wade? That ex?'

I faux tut. 'Don't be like that. You know he's completely legit. Anyway, you know his new partner?' I choose my words carefully and keep my voice even. 'Jem Carter.'

He laughs loudly now. 'Jem as in "truly outrageous"?'

He's not far out. She *is* skinny and her boobs *are* disproportionate to her waist. I laugh too.

'More Barbie crossed with Taylor Swift. Anyway, to cut a very long story short, she doesn't much care for me. And I am not her biggest fan.'

'So, she wouldn't piss on you if you were on fire?'

He's enjoying this a bit too much, but I press on. 'Something like that. Well, the other night, I received a text. Saying *Lauren. You've got to help me. Please.* Then the kids came back, and Daniel told me she had gone to visit friends. I texted her back but got no reply. Daniel showed me a note, saying she had left it. But I'm worried, Dave. She never goes anywhere without Pepe.'

There is a lull in the conversation, and I realise how trivial this is next to what he could potentially have to deal with right at this moment. Yet I am continuing my whining narrative about bloody Jem. To the police. Dave regains his composure.

'Okay. Look, there's probably nothing to worry about. But I'll make a note you rang this in and if anything does crop up...'

I laugh. 'Thanks. I know it sounds weak, but I'd rather have said something.' It doesn't sound weak; it sounds like I am trying to frame Daniel for her disappearance. 'By the way, I'm not trying to blame Daniel. He wouldn't do anything... like that.'

He's more serious now. 'Like what?'

I pause. What do I think has happened? What do I *really* think?

'I don't know. All I know is she's not around and it's the first time since–'

He interrupts. 'Look, love, I know you're worried but I'm a detective, not social services. I'll make a note, but seriously, unless you think there's a crime committed and you have some evidence, I'd hold off.'

I want to ask him why she would ask for help, from me. But he is right. Who knows? She could be at a mate's, drunk and...

Dave is saying goodbye and laughing again. I laugh too.

'Yeah, you're right. But better safe than sorry, eh? Anyway, if you're ever in town at the weekend let's have a chat. I'll buy you a drink. I know Lisa would love to see you!'

Lisa chased Dave for about a year after he got divorced, and he put equal effort into avoiding her.

We end the call. I order another coffee and deactivate the camera app on my phone. This is it. A new me.

CHAPTER SIX

I spend the rest of the day engrossed in my work. No distractions because from now on I am not dwelling on the past. I set myself some alarms on my phone. I want to organise my life better. I feel tearful that I have finally reached a decision to leave all this behind.

None of it will be easy, but if I can make a difference and earn good money while I am doing it, I should be able to manage. Get things on a more even keel with Tim. I know I can do it.

I collect Ben and Angel and drive home. They have homework, and we sit on the high kitchen stools and do it together. I cook lasagne and home-made chips and we tuck in. Ben tells me about his jungle project at school and how Daniel said he would help him.

'And did he?' I temper it with kindness. 'If not, I can.' He nods.

'Yeah. He did. He got the tape stuck to him and Jemi...'

He stops and looks at Angel. She is frowning. I intervene. My God, they are stopping themselves talking about her. I fight back tears and speak gently.

'It's okay. I don't mind you talking about Jem. She is Daddy's partner and part of your life.' It's the first time I have spoken to them about her, beyond asking probing questions. 'If you like her, I like her.'

Angel relaxes. Ben continues warily. I fix a smile.

'Okay. So, Jem had to get the scissors. Then she helped too. But she wasn't any good either and she got the glue in her hair.'

Angel was laughing as she dipped her chips in ketchup. 'Daddy said it was okay because she could get new hair.'

I stifle a laugh. Hair extensions. I knew it. *Stop, Lauren. Stop.* Ben picked up the story.

'Daddy says we can go on a safari. To the real jungle. We can go on holiday.'

Angel pulls a face. 'But Pepe would have to go to a kennel. Unless...' She looks at Ben and he nods. 'Unless you would look after him for Jem while we go?'

I take a very deep breath. It all seems ridiculous. Ludicrous. I need some boundaries. They stare at me, blinking into the artificial brightness of the kitchen. Do other exes do this for each other? I've heard of amicable arrangements but just how amicable?

On the other hand, what's the harm?

'Yes. Yes, Pepe could come here. It's not like we haven't got the space, is it?'

I think about getting a dog but dismiss it immediately. I can barely manage financially as it is. But two weeks with a chihuahua wouldn't be so bad. I need to make this more about what the kids want.

Angel claps her hands and grins. Ben smiles into his bowl of frozen yogurt I serve as a healthy alternative to ice cream. I nod as he scrapes the bowl. I am super-mum. But I must stay super-mum. I must keep believing that nothing has changed and my children love me just the same. That Jem isn't the competition.

That's the problem. It's hard not to look backwards at the carnage of the past. So, I will look forwards.

I tuck my children into bed in their lovely bedrooms and hope again I can keep the house. Maybe if Daniel sees I am serious about that, he will raise my maintenance. In the meantime, I can enjoy this place as much as possible.

I go through the kitchen to the garage and move some paint around until I find what I am looking for. I grab a plastic container of paint thinners and take it into the kitchen. I fill the spray bottle I use to water my plants with soapy water and grab my hairdryer from the drawer. It's time to put this right.

I march along the landing to what was our room. I hesitate at the door and wonder if I should leave this for another day. But leaving things for another day is what got me into this mess. I lean on the door, and it opens. Incredibly, the room still smells of her, but I guess that's why her particular brand of perfume costs so much. I look at the bed, still crumpled in exactly the formation it was when I discovered them. The speakers still show a blue light, and the curtains remain open still.

Daniel has been in here. The day after he left, he came back. I heard him pull up on the drive. I remember thinking how odd it was that I hadn't cried. Or lost my temper. I just felt numb. Shouting wasn't in me. Instead, there was a deep hole that all my emotions were falling through and resurfacing over and over. He'd walked into the kitchen and looked around.

'I'm taking some of my things.'

I nodded. 'Fine.'

He looked at the lounge door. 'Are they in there?'

My heart had skipped a beat as I realised what he was about

to do. Telling our children was the final confirmation. There was no going back.

'Yes. Are you sure about this, Dan?'

He moved closer to me. He took off his wedding ring and placed it gently on the stone worktop.

'I am. I really am. It's no reflection on you. I just fell in love with someone else. With Jem.'

I could hardly breathe. I heard the words come out, echoing inside me. 'But you barely know her.'

He sighed. 'I've known her a while. We didn't sleep together at first. She was a friend. But I fell in love with her. I want to be with her. Don't make this more difficult than it already is.'

I laughed. 'So, you admit it's difficult? You haven't even said you're sorry.'

I sounded like a whiny child. I hated myself in that moment. And I hated her. She knew about me and our children, yet she went ahead and took him. He waited for a long moment.

'I'm not sorry. Well, I'm sorry for Ben and Angel. But they will get used to it. Like thousands of kids do. We'll be sharing parental responsibility. I've already looked into it.'

My blood ran cold. The thought of my children not being here. Just me, in this big house. Alone. It chilled me. This was supposed to be a family home. I waited for my temper to rise. For the inevitable row. But it didn't come. He looked at me for a long moment. I could see his brain ticking over with impatience as he awaited the inevitable scene that never came. Then he went into the lounge.

Twenty minutes later, he came out and went upstairs. I sat with Ben and Angel until he brought down some cases and suit bags.

'I'll get the rest another time. I said I'd take them out for tea, you know, to...' His eyes strayed to his car on the drive. I hadn't even thought to look. But there she was. Waiting. 'It'll give you some time to...'

I just nodded. Ben and Angel ran outside towards the car. I watched her get out and give them an exaggerated handshake. Daniel looked too.

'You'll get used to it. We all will. We'll talk about this place through our solicitors.' He moved very close to me. 'But I just want to say that I know what you are like. That little jealous streak.' His lips were close to my ear. 'You harm one hair on her head. Say one wrong word to her and I'll drag you through court for the kids.'

He sauntered away and got in the car. She looked at me standing in the doorway and smiled. Me? I was broken. Completely broken. I was struggling to understand what had happened in those twenty-four hours. Only two weeks ago we had sat together in our family home and planned a family Christmas. Daniel's parents. His sister and her husband and children. My dad was invited. Friends, Angel and Ben's school friends. Now, I was here alone.

I watched him drive away and when he turned left at the end of the drive towards the city, I went to the garage. I pulled out a selection of cleaning implements and threw them into an old cloth bag from the boot of my car. I'd slept on the sofa the previous night. If I was going to sleep in our room, I needed to clean it. Clean him from it. And her.

I hurried upstairs and, just like today, paused at the door. It was still raw. I often wonder if I had done what I had intended to do that day if everything would have turned out differently.

I stand now in front of my handiwork. RIP. In huge sprayed black letters on the pristine white wall. RIP. Underneath it I sprayed BITCH. It's shocking now. The beautiful room defiled. I can't believe I did it. Only a sliver of the depth of the hurt I felt in the moment I sprayed those walls remain now, but it still hurts more than anything, except mum dying.

I set to work with the turps and soapy water. I scrub at the paint, but it won't budge. The paint thinner soaks in and just makes it sticky. After an hour I stand back. It's worse than ever. Smudged at the edges and tacky. I look around the rest of the room. I'm going to have to paint it again. I can't afford to get anyone in, but I will do it. This is my room.

I am exhausted. I would usually spend at least an hour before I go to bed scrolling social media. That, I admit to myself, has become a bit of an obsession too. Scouring social media for any sign of Jem. She appears from time to time on other people's Facebook feeds. Out to lunch. Smiling in a group. Posing in front of a landmark. Never with Daniel. She has her own profile but never, ever posts.

On Twitter and Instagram too. She has a curated feed for her coaching business. Very classy and clearly done by a professional. She claims to have high-profile clients, and it all has the hallmark of being "apart" from the de rigueur of run-of-the-mill. She follows the general rule of social networking by sprinkling a touch of her personal life between her business posts. And that personal life consists of cosy scenes in The Rosarium with my children. Perfectly curated round-the-table scenes. I had called her a pound-shop Brené Brown to Lisa, but deep down I am not so sure. I have to concede that she is making money somehow.

But tonight, that is of no consequence. Tonight, I am going to read a book. I have a pile to be read beside my bed in my makeshift bedroom. Lisa is an avid reader and recommended them. I'd bought them and then piled them up because my mind was full of Jem. Jem, Jem, Jem, Jem bloody Jem.

I pick up the top book and begin to read. It's a thriller about a psychologist who wants revenge. Probably not the right one for me just now. I take the second book. I am gripped from the first page. For the first time in a year, I read and listen to the silence. Our previous home was on a busy road, and part of the attraction of Sturgeon Hall was the long driveway.

It's suddenly perfect. What had been my prison had a glint of light shining through. My prison is in my own mind. With a bit of time, I can do this. I can get over it. I am sure of it. A bit of peace and quiet. I hear an owl call and, for the first time in ages, look forward to tomorrow.

CHAPTER SEVEN

I blink into the morning sunlight as it streams through the window. The book is on my pillow, and I feel warm and calm as I remember my resolve. I pull the quilt around me and promise myself just five more minutes.

I can hear Ben and Angel laughing in the room next door and Angel walking along the landing to the bathroom. If they are unsettled by all the changes in the past year, they don't show it. Everyone says kids are resilient, but I sometimes wonder if they just don't tell me how they are feeling. Every question about how they went on at Daniel's is answered by a "fine". I worry about them, and this has been a big part of why I have done the things I now regret.

But I can hear them now, chirpy and giggling. It warms my heart. All as it should be. It's a school day and I will cook them something nice for breakfast. I pick my phone up to google "recipe for pancakes" and see there are nine missed calls. From Daniel.

I jump out of bed and pull on my dressing gown. The first call is at six o'clock, followed quickly by the others. I check my messages. Nothing. My fingers fumble to press his contact to ring him back. It rings and rings, then goes to answerphone. I end the call, then ring again. It must be urgent. His mum. She has heart trouble. It might be his mum. Or Jem? No. No. I mustn't get carried away.

I listen as it goes to voicemail again. This time I leave a message.

Dan, I don't know what's happened but please ring me back. I was asleep.

I cringe at the stupidity of my message. Of course I was asleep. He'll know that. I pull on some leggings and a T-shirt and tie my hair in a scruffy bun. I double check my phone, making sure the volume is up, and wait.

Ben and Angel are in the kitchen, and I open my laptop. I google "recipe for pancakes" and collate the ingredients. They are watching children's TV on the wall-mounted flat screen. I feel guilty about the amount of TV they watch and that is something else that is going to change. I pull out the electric whisk from under a bottom cupboard and everything spills onto the floor.

I feel the spike of stress. *No, Lauren. No. It's fine.* I tell myself it will take time to fix everything. Get everything in order. This is just the start. Positive. *Be positive.* I pick it all up and shove it back into the small space, extracting the whisk. I plug it in, and the whirring attracts the children's attention.

I finish and pour the liquid into a glass jug. Just like my mum did. She made pancakes, and they were the perfect days. The days I always remember. The days I want to make with my children. I collect everything I need. The oil. Sugar, lemon, maple syrup. I cut some strawberries and banana and put them in a bowl in the centre of the breakfast bar.

I am just lifting a heavy cast iron frying pan down from the brass hanger when I hear it. Shouting. Outside.

'Lauren, come outside. Now. Lauren.'

I know it's Daniel, but I rush to the lounge to confirm. He is looking up at my bedroom. I open the window.

'I'm making breakfast for our children. What do you want? Why were you ringing me?'

He looks dishevelled. He hasn't shaved and his longer-than-usual hair is product free and unevenly curly. His eyes are bloodshot, and I can tell he hasn't slept much. He moves towards the window.

'Where is she?' When I cower back, he screams at me. 'Where the fuck is she?'

I stare at him for a long moment. 'Dan, the kids. Don't do this. Look. Come inside.'

He fumes at me but walks around the side to the back door. I run to the kitchen.

'You two, go and watch TV.'

Angel whines. 'But the pancakes. I want pancakes.'

Ben gathers his homework and goes through to the lounge.

'I'll make them before you go to school.' I pour her some Coco Pops and splash milk on them. I hurry her through to the lounge and shut the door. Then I unlock the back door. Daniel bursts in.

'I knew it the other day. I knew it. This is down to you, you crazy cow. What have you done with her?'

I can't breathe. I feel like I am going to collapse and back up to lean on a kitchen stool. 'Hang on, what's anything got to do with me? What's happened?'

He's screaming in my face. So close that I can feel tiny drops of saliva on my cheek. His breath smells and the musky overnight odour I know so well tells me he hasn't showered.

'Her car. They found it on a bridge. On a bridge. Over the brook near Lees Valley. The door's open and her driving shoes are still in it.'

I hold my hands up. 'Look, back up and calm down. When did this happen?'

'Overnight. The car's been there ages but only just reported. Soaking wet inside.'

He starts to cry. Deep, childlike sobs. I walk over to the worktop and flick the kettle on. I get two mugs and make hot, sweet tea. I hand him some kitchen roll. And the tea. He takes it.

'What sort of bridge? What kind of bridge? You don't think...?' I panic inside. *Did I drive her to this? Did I?*

He shakes his head. 'No. Not that kind. There is water at the bottom, but it's a disused canal. Shallow and still. If she had... jumped...' His voice breaks as he says it. 'If she had jumped, she'd still be there. But she isn't. The police have searched. They were there all night. Then early this morning they told me. No sign of her.'

'But she sent me the message. On Monday afternoon. It was late on Monday night when I saw it. I was...' I flashback to Tim and him holding me tight and kissing me. 'I was busy.' The crease appears in his forehead.

He ignores what I say and rambles on. 'I took the kids over to Mum's on Monday. She knew it was inset day and she wanted to see them. We were there most of the morning, then I brought them straight here. When I got back from Mum's she was gone. The note was there.' He talks into the ether. 'To be honest, I was a bit surprised. It's out of character. She didn't say anything and I've no idea who this friend is. But I've no reason not to trust her.' He shakes himself out of it. 'I've no fucking idea why I'm telling you this. I swear if you have anything to do with it...'

I shake my head. I need to stay calm. 'Nothing whatsoever to do with me.'

He grabs my phone. It's locked, and he throws it across the

worktop. 'Forward that message to me. I'm showing it to the police.'

I stare at him. 'Dan, I already phoned it in. I was concerned. Does that sound like someone who has harmed someone else? Does it?'

He doesn't answer. I expect he's recounting all the peering through his windows and the silent phone calls. The drive-bys and the snarky comments. The turning up to 'speak to the children' in his shared custody time. The staring Jem out and the refusals to go to mediation with them. Just like I am thinking how he betrayed me with her.

'And what did they say?'

I snort. 'They said they weren't social services, and she'd probably got drunk at a mate's.' I paraphrase and don't add that Ms Goody Two Shoes didn't do that sort of thing, did she? It's not the time. 'But I guess they will have another look at it now.' I pause. I've seen this before. My dad used to talk about Reginald Perrin syndrome. And then there was that guy from that TV programme. The one who faked his death in a canoe. Abandoned everything and disappeared. 'You don't think she's done one, do you?'

He wipes his face. 'You'd love that, wouldn't you?'

I shake my head. 'No, I wouldn't. But it's a possibility.'

'No, it isn't. We're close. She would have told me if she wasn't happy. And if she was just leaving, she would have taken that bloody dog.'

I raise my eyebrows. He was right. She loves Pepe. She buys clothes for him and dresses him up. Angel told me she feeds him scraps under the table and 'Daddy doesn't like it'. I know he wouldn't have put up with it if I did it. That he did, and the state of him now spells out the depth of his feelings for her. I feel panic. But this really isn't the time for this. I focus. Where is she?

'Mmm. Can you think of anything that anyone would want from her?'

He pauses. He's weighing up whether to tell me something. He scrutinises my face. 'Her parents are loaded. Her dad invented some kind of coating and it's gone international.'

Everything falls into place. Rich parents. Beautiful. Good in bed. Pliable. That's who I was when he first met me. Fast forward to when Mum died, and you could almost cut the rage in the room when he found out she hadn't left anything to me. He didn't say anything because Dad inherited the lot. All her legacy from the mill her father owned. She'd given us the deposit for Sturgeon Hall and some of the money to renovate it. She'd also given us the deposit for our first home, a large Victorian terrace.

But when Dad married Chrissy, Daniel hit the roof. He shook me and asked me if I realised that our kids had missed out and her scruffy offspring would get everything. I tried to explain that our house was their legacy. That Mum had a living will; she had told me more than once that the money was better spent than in the bank. But he wouldn't listen. It was the only time I was ever scared of him. A year later, he was chasing an heiress.

It all made sense. Some people will do anything for money. I'd deluded myself that Daniel wasn't one of them, but clearly, I was wrong. I nod at him now, loaded with this new knowledge about the man I thought I knew everything about.

'Oh. Right.'

He sniffs. 'Yeah, I told the police. They'll follow that up, too.' I nod. He continues, 'They're going to try to find out her movements that day. I have to give a statement later on. Will you be available?'

I frown. 'I'm working. But why will they need me? I haven't seen her. I wasn't there.'

He looks at his shoes. 'But I mentioned the message. And that you'd been round.'

I nod and sigh. 'Okay. Okay. Tell them to ring me. I'm not waiting in.'

He starts to panic again. 'You're not taking this seriously. She's missing. Missing, Lauren. Not just popped to the shop.'

'Or her friend's,' I snipe back and instantly regret it. But he needs to know how things are. 'Look, Dan, this is your mess. You traded me for her. You've ignored me since then, but now you want me to sit around here because you said so. No. If they want to speak to me, I'm available. Tell them to ring me.'

My insides shake and I wipe the sweat from my forehead. The pancake mix is congealed and has separated in the glass jug. I feel sick to my stomach looking at it. I touch his arm, but he pulls away. So I end the conversation.

'I hope she is okay, Dan. I really do. But it's nothing to do with me. Nothing at all.'

CHAPTER EIGHT

He's gone. As he leaves, the shock drains through me and changes into sorrow as the reality hits me. Oh my God. I know exactly the place her car was found. On the edge of a country park. I read a pollution story about a chemical spill near there a couple of years ago. That place is a patch of sprawling forest in the middle of an urban area. It stretches miles. A river runs through it and there are the remnants of a factory there with steep walls and plenty of places to make a mistake and fall.

But it wasn't dark when she left. It was daytime. Maybe she broke down? Or her car was stolen? Maybe she *is* at her friend's, who picked her up. They just didn't know which friend. Daniel didn't seem to know a lot about it. There are a million potential explanations, but none of them make sense. I have so many questions but no one to answer them. But I will leave it to the police to do their job – this is none of my business.

It's school time. I open the lounge door and the kids are oblivious to what happened. I'm surprised they didn't hear Daniel's shouting, then crying. I do feel sorry for him, but we need to carry on as normal until we know what has happened. I don't know why, but I still feel like this is some kind of trick. An elaborate way to leave. Or to get at me.

Angel is humming to herself and Ben is sorting through his homework. I check myself. How self-centred of me. They have spent half of the last year with her and, even if I protect them, this will have wide-reaching effects. I can't keep it away from them forever.

I retrace my conversation with Daniel. The police are involved, so it's only a matter of time until the press and media start to report it. I don't let the children watch the news, but other children might. Even if I kept them away from every source of information, I can't keep them away from school. Or from Daniel. I know better than anyone that once the news is out, there will be regular updates until the story fades. Or is resolved. A chill goes through me.

Whether I like Jem or not, she is part of our children's lives. She has looked after them, cooked for them and sat with them. Even laughed with them. Her disappearance will disturb them. Upset them. And if – I don't even want to think about anything worse – they will be devastated. Explaining where Granny had gone was heart-breaking. But this.

I feel the tears come. Thick and fast. She is so young. This only underlines how much I don't know about her and Daniel. How much I have assumed. Maybe she was really unhappy, and she really has done something to herself. I know that area. She might not have jumped. She could have wandered around there and fell. Or taken an overdose. Or...

I wipe my eyes. I can't let them see me upset. I must be strong. For them. I have seen them look at each other when I have been anxious and irate months ago. They are close, and I wonder what they have made of me over the past year. I hope they have understood. I wish I had been more like my mum. She was serene and calm. I only saw her cry a few times, and those were times when it was entirely appropriate for tears. When Gran died, at her funeral. And when she found Bobby, our ginger cat, curled up very still behind the sofa. No. She wasn't like me, suspicious and worried. But is it any wonder?

I bat away the *you've been through a lot* that buzzes around my head and presses down on my soul. I should be able to cope. I should be able to walk away from the marriage I had the highest expectation of unscathed. I shouldn't have done any of the things that now loom large in front of me.

Ben switches off the TV, and they get their bags. By the time they are in the kitchen, my tears are wiped and I am smiling. Angel looks at me mournfully.

'No pancakes, then?'

I shake my head. 'Tonight. I'll pop the mix in the fridge, and I promise. Tonight. With ice cream.'

She looks satisfied as I push the glass jug into the fridge. I am not sure I can drive. I am shaky and vague with shock, but I have to. I must carry on as normal. Once the kids are safely in school, I can think this through properly.

Half an hour later, I am heading home. I can only hope they don't hear about this from someone else. I call Lisa as I drive. She answers in one ring.

'You heard then?'

She sighs. 'I did. But as far as I can see, they are treating it as MisPer. She wasn't reported missing at the time, but I expect Dan has now.'

I catch my reflection in the rear-view mirror. My eyes are bloodshot red. I need to work.

'He's been round to mine. Shouting at me. Asking me what I've done with her.'

Lisa tuts. 'Right. The message.'

'I rang it in. Yesterday. To Dave Pilcher. I still had a funny feeling about it.' I turn into my driveway and park up. I switch from in car to mobile. 'Bloody hell. I hope she's okay. Dan reckons her parents are loaded.'

Lisa perks up. 'Right. Gets you off the hook, then.'

I am shocked. Off the hook? Off the bloody hook?

'What does that mean? You don't think I...'

She laughs. 'Ooh touchy. Of course I don't. But I'm not the team who will be looking for her. Especially if Dan and her folks are pushing. You have to admit you've pulled some crazy shit.'

Crazier than you know. I can't even think about that now, though.

'No worse than other people. Remember that woman who burned her ex-husband's clothes in the middle of the M60? Or the one that dumped all the white goods in her ex's girlfriend's front garden? I might have been a bit upset, but this is nothing to do with me.'

She sniggers. 'Yeah. Or the one who sold all his stuff for a quid on eBay?'

'Yeah. At least I'm not the only one.' I rationalise my behaviour to myself. I know full well I'm not the only woman who has pulled this kind of shit, but that is no excuse. I have a horrible feeling of doom. 'God. I hope she's okay.'

Lisa sighs again. 'Me too. For everything we've said over the past year, I hope no harm comes to her.'

There is a long moment of silence and I choke up. I'm in the kitchen now and this morning floods back now I am alone.

'Look, Lisa, I'm going to go. I need to think about this. I've got to go to work as well. But if you hear anything, let me know.'

We end the call. Doom sets in. Lisa is completely right. I have done some crazy things. As well as the main events, there have been smaller indiscretions. Small acts of madness that, when you add them all together, they look bad. But I was in a lot of pain.

The worst one was the decision I took to break into The Rosarium. I was convinced that they were going to keep the children. Freeze me out. Underlying that was my suspicion that they were calling her mummy. I was devastated. I asked Daniel to go to the family courts and sort out a legal separation. Family arrangements. He said he wanted to do it out of court.

I panicked. I was so sure that he was stalling so they could move the children in with them. He had told me he wanted them to stay four nights one week and three nights the next. Their main home would be with me still. So I could claim benefits. I knew this was exactly what would be awarded if we went to the family court.

I agreed. He was living in a small rented flat with no space for a nine-year-old Angel and an eleven-year-old Ben. I was happy with them going one weekend night. Then they bought the house almost immediately. They had it renovated quickly. I would drive past and see building materials stacked in the garden. Her car, a vintage silver convertible Daniel had no doubt written off as a business expense, was in the drive.

Stopping outside got to be a bit of a morning habit, and one day I saw beds being delivered. A double and three singles. My mind burned with possibilities, scorched with the image of Ben and Angel in that house, with her.

They had them stay over for half the week before the house was finished. I tried to object, but Daniel just said they were helping to decorate their own bedrooms. I was mad with envy. Mad. Blinded. I had to know what was going on. With my children. I had rights. She didn't. She wasn't their mother.

I phoned an ex-colleague of mine and Lisa's who knew people in the hacking business. He was the king of exposing all dodgy dealings and could find anything out. I steered clear of anything unethical at work. That wasn't my MO. But this was different. Personal. I asked him for four high-performance cameras. Tiny. Discreet. Wifi. Motion sensor. Long battery life, with a backup. I gave him some guff about protecting my property with surveillance. It was expensive. It wiped me out. But I had to know.

Even now my heart is in my mouth when I think about what I did. I waited until the next time the children stayed over. I'd watch them drive the kids to school together, her taking them to the school gate and waving to them. That's when I started to think she was just a replacement. Just stepped right into my shoes. A younger, thinner model. Like one of Daniel's luxury cars. It destroyed me. Because where did that leave me?

I watched them drive away. I'd brought some tape and some scissors. And some rubber evidence gloves. I'd parked up the road from The Rosarium. It wasn't posh. Oh no. It's in the middle of an urban area. But it is a lovely property. They had decided to retain all the original features. More expensive, but, it turned out, easier for me to get in. I simply smashed a small pane of glass in a side window with the scissor handle, just big enough to get my hand through. It cracked in one piece and I flicked up the brass latch. It was quite firm but moved easily. I heaved myself up and climbed through.

The house was only partially finished. I managed to place a tiny camera on top of a finished cupboard, its eye just peeping through the space between the glo-white high cabinets. I padded on their new carpets into the lounge. This was finished. It was beautiful, I had to concede. Not to my taste, but I have never gone for pink. I placed a camera on a shelf behind the TV. It already held Daniel's books. A collection that he has never read and keeps only to impress. I noted they were joined by some of her preferences. Jackie Collins. Jilly Cooper. My stomach lurched at the hint of sex with my husband.

I climbed the slightly bending staircase and hesitated on the landing. I didn't want to spy on my children. No. But I did want to see they were okay. I taped a camera under the black steel arm of a faux-flickering gas lamp. I stood back to make sure it wouldn't be spotted. No red lights on this kit. I tapped on the app on my phone, and I appeared on the screen, looking at my phone.

Next was their room. I stood outside the door and suddenly my reasoning faltered. Why their room? What would I gain by seeing them...? Something inside me froze and right there, in the heat of the moment, I doubted myself. What the hell was I doing? Yet I carried on. I hurried into the unfinished room and the first thing I saw, in the bare plaster was a heart scraped into the wall and *Jem + Dan forever* scratched underneath. Forever.

It was this kind of thing that sent me into the little space between the end of our relationship and me functioning on my own. Like a void where all reasoning is abandoned and everything is up for grabs. It pulled me two steps back from the forward pace I was making towards moving on. Right in that moment I felt it, like I have felt it less and less since then – a fleeting yet irresistible urge to get even regardless of the consequences. I stood on tiptoe, balanced the remaining camera on top of the wardrobe facing their bed. Like the kitchen cupboard, the join just accommodated the camera eye.

This time I didn't appraise my work or test the tech. I just ran. Through the house and into the kitchen. They had left a key in the back door. I hurried back and locked the window, clicking the catch into place. Then I left and locked the door behind me, pushing the key into my pocket. Once outside, I pushed the broken piece of glass back into the window and taped over it with the same tape I used to secure the cameras.

My heart thumped as I hurried back to my car, and once safely inside, I removed the gloves. Then I tested the phone. The kitchen camera was a little high, but the others were perfect, their fisheye lenses capturing a wide panorama. My contact had assured me that the battery life was exceptionally long because they had motion sensors and no visible lights. The only thing that would drain it was connecting it to view.

There was no real need to go back after that. No need to sit in the back garden watching them through the window. I could watch them anytime I wanted to, which, at first, was often. I went back a few times. Mostly when I was *really* hurting. Like the first time I saw Angel run up to her and hug her. Or the time she drove Ben to football practice – when I didn't even know it was on – and stood and watched him. I went back, and I cut the heads off all her roses. I wanted her to hurt the way I hurt. It was just the once, and it didn't feel good. But when I watched her face crumple the next morning as she looked out of her kitchen window, it reminded me of the nights I'd lain crying because of what she had done to me.

I completely see now that it all got out of hand. I gathered the roses up and pressed them between the pages of my books. I'm not the only person who has done these things; I know it goes on. If I could turn back time I would, but I can't. And most of it is old news; tiny events that came and went. But I have a horrible feeling that the one remaining thing – and the worst – is going to come back to haunt me. It feels treacherous to think about myself at a time like this when Jem could be in danger, but I have to get those cameras back before this goes any further. I have to.

CHAPTER NINE

I need to go to work. It is starting to feel secondary to everything else now, but I remind myself of my new plan to forge forward. On the way there I try to think of work, but the spectre of Jem's disappearance and how upset Daniel was replays in my mind.

I still can't understand why she would message me. She must have lots of contacts in her phone. And why not Daniel? I try to remember if there was a single moment he seemed insincere. But there wasn't. It is true that he could sell sand in a desert, but I could usually tell when he was lying.

Except I couldn't, could I? He lied about her for months. He'd been seeing her for six months before I caught them. And, it came to light, lots of people knew about it. All his work colleagues. He'd even taken her to the nightclub we used to go to. I'd seen it happen with lots of guys. They'd married and had kids and had a really lovely home life.

But that was never enough. Their wives were there to look after them and their offspring. Their girlfriends were there for drinking and sex. Some of the wives knew about it and tolerated it for the lifestyle – the richer the husband, the more tolerant.

But none of them were happy about it. They either got a bloke of their own, or the ones who objected caused a drama followed by divorce.

Linda and Stuart Donnelly were close friends of ours at the start of our relationship. They were inseparable. Linda would tell me all the lovely things Stuart did. Diamonds on birthdays. Weekly flowers. Each trip he went on resulted in a shining description of the extravagant gift he had returned with. I wasn't jealous, because my gifts were my children. Linda told me they were waiting. Waiting and waiting and waiting. Until, it turned out, he had time to spare from a parallel relationship he was running.

The details of it seeped out through Linda's pores as she sat, ashen-faced, in my lounge, amid toys and baby bottles. He had been living half the week with another woman. Like an overgrown toddler, these women had shared custody of this man in the same proportions my children now go to Daniel's. Each thought he was on a business trip. He was surviving on an inheritance his father had left him. Linda didn't even know Stuart's father had died.

Worse, he had two children with the other woman. Linda went over to her house and demanded to see their marriage certificate. Once she had established that she was married to him first, she reported him to the police for bigamy. She changed the locks on all the doors and emptied their joint bank account. She called his boss and told him what he had done. Then she gave up her job and went on a round-the-world cruise. I watched, open-mouthed, as she destroyed their life shred by shred.

I wondered how she could live like that, with the knowledge that the consequences would be much further reaching than the divorce courts. But now I know. Now I know the reckless feeling that takes over. The sudden disregard for houses and possessions. The stripping down to the bare core of the marriage and throwing the debris in a skip, and setting fire to it. Linda and I weren't the only ones. But I didn't do it so publicly. I wasn't as brave as some. I did it in secret. Creeping around and hiding. But all secrets come out in the end, don't they?

Some of the things those women scorned did were outrageous. Cars set on fire. Cat fights with girlfriends in nightclubs. Having them followed. But there were just as many happy marriages. Men whose whole lives revolved around their family and work was just an inconvenience. Wives and girlfriends who knew they could trust their partners with their lives.

I thought me and Daniel were for keeps. I thought he was one of the guys who was committed to his family. But I was wrong. As far as I know, Jem was the first, which in many ways hurts more, because it makes her special. In my more rational moments, which are definitely on the increase, I think that I just wasn't the right one for him, but she is. He should have met her first. I wonder if he has said that to her.

I am punishing myself for nothing. He is devastated right now, and I want to help him, but I can't. He is out of my reach. He'll have to get that help elsewhere. And meanwhile, I need to make a living.

I sit down in my office and set my smart watch for ninety minutes. A moment later the receptionist buzzes through.

'Your client just phoned to say she can't make it.'

I sigh. 'Okay. Thank you. Did she pay in advance?' I feel awkward asking but I need every penny I can get.

'Oh yes. Yes, she did. She paid up front for four sessions. She said she had a cold.'

She leaves and I am alone with time to kill. I check my phone. No reply from Tim. I text him again.

Hey lover boy! How's things? Coming round tomorrow night or what? 😊

I dither but eventually press send. Everyone expects automatic responses these days. I stare at my phone for a while and then I lay it face down on the desk and open my laptop. I want to move on to the next stage of this relationship but I think it might take some effort. We seem to have fallen into a pattern of only seeing each other when it's convenient. I panic for a moment and think that the honeymoon period is over, then realise it hasn't even begun in earnest.

Tim is so organised. He's one of those people who is always on time. If we are going anywhere, he has a route planned and everything booked in advance. I have his undivided attention at all times. He switches his phone off and isn't constantly checking it. He makes sure we have the best tables in the best restaurants. But none of it is spontaneous.

Our first date, the one after the day we met in the café, was at a little Italian. He wasn't nervous, he was very sweet. Very attentive. I was in pieces. I had never in my wildest dreams imagined myself dating again. Even though I was very early, I'd waited around the corner until Tim arrived and went inside. I couldn't have stood the embarrassment of sitting there alone and him not turning up. But he did.

My temporary desperation at the end of my marriage was easing by then, but Tim's kindness gave me the confidence boost I needed to try to start again. I was excited. I wanted to shout from the rooftops that Daniel might have run off with a younger version of me, but someone was attracted to me and someone was interested in me. Someone cared. Someone good-looking with a decent job and great taste in food.

I remember posing for a selfie in the restaurant. Tim blinked at me and was suddenly very serious.

'Oh, can you not. Only I'm not really...' I'd positioned him in the background. He leaned sideways out of shot. 'I don't like having my photo taken. I don't like all that online stuff.'

I don't know why but my heart sunk. I'd made an assumption that everyone liked showing off their new love on social media. Even us older daters. I mean, I am thirty-six years old and Tim is forty. I'd felt childish and attention-seeking. Cheap and nasty. He rushed to my defence.

'Oh no, I didn't mean... it's me, not you.'

We'd both collapsed into laughter. The cliched phrase had eased the mood and I pushed my phone back into my handbag. I made a promise to myself to extend the no phones when the kids are around to no phones when we are together. It made sense. And as the weeks and months went by, it became increasingly obvious that when we were together, we only needed each other.

It was true that when we were apart, I reverted to my former Jem-hating self. But Tim was the antithesis to that. So it made sense now that I see more of him. Replacing the bad with the good.

The only way we communicate is by phone or text. I can't ring him at work, except at lunchtimes and he rings me on the evenings we aren't together. He doesn't ring me so much when I have the kids. There was only once in the past four months that he hadn't been around when the kids were at Daniel's. He apologised profusely for it, saying he had to go on a stag night. He told me it was in Amsterdam, then later he told me that had been moved to Bradford.

I'd told him that seemed a bit extreme and he'd seemed distracted.

'I don't want to be away from you. I don't really want to go. But it's my mate and...'

I laughed. 'It's okay, I'll be able to see you on the pictures.'

It was his mate, Pete, who was getting married. I'd waited and waited for the invite to go with him to the wedding. It hadn't materialised and it was in two weeks. I knew Pete was on Instagram – he was a workmate and somehow the algorithm had sent Pete's profile my way, probably because I had looked at the company website so often to see Tim's only internet picture. I'd scanned Pete's profile for Tim, but he wasn't there. He really wasn't anywhere.

'There won't be pictures. What happens in Bradford stays in Bradford.'

I didn't like the sound of that and it must have shown. Tim tensed. I couldn't help it. I had to say it. 'What about the wedding? Surely there will be wedding photos?'

He shook his head and looked hurt. 'Yes, there will. In Barbados. They're getting married on a beach in Barbados. That's why Amsterdam's off.' He sat in front of me and took my hands. 'Oh my God. You think I'm hiding something from you.'

It was in that moment I knew this was different. Daniel and I had been together a long time, but it was always a game. Always a stand-off. Daniel would never, ever have sat close to me and seen into my world. He had watched me give birth twice, but the empathy was missing. If I did complain, he would walk away. Brush it off. Even laugh. But never witness my concern, like Tim did that night.

He'd moved really close. Close enough that I could feel his breath on my face. I'd tingled and smiled. He smiled too.

'I promise you I will never lie to you. I have things to do, but they are just things. This is what is important, me and you. This stag night has been planned since before I met you, or I would never have agreed to go.' He touched my cheek. 'You have to understand, I am a very private person. I like to keep myself to myself. There's nothing to worry about. Nothing at all.'

That's when I told him about Jem. I'd already told him

about Daniel and that he had cheated. Glossed over the detail to avoid saying he chose someone else over me. Made it seem like Daniel had a fling and I threw him out. But that night I told him what really happened. That Jem had moved into their new home. That I didn't like her. I played it down but I told him the facts. He'd nodded.

'But you're okay now? She hasn't hurt you, has she?'

I wanted to tell him she had hurt me, but not physically. She had hurt me deep. But I didn't.

'No. No. It's not like that. Anyway, it's over now. Settled down.' I lied. Since then, he'd seen me become upset and asked me why. I'd shaken my head and he'd nodded. He understood, I think.

The weekend of the stag party passed with me staying home in my huge, cold house and him calling me the moment he got in. I'd checked Pete's Instagram but, as predicted, no party pictures appeared. After that, we'd fallen into a sweet routine of romantic rendezvous. But I will change that. I will inject some fun. I tap my fingers on the table and wait for a reply. When none comes, I open my case notes and begin to work. I will wait. Because he's worth waiting for.

My smart watch buzzes ninety minutes later and I close the notes. It feels good. I made progress. I know that giving my day some shape will stop me being distracted by Daniel and Jem. I'm getting there, but right now I need to know what has happened. If the news has broken yet. If it will at all.

Jem. I google 'abandoned car' and both her and Daniel's name. Nothing. I think about what Lisa said. I know from my own experience that unless there is evidence that she has been harmed, this will be a missing person case. People walk away all the time and the police don't have time to investigate every single one of them. She left a note saying she was going away. But she messaged me. It doesn't make sense.

I get my car and drive home. It's still hours until I need to pick the kids up. As I turn into the drive, I see a red Ford Focus parked outside my house. As I get nearer, I see a woman with red hair sitting in the driver's seat talking on her phone. In the passenger seat, a man is reading some papers.

I pull up beside them and get out. The woman winds her window down.

'Lauren Wade?'

I nod. 'Yes. That's me.'

She pulls in her lips. 'DS Bradley. And this is DC Sharples. Shall we talk inside?'

CHAPTER TEN

My heart is thumping in my chest even though I know I haven't done anything. Jem is nothing to do with me. I lead them around the side of the house and unlock the kitchen door. They follow me into the kitchen. It's only when strangers come in here and look at the huge stone worktops and breakfast bar, I realise how fabulous it is.

DS Bradley stands by the breakfast bar and DC Sharples' eyes scan the room. He is tall and lithe with a haircut that doesn't belong in the police force. She is very pale, her skin almost translucent, and she has long auburn hair that has a curl. I muse she looks Elizabethan until she stares at me. Her eyes are dark blue and pierce me.

'Sorry to turn up unannounced. We're investigating the disappearance of Jemima Carter. As you probably know, your ex-husband...' she checks her notebook, '...Daniel Wade has reported her missing. After her car was found abandoned. He told us she sent you a message?'

I nearly laugh. Jemima? Bloody hell. I bet she hates that. I compose myself. *This is serious, Lauren.*

'Yes. I rang it in. To Dave Pilcher.'

She writes it down and DC Sharples touches the breakfast bar, feeling the surface. DS Bradley continues. 'May I see the message, please?'

I fumble for my phone. Thank God I deactivated the camera app. I press Jem's name in my contacts and her smiling face appears. I suddenly feel tearful. What if something bad has happened? I realise I haven't had anything to eat, and I catch hold of the worktop. DS Bradley lunges forward to catch me.

'Are you okay?'

'Yes, yes.' I hand her the phone. 'It's just so upsetting. I'm a bit shaken to be honest.'

She nods and looks at the message. She makes a note of the date and times. Then she scrolls down to see previous messages.

'So, you weren't close then? Only it doesn't look like you've been keeping in touch.'

I breathe deeply. 'Look. There was no love lost between me and Jem. If we needed to say anything to each other, it would be when the kids were dropped off.'

She glances at the fridge. Photos of Angel and Ben. Me and Daniel. Drawings.

'So they live with you, the children?'

I nod. 'Half the time. Shared parenting.'

'Okay. And where were they when Jemima disappeared?'

'When did she disappear? Only Daniel showed me a note saying she was going to a mate's.'

'So, you saw Daniel after she'd gone? To collect the children?'

I am flustered. 'No. No, he brought them back Monday. They were with him. Inset day. I went round Tuesday morning. I was worried about the message. But he showed me the note and...'

'You weren't worried? So why did you call Dave?' She stares at me and taps her black biro on her teeth. I sigh heavily.

'I was still worried. I just couldn't see why she would have messaged me.'

She nods and looks around the kitchen. 'This place is lovely. Was this the family home before...?'

'Yes. Me and Daniel bought it for next to nothing and started to do it up. It's about a third finished. I probably won't be able to stay here, which is a shame.'

'It is a shame, but renovations are expensive. I've been doing up a cottage in Saddleworth. Should have taken six months. We're on year three now.' She pauses. She leans back onto a kitchen stool, hands on thighs. 'So, what do you think's happened? To Jemima?'

I rally. 'I have no idea. But this doesn't make sense. Much as I don't like her...' It slips out, and I try to catch it in a heartbeat but don't manage to. 'Much as I think she shouldn't have broken my family up, I don't wish her any harm. I just can't see why she would leave Daniel. And the alternative doesn't bear thinking about.'

I shrug. I'm only just realising that something bad could have happened to her. Until now I've thought it was drama. A way to get attention. I'm shocked that I, a considerate person, could actually think that when it could be so much worse. But I must focus.

'Daniel told me her family are loaded. He thought it might have something to do with that.'

She raises her eyebrows. 'When did he tell you that?'

'This morning. He was round here early, upset.'

'To pick the children up?'

I feel my hackles rise. What is she saying here?

'No. He was upset.'

She taps her pen again, this time on the workshop. It echoes into the high ceiling.

'You see a lot of each other then?'

I remain calm. I don't know what she is getting at, but I know from my media training at the station when I had to sit in on missing person appeals to stay on message.

'Not usually. Just about the children. But I expect he was upset.'

'Yes, he was upset. Wasn't he, Mike?'

DC Sharples nods. 'Yeah. Devastated, in fact. He mentioned that you and Jemima had some... run-ins. Said you two hated each other. That you'd screamed her out at some party and threatened her.' He watches my reactions, then adds, 'You have to understand that we need to look into everything. So we can rule things out.'

I shake my head. Daniel. Of course he told them that. And everything else. I can feel tears rising. How could he say that about me? After he knew what he put me through.

It was true. Not long after the split, I'd gone out with Lisa. In fact, it was my first night of freedom. The kids were at Daniel's and there was no reason that I couldn't go to the swanky party she had invited me to. She was surprised when I agreed, and even more surprised when she came to pick me up.

I'd dropped ten pounds and had my hair cut. Even I admitted I could still cut it and, for the first time in months, I felt confident. We got a cab into the city and in no time, I was sipping cocktails on a rooftop bar. The party was held by mutual friends, but I assumed that, as Daniel was looking after the children, he wouldn't be there.

I was wrong. I spotted her first. In a black backless dress, laughing with Janet Brown, someone I'd known for years. It hadn't registered until that moment that she hadn't just stepped into my place with Daniel, but into my social life. Dinner, barbeques. All the things me and Daniel used to do. She was doing it now.

The guy I'd been talking to followed my gaze. 'She looks like a young Claudia Schiffer, doesn't she?'

I caught a reflection of myself in the plate-glass windows that led to the bar. The same, but different. Two children and baby belly different. It shocked me. I was an older version of Jem. He had literally traded me in for a new model. Of course, the three boozy cocktails that I wasn't used to hadn't helped my reasoning.

I turned my back, but I was aware of her now. Simpering with Janet. Then I saw him, Daniel. His hand on her lower back. The way he looked at her. I'd told myself over and over again that I would, at some point, bump into them, but I wasn't ready. I looked around for Lisa, but she was already heading over.

'Do you want to go? Or we can go inside...'

I nodded. I didn't want to let her down. 'Let's go inside. Round the bar.' She looked concerned, but I waved it all away. 'Inevitable. It will be fine.'

But it wasn't fine. As we headed to the doors, they started to dance on the makeshift dance floor. So close, his lips on her ear. I literally could have murdered her then and there. Hate was not a strong enough word for how I felt. I skirted around them, but my coat brushed her, and she cowered into Daniel as if I'd struck her, both of them turning. I held it down, taming my temper.

'Oh. Hi. I'm just...'

She was rubbing her arm. Daniel was looking at me, eyebrows raised.

'Why did you have to do that? Can't you control yourself?' He said it very quietly.

'I didn't do anything. My coat just brushed her. Anyway, why are you here? Where are our children?' I realised I was shouting. The room was quiet. Daniel hugged her to him.

'They're at my mum's. They wanted to see their grandmother.'

I knew in that moment that it all sounded normal outside my rage. I was ready to walk away, but she spoke. Not to me, oh no. To him. A simpering whine.

'She dug me in the arm. Look.'

She showed him, and everyone else, her arm, which she had rubbed red. I blew.

'I didn't dig her. I brushed her with my coat. But you all know she's a liar, anyway.'

She looked at the floor. Daniel blew out his cheeks.

'That's enough, Lauren. Go home.'

I laughed loudly. 'No. You don't get to tell me what to do anymore. I'll stay if I want to.' Out of the corner of my eye I saw a bouncer hurrying through the bar area. I moved closer to Jem. 'And you. You can fuck off. Away from me and away from my kids,' I screamed in her face. 'Fuck. Off.'

I felt a hand on my arm, and I spun round to shake myself free. But it was Lisa.

'Come on, love. Let's go. He's not worth it.'

I backed off and saw Jem flash a grin at the floor. She was loving this. And I'd fallen for it. Lisa was dragging me away, and I was shouting back at Jem.

'You won't get away with this, you cow. I'll hunt you down.'

I hear DS Bradley repeating this now. She is reading from her notebook.

'I'll hunt you down. Is that what you said?'

I shake my head. 'It was a stupid argument. I was very upset. We'd just split up. I really didn't mean it.' I look her in the eye. 'If you are asking me if I have done something to Jem, the answer is no. No, I haven't. Daniel asked me this morning. I can see why you think I have. And yes, I don't like her. Obviously.

But I have my children to think about. I'm over it now. I've got a job and a life.'

She stares at me for a long moment.

'You do understand we have to check, though? Can you think of anyone else who would want to harm Jem?'

'I'm the wrong person to ask. I barely know her. Ask Daniel.' I want to tell them to ask about his dodgy cash car deals and his dubious clientele, but I don't. Let them find out. I need to get them out of here before they ask for a tour of the house. 'But what I do know is it's nothing to do with me. And I have no idea why she asked me for help. As you can see, I reported it to you guys.'

'Much later.'

'Yes. I'd been out with a friend. The night before. We'd been for a... break. At a lovely hotel. You can ask them.'

She smiles. 'That won't be necessary at this point. We're just covering all bases. Ruling things out.'

I feel my face flush as I realise my two lives might merge. My exciting new relationship laid bare beside my two-kids-and-a-job.

'I am genuinely sorry if anything has happened to her...' I hear my voice break. 'You have to understand that I will need to tell my children. They are close to Jem. I feel very sorry this has happened.'

'And Daniel, of course.'

I frown. 'What about him?'

'Well, you still care about him, don't you?'

Her eyes are on the photo of us on the fridge. I look at it too.

'We were married for years. Of course I still care.'

DC Sharples makes for the door. DS Bradley stands.

'Right then. If you remember anything or she contacts you at all, get right back in touch. I'll get your number so we can call you if we need anything else.' She reads my number from my mobile phone, which I had completely forgotten she still had, and hands it back to me.

I open the door and follow them around the front of the house. They look through the lounge window and DS Bradley says something I can't quite hear to DC Sharples. I hug myself. I tell myself it's fine. Fine. They are just asking questions. Of course they are.

But I can't help thinking there is more to it.

CHAPTER ELEVEN

I spent the rest of the day picking the kids up and making food. I made a cheese pie and some home-made potato wedges, followed by pancakes and ice cream. Angel's face lit up, and I felt good that I had done what I said I was going to do. Yet in the background was a silent ticking. A metronome of utter doom. A building panic that none of this could ever turn out well.

When they went to bed, I turned my phone back on. Tim had replied to the message I sent.

I can come over tonight if you want.

I thought about it and then texted him back.

Now would be good 😊

I needed a hug. Twenty minutes later, he was pulling into the drive. I watched as he got out of his car and raced to the back door to open it before he knocked. I still didn't want the children to know. Tell Daniel. Even though I know I will have to if I take things further.

Tim stood in the kitchen hands in pockets, looking awkward. I smiled and moved towards him. He took a step backwards as his phone beeped a message. And another one.

'Oh. Mr Popular!' My voice was high-pitched and nervous. This was all wrong. I backed off. 'Look, shall we watch a film or something?'

His gaze moved from me to the lounge door.

'Are your children here?'

I nodded. 'Is it a problem?' He shook his head, but his expression told a different story. His phone pinged again. I snorted. 'Is there somewhere you need to be?'

His phone was usually off. I wondered if this was why. He perched on a high stool at the breakfast bar.

'I just... I just think we could keep things how they were. I like to know in advance what I'm doing.' He paused. His phone pinged. 'You know. Work and that.'

I'd never seen him so uncomfortable. He is usually in control of the situation. Up to speed. I change the subject.

'Yeah. I know. That's fine. Are we still on for dinner at yours?'

His expression softened. 'Yeah. Sure. It's just coming here in the week. It's difficult. I've got football and early starts.' He crossed the room and put his arms around me. 'Things are good between us. I don't want anything to come between us and what we have. Let's keep things the same for the time being?'

I nodded into his shoulder. I felt suddenly tearful. I wanted to tell him about the day I'd had. A problem shared and all that. But it didn't feel right. His phone kept pinging and I wondered if he was merely slotting me in. But wasn't that what I'd been doing too? Fitting him in between managing my divorce.

I pushed down my annoyance. He'd told me what he

wanted and nothing had changed. I held him tight. Over his shoulder I could see a long curly red hair that DS Bradley had shed earlier lying across my clean worktop. Had he heard about Jem? Was he holding me at arm's length?

I held him tightly, his warmth comforting me. He kissed me gently and held me away from him.

'I'll pick you up. I'll cook you a meal like you've never had before.' Then he said something strange. 'You don't have to worry about anything else.'

I froze. 'Like what?'

He shrugged and we were back at the beginning.

'I don't know. Whatever's worrying you.'

His eyes pierced into me and I felt exposed, as if he could see the corner of darkness in my heart. Then he was gone. I hurried to the front window just in time to see him get into his car, check his messages, answer one, then drive away.

This morning I feel foolish. I feel like a demanding girlfriend, eating into her boyfriend's football time for attention. Tim has no reason to lie.

I'll be dropping the kids off at school soon, then they will be with Daniel for the weekend. How will he cope? Will he be able to? I take my phone out to ring him, but then I remember DS Bradley's insinuation that I saw a lot of Daniel. Maybe I should steer clear for a while. Let things settle. He has his friends and his parents.

I recall DS Bradley's line of questioning about the party. And me threatening Jem. Daniel must have told them that. I know he's upset, but I am sure he knows what is really going on, even if he chooses to ignore it. Yes. Staying away is the best thing.

I round the kids up.

'Come on, you two. Let's have a hug before you go. I won't see you until Tuesday.'

They run at me. Bigger now, they still fly at me like they did as toddlers. We've always had a tactile relationship and their hugs are the best. Ben finally pulls back.

'Mum, is Dad okay?'

'Yes. Why, love?'

'I heard him shouting at you yesterday. He's been doing a lot of shouting lately.'

Angel flushes. 'Ben...'

I stay calm. 'Shouting? At who?'

They look at each other.

Ben looks at the floor and speaks. 'At Jemi. She was crying.'

I frown. 'What, in front of you?'

'Yeah. It was no big deal, really. She'd just burnt something.'

Angel looks earnest. 'She's not a very good cook. We get takeaways.'

Ben continues. 'She'd made a pie. But she was playing with us. She was chasing us in the garden, and it burnt. He called her a silly bitch.'

I am shocked. Ben is a quiet child and I have never heard him swear before. He looks embarrassed. My insides clench. I always have to clear up after him.

'Look, everyone argues sometimes. Even the closest couples. I'm sure they made up.'

I am sure, but I don't want the details. I hurry Angel into her coat and she speaks to me earnestly.

'Is that why she went to see her friend, Mummy, and left Pepe?'

I hug her. 'No, sweetheart. I don't think so. I don't really know. But let's see what happens.'

Ben grumps. 'But he was shouting at you. I don't like that, Mum. You haven't done anything wrong.'

I look at my laptop on the side. Its screen that was alive with my children walking over the landing with Jem. Me watching, crying my heart out.

'He's just a bit upset. I'm sure he will be fine.'

But I am on red alert. I'm not sure Daniel will be okay, and Ben is hesitating near the door. He doesn't want to go. Something was wrong before Jem left. Daniel is not a shouter.

We drive to school, and I wave them off. There are stares at the school gate. Some of the other mums must have heard about Jem. I wonder who else the police have spoken to. Shit. I style it out and soon I am back in my car, the kids safely in school. What a mess. I call Lisa.

'Hi. It's me. The police came round.'

She sighs. 'Who was it?'

'DS Bradley.'

She whistles. 'Bekah Bradley. Bloody hell. Posh 'n' Becks.'

'Posh 'n' Becks?'

She laughs loudly. 'Yeah. He's from some Cheshire hoity-toity place pretending to be a Manc. She's... well. Bekah. Very. Erm. Pointed.'

I snort. 'Yeah. She asked some weird questions.'

'Big guns. But like you said, loaded parents. Was she okay?'

I laugh. 'Well, apart from insinuating that time at the party was a direct lead up to the moment Jem disappeared, yes. Fine. Oh, and Dan told them I was a psycho bitch from hell. So yes. All fine.'

She laughs too, but we both know it isn't funny.

'They would have arrested you if they thought you had anything to do with it. Bloody hell. I wonder where she is?'

I sigh. 'You know, it didn't hit me until yesterday. What if she's...' I sob. It surprises me. 'The kids told me he'd been shouting at her. They asked if she'd left because of that.'

Silence. Lisa is never silent.

'Dan, shouting? Are you sure?'

'Yeah. He was round at mine yesterday morning too. Shouting and carrying on. I thought it was just because of Jem, but Ben said he'd shouted at her in front of them for burning a pie.'

We'd normally be joking about trouble in paradise and laughing, but it suddenly feels very serious. Lisa sounds worried.

'I've got a bad feeling about this. Are you okay?'

I glance at myself in the rear-view mirror. I don't look okay. I look tired and drawn. Am I okay?

'I'm not sure. And he's got Ben and Angel over the weekend, so I'm going to have plenty of time to imagine her dead in a ditch.' Silence again. My throat is tight, and my breath staggered. 'I just hope she's–'

Lisa interrupts. 'Look, she's probably broken down and gone off somewhere. You don't know where she was heading.'

'She left that note.'

'Yeah, but maybe she was just stalling for time. She left the car. Maybe she wanted a clean break? But he's not going to twig that, is he? Too busy looking in the mirror.'

I suddenly snap back into reality. I feel a stab of indignation that she is calling Daniel out. It takes me completely by surprise.

'He does care, though. He was crying when he came to see me.'

She sighs. 'Yes, yes. Okay. Maybe I'm wrong, but you have to admit he does love himself.'

I prickle more. I'm usually up for complaining about Daniel. But not today. Something feels wrong.

'Mmm. You should have seen him, though. He was very upset.'

She pauses. I can hear her breath. Then she says it. I've sensed it hanging in the air. With Lisa. With the school mums. Even the kids. She says what I guess I've been thinking too.

'Lauren, you don't think Dan's got anything to do with this, do you?'

Her tone is gentle. She's not name calling now, she is genuinely concerned. I return service.

'Well, you've known him as long as I have. What do you think?'

She pauses again and I know she is screwing her face up in indecision. I know Lisa well, too. She's always been indifferent about Daniel. She put up with his possessiveness, and him accusing me of an affair that time Lisa and I missed the last train home.

'I don't know. You were married to him.'

I roll back over our life together. He was never aggressive. Never. He was firm, but he never laid a finger on me. He never had to. I knew from the beginning that if I disagreed there was no bend in him. He would just go ahead and if I argued, he would shrug in a kind of 'I'm making the money to spend' way – even though back then I had a decent salary. It was how it was.

We argued occasionally, but he was never unkind. If anything, I was worse than him, shouting and swearing. He only raised his voice when it was very serious.

'Yeah. And I just can't see it. He barely raised an eyebrow most of the time. But he's shouting at her over a pie. And with the kids there.' We'd never argued in front of the kids. Never. 'Doesn't make sense.'

But inside I'm in turmoil. I want to shout at her that Daniel would never do anything like this. He'd told me he loved Jem, and I believed him. I don't and it weighs heavy in my chest; he told me he loved me. He married me and told me it was forever. Then he went off with her. Goodness knows how many others there had been. The thought sneaks up and ambushes me. If this is something to do with him and he did lie about loving her, then it might all have been a lie about me, too. I gasp. Something deep inside of me cracks open. Have I been living a lie? Have I? Lisa rallies.

'Well, if you can be sure of anything, it's Bekah Bradley. She does her job. She is pretty thorough, and she'll find out who's bloody done this.'

We end the call and I sit in my car outside school. I can't help but hope it's a kidnap plot. Someone after Jem's parents' money. Nothing to do with Daniel. Then I realise that I have just wished something bad on her instead of her safe. I cover my face with my hands. This is all too much. I don't know what Daniel will tell the kids. It's a complete mess.

I pick up my phone, tempted to open the camera app and see if they are okay. But that just drives my next fear. If Bekah Bradley is so thorough, so good at her job, then it's inevitable that the cameras will be found.

CHAPTER TWELVE

I'm halfway home when my phone rings. I miss the call and pull over. It's Daniel. I wait for a second to see if he leaves a voicemail. I pray to God that Jem has been found alive and well.

He doesn't leave a voicemail. Instead, he sends a Facebook message.

Ring me. I need to talk to you.

I message back.

What is it? I'm working.

Technically true, as I'm thinking about work. Thinking about going into the surgery and organising my client rota for next week. I can see the availability list ever-longer on my phone screen and other clients added all the time. I look at my bank account. It isn't good. He rings anyway. I answer immediately.

'What is it? Have they found her?'

He laughs. 'Like you bloody care. No, Lauren, they haven't found her.'

His emphasis is on *they* and I shiver. There's a scathing note in his voice.

'What then? What's so urgent?'

He is silent for a long moment.

'When I pick the kids up from after-school club, I'm taking them to their grandma's. We're staying there for the weekend. This is no place for them to be at the moment.'

I imagine police crawling all over The Rosarium. Their heavy boots on Jem's pink sofas and carpets. Hands up the delicate wallpaper and on the white and pink linen. Reaching up until they find the cameras.

'Oh. Is something going on at the house?'

He sighs. 'No. If you're asking if I'm a suspect, then I'm not. I just think it'll upset them Jem not being... anyway, Mum said it was okay so... just letting you know.'

Silence again.

'Okay. But I'd like to talk to them tonight, please.'

'Of course. Oh, yeah, I meant to ask. Did the police come round?'

I snort. Meant to ask. He's probably wondering why I'm not round at his house kicking off. But this is the new me. I stare at the cars speeding past me on the dual carriageway. The dust on the copper beech bushes at the side of the road. Grubby. Just like all this. And now I face a horrible weekend wondering what has happened with no one to ask.

'Yes. They asked me some questions.' He waits for me to continue. 'And then they went.'

He's suddenly more tense. I can somehow feel it. I picture him tapping his fingers and nodding to himself. He used to do this when he was insisting I'd had an affair. Wait. Until I lost my temper and then ask question after question. He finally asks me.

'And did they mention what I said?'

I laugh. 'Yes. But like every other rational human being,

they can see the situation. That I was upset, and it was an accident. So, no, Daniel, they didn't arrest me on the spot. They didn't even ask me who I was with.'

His tone changes. 'Oh. Out, then, were you?'

My hackles rise. He has no right.

'Yeah. Most of the day and evening. And then...' I flashback to Tim in bed in the hotel and me emerging from a hot shower, naked. 'Well. It's none of your business.'

I am sweating. I have dreaded this moment. when I have to explain to him. Somehow, it still feels like cheating. I've gone to great lengths to never let the kids and Tim meet, yet they practically live with her. I know it's double standards, and I thought it would get better with time. But it hasn't. The moment is here, as dirty as the layby and the copper beech leaves.

'Got a boyfriend, then, have you? Ben and Angel never mentioned it.'

I feel my breathing quicken.

'It's not the time, Daniel. We can talk about it when we know Jem is okay. I'm very worried about her.'

He ignores me. 'They haven't met him, have they?' He laughs loudly. 'Bloody hell. I can picture the scene. Single mum. Big house. He's a freeloader, isn't he?' His voice is scornful, mocking. 'After what he can get. I know that kind of man, Lauren. Just be careful.'

He's talking to me like I am a child and it's too much.

'It's none of your business.'

He cuts in. 'Oh, but it is. I have a right to know who is around my kids. Check him out. Who is it, Lauren? Anyone I know?'

My phone buzzes. Someone is trying to call me. I look at the screen. It's the surgery.

'I have to go, Daniel. I have a work call. And you'd be better worrying about what's happened to Jem rather than who's in my bed.'

I end the call and I'm shaking. I said too much. I promised myself I wouldn't ever tell Daniel, or the kids, about a man until I was serious. Is it serious? I'd tried to move to another level, but the other night, he treated me like I was nothing. We'd been away for the weekend lots of times, but now I look back it had been a lot of nice food and good sex in lovely hotels. Or fun, as I thought it was. Fun but hardly normality. Hardly the mundane parts of relationship that allow for closeness. Until now I'd thought of it all as Tim being considerate and treating me well. But how did it look to everyone else? To Daniel?

I suddenly feel like Tim is compartmentalising me. He was clearly uncomfortable last night. But calling it out would make me look hysterical. And I have so much going on at the moment.

I drive to the surgery and I am greeted by the receptionist, Sarah, and the practice nurse, Pam, beaming at me. Sarah points at a huge bouquet of flowers on the side.

'Those are for you.'

Their anticipation is infectious. My heart leaps and I feel guilty for all the things I thought about Tim after last night. He has no agenda. He just wants to take it slow. Sarah beams.

'Off your new man?' I raise my eyebrows but my grin gives it way. She tuts. 'We've noticed. You've been a lot more chirpy recently. Who is he then? Tell all.'

I weigh it up. I've decided I need to be more open about Tim. Now's my chance.

'He's called Tim. I've been seeing him for a couple of months. Just now and again. Taking it slow.'

'I'm made up for you. Especially...' My smile fades and her eyes widen. 'We heard it on the local news. I said to our Julie, isn't that Lauren's...'

I look from one to the other of the women. They aren't

gossiping, this is genuine concern. Yet I feel like it is a huge intrusion.

'Yes. Daniel told me what happened.' I don't mention the police or the message. 'He's devastated and her parents must be too. Goodness knows what has happened. Poor Jem.'

They nod and frown and I am holding a huge bouquet, teetering backwards. I back through some swing doors and into my office. I set the glass jug they have stood the flowers in on the table. They are lilies and tiny daisies and some carnations. All pink. In the centre is a perfect pink rose. My heart beats fast as I tell myself not to be silly. I scramble to open the card, but it is a larger envelope tucked in between the stems. I rip it open and read the card.

Tim x

Brief and to the point. No apology. But I guess all relationships are strained at times. The flowers are an apology. He took the trouble to send them to work. I love that. The smell of the blooms fill the room and I know Tim has won a little bit more of my heart.

I desperately need to do some work but I find myself googling 'Jem Carter' and 'missing car'. There is one line in the local news and a soundbite on Twitter. Both are framed in the context of Jem's parents. *Mining magnate Ian Carter's daughter missing* is the central message. I quickly bring up her Instagram page and there are dozens of messages underneath her last photo, one with her holding Pepe and wearing the shortest of shorts in the garden of the Rosarium. Lots of people telling her to *get in touch, babe* and *please be safe.*

I go back into reception. Sarah and Pam are talking and stop when I appear. I laugh.

'It's okay. I know all about what's happened. I just wanted

to know how you heard?' They blink at me. It came out like an accusation. 'Only I'm worried that my children will hear something bad.'

They relax. Pam folds her arms.

'Well, the woman in the greengrocers knows her mother. She's put a post on Facebook appealing for anyone who knows anything to come forward.'

She scrolls her phone and holds it up. I move closer. Jem's mother, an older version of Jem, has posted a picture of her abandoned car. A chill goes through me. It is real. She needed my help and I didn't read the message. Then I didn't take it seriously. But how could I have helped? My head swims with questions as I stare at the picture. Pam lowers her phone.

'It's gone viral on one of those local sites. I wouldn't have put it together except she's mentioned your Daniel. He must be out of his mind with worry. You all must be.'

'Yes, we are. All of us. But I'm worried the kids will be upset. And it's Dan's time to have them.'

She nods. They both look solemn. Sarah shakes her head.

'What sort of person would harm a lovely girl like that?'

And there is my conflict. Right there. I feel angry that something might have happened to her. But equally angry that Sarah thinks she's nice. After what she's done to me. And the icing on the bitterness is the selfish fear for myself because I know full well that any possibility of me putting my past actions to rest are looking more and more remote.

But I cannot afford to worry. I need to keep life on an even keel for the kids. And keep reminding myself of the fact that apart from that, none of this is my business.

I ring Daniel's mother's house and talk to Ben and Angel, who are distracted by her cats. I vaguely wonder how Pepe is getting on with them, then remember I have to detach and stop worrying. Focus. Be strong. A million platitudes I tell myself every day.

They are fine and they tell me they love me and will see me soon. I am envious for a moment. They are oblivious to the seriousness of Jem's disappearance, still thinking she is at her friend's house. Daniel's mother, Belinda, is the queen of pretending things are fine when they are not.

I had a wobble. Pre-marriage nerves. While my mum got caught in the *will-she, won't-she* drama, Belinda just carried on as if nothing had happened. As if I hadn't wavered about marrying someone who refused to take my point of view into account. I was in so deep that when the day came, I just went along with it.

I stop. It's the first time I have thought about that for a while. I'd wiped it from my memory and replaced it with a strong marriage built on strong foundations. My breath comes hard and fast as I realise I was right. I shouldn't have married him. It feels so wrong to think it. So strange to question it. Because I had defended it so hard when Jem came along and smashed it so easily.

I have known Belinda is Daniel's closest ally for a while. She never questions him and always supports him. She switched from Lauren to Jem in the blink of an eye, replacing me so easily. Creating a perfect world around herself, a bit like my kitchen – too perfect in the middle of a swirling mess.

I blink into the afternoon sunlight streaming through the window. Is that what the illusion is? The same women are creating a tiny spot of belief that they are okay, safe. Equal. But really, the truth is nothing like that and we are not, in fact, irreplaceable?

CHAPTER THIRTEEN

I fell asleep around nine thirty and, for once, slept all night. I dreamt about Ben and Angel and a picnic. When I opened my eyes at half-past eight, I knew what I had to do. One of the things my mum used to say to me was, 'Control what you can control'.

I can't find Jem, or even help Daniel. It's not my battle. Much as I wish I could, I need to leave it be and use the time I have constructively. I have written up most of my client notes and now I can get completely up to date and make some more appointments. I feel a flash of normality as I imagine myself in my practice room, face to face with a client.

But I can't think because something is blocking my mind. Irritating me. I know I will never rest until I have removed those cameras. I have no idea if the police have searched The Rosarium. Or if they plan to. Daniel would probably have told me, accusing me of it being my fault. It's the only thing that is stopping me moving forward.

It was a bad decision. Very bad. But I was in a bad way. I try to forgive myself and, for a few minutes I concede that it's unlikely they will ever find them. But I know they might, and I have to do something about it.

I consider ringing Daniel, just to check they haven't encamped back at his place. But why would it matter? I could just turn up and if they were there, tell him I wanted to see my son and daughter. My stomach turns over at the thought of it, but this is a now or never situation. I never meant it to go so far.

I shower and pull on black leggings and a black light fleece. I put on my cycling gloves and a beanie hat, tucking my hair in carefully. My cross-body bag is hanging on a brass hook behind the door, and I pull out the contents onto the kitchen worktop. I grab a pin hammer from the bottom drawer where I keep screwdrivers and the like, and some tape. Then I feel along the back of the fridge-freezer. My hand touches the large brass key and I tug at the tape holding it in place.

Once in my bag, I tell myself that if the locks have been changed, I will go in through the window like last time. I pause for a moment and look at the photographs on the fridge. Once this is over, I will make a clean break. I will have nothing to hold me to this terrible situation. To Daniel. It will be over. Properly over, this time.

Half an hour later, I am sitting in my car on a road adjacent to The Rosarium. I can see the house through some dense bushes when the wind blows. My legs are jittery with fear, but I remember what Daniel said about staying away from here. It could mean anything, but if it means this, then I need to put it right before the police find out. My addled mind cannot work out how anyone could find out, but I am not hedging my bets. While this hangs over me, I can't move forward. I want it done with once and for all. I know I was wrong. I want to put it right.

I have a perfect vantage point from here. If the police are watching the house – but why would they be? They don't think Daniel is responsible for this or they would have arrested him –

I would see them. Maybe he told them he was going to his mother's. Taking his children to safety. I catch myself sneering at the thought. I ambush myself with another realisation. Daniel does things for Daniel.

I brush it away. This isn't the time. I need to focus. I get out of the car and walk up the road towards the back of the house, retracing my footsteps from when I made this mistake in the first place. The fear is worse this time because I know what is going to happen. What I have to do.

The wrought-iron gate to the back garden squeaks loudly as I push it. This time there is a thick chain and a lock. I pull up the panel of the fence to the left of it and slide underneath – Daniel's love of these panels, cemented-in posts but so easy to lift, has served me well when I have forgotten my keys at our first home. I'm in the garden and I see the makeshift enclosure for Pepe is still there.

I hurry over to the back door. The pristine kitchen looks dull without the spotlights on. I peer through and see the light of a burglar alarm and panic. But it's green. It's the same alarm I have. Of course it is. Daniel likes things to be the same, I am quickly discovering. Green means not set. Red means set. Unless he has changed it.

There is movement. A slight flash of white. Then gone again. I hear my pulse banging as I try the key in the door. I jump back as it opens and Pepe comes running out, yapping. Shit. The dog's here. Why would he leave the dog here if he was going to his mum's? Pepe sniffs around me and stops barking as he recognises me. I stand completely still and look into the house. I would be able to see any lights on from here – downstairs is open plan and has an open staircase.

There are no lights, so I go inside, shutting the door behind me. I reach up onto the kitchen cupboard and tug at the thin camera tube. It is firm but comes away easily. One down, three to go. My heart lifts as I realise this is possible. It won't take long at all. I move into the lounge. Her signature is on this room with a huge Biba style rose on the feature wall. There are framed photographs in silver casings everywhere, glinting even in dull light through the window.

I am mesmerised. Family snaps, almost identical to the snaps we had in our home. Except she is in my place, her hands on my children's shoulders. I almost forget she is missing and could be in danger and hate her again. I check myself. I need to keep my focus.

I reach up and pull at the second camera. The cupboard underneath it opens, and papers fall out. It's not as neat in there as you would imagine. I scramble to pick them up and push them back inside. This is turning into a nightmare. At least I remembered the gloves. I push the door and it clicks shut. I have the second camera. I feel a slight thrill. I am halfway through. I sit on the pink and white sofa gently to collect my breath.

Now I am in here, I am hypnotised. I look around. This is where Daniel lives. One of Jem's pink sweaters is folded neatly on the edge of the sofa. I pull it on. It still smells of her perfume. It fits, and I am surprised. I hug my arms and wish I was her. I wish I was living in this house with Daniel and my children. It's mad, I know. Just being here is mad. But this is how it has me at times. Something takes over and I am crazy with envy.

But this is Jem's territory, and I can only borrow a tiny part of it. It's so different from the dark wood of our former home, and the red of the lounge in my house that we designed together. I am surprised he would like this. But again, I realise that there are so many things I don't know about Daniel. I had been tied up with small children and my job. So busy. No time to pay attention to feature walls or the particular sheen on the kitchen units.

A memory catches me unawares and I feel tears rise. Angel

had been sick on our old sofa and Daniel had arrived home with swatches for a new one. I was breast feeding, and he tried to push the swatches in my face.

'It stinks. Really stinks.'

I'd shrugged and frowned. At one time, we would have laughed at something like baby sick. When Ben was small, we were grossed out at lots of new things. But the mood soured somehow, and I had a feeling it was to do with my ever-expanding waistline. Two pregnancies on the run had not left me time to get into shape, and his critical eye and the fact that our lovemaking became routine was telling. I constantly told myself I would get to the gym, but there wasn't time.

'Okay, Dan. Okay. Just pick one.'

Two weeks later, it arrived. A huge purple sofa. It didn't go with anything, and I hit the roof.

'It's... ridiculous. I'll never get anything to cover it. We'll have to keep the plastic on.'

My baby brain was ticking over and only a year previous, he would have rolled his eyes and ignored me. But he dug his heels in.

'Don't be silly. We'll redecorate.'

I'd laughed, a high, pretend roar. 'Yeah. Redecorate. I hardly know my own name, Dan. I'm so tired. It's not the time.'

He'd stared at me for ages.

'It never is, though, is it? This place is a tip. It needs a woman's touch.'

I'd stopped stroking my baby's head.

'I am a woman, Dan. In case you hadn't noticed.'

I was shocked. I looked at him for reassurance, but his expression said one thing. A proper woman. I knew what that meant. Someone who cooks and cleans and who doesn't work. He told me I didn't need to work. He would take care of things. But that made me afraid.

Now, in this room, with the family photos and the neatness and attention to detail, I feel even less. Jem is a proper woman. Even if she burnt the pie, she is more of a woman than me. I concede. He wants her, not me.

I need to get out of here. This is doing me no good whatsoever and I need to finish this. I pad up the plush stair carpet. There are huge canvases of Ben and Angel hung on the double drop landing. This house is small but the extensive use of stark white and its open-plan layout makes it look bigger. I reach the top of the stairs and locate the third camera.

I turn around and catch my breath. The bathroom door is open, and I see myself in a full-length mirror. Then I see it isn't me. It's her. She is naked, back to me, looking over her shoulder. I duck back and peep around the corner. She doesn't move. Because she is a photograph. A huge, naked Jem. Made to look like a mirror reflection.

It shakes me to my core. The fact I thought the image registered as me is disturbing enough. But my second concern is that Ben and Angel have seen the picture. Who would do that? Then I see there is another door leading to their bedroom. It's en suite. I scope the layout and see a door at the end of the landing that says, 'family bathroom'. It's cramped and no real space for two bathrooms. I am overthinking this. My children were safe here, but I had to know for sure.

But why? Why don't I trust Daniel? I blamed it on her, but with every passing moment I am starting to understand that things were bad before she arrived on the scene. And every time Daniel was in the firing line, Belinda appeared.

There was a particular time that he had had some trouble with a car and some guys had come to the door of our old house. They were swarthy and tough-looking and when I told them Daniel wasn't in, they looked past me. They eventually left, but sat waiting in a car outside our house.

I called Daniel and an hour later Belinda arrived.

'He's had to go on a job, so he sent me. So you'll feel safe.'

I believed her. She was a little bit posh and straight talking. All an illusion, of course, but most people bought it. She stood at the door, arms folded, until dusk when the men drove away. Then she settled on the sofa and watched TV. Silent. Waiting. Waiting to protect Daniel.

I stare out of the window at the top of Jem and Daniel's stairs, over the garden. She protected him lots of times. She was always turning up when things got rowdy or when there was trouble, rolling up her cashmere sleeves and claiming to want to help.

So, what was she helping with now? How was she helping Daniel now?

I hear a door slam and laughter. A woman.

'Daniel!'

She's giggling. Pepe runs past me and downstairs. He isn't barking. He knows them. It's them. Jem and Daniel.

Half of me is relieved that she must be okay, and half of me is terrified. I back slowly into the room behind me and shut the door as quietly as possible.

CHAPTER FOURTEEN

I turn around and, in a split second, I scan the room. Pink. Not rose pink, a lot paler than that. There is a pair of angel wings on the wall, and on the wall opposite a panel of framed photographs. Two smiling people. All white teeth and blonde and red hair. Huddled together. Another one of them with the angel wings behind them. Jem and Angel.

A smaller photograph of her and Ben and Angel, again, laughing. I look around. The room is beautiful. This is where my daughter sleeps. I brush my hand over the soft quilt cover and open a jewellery box on the bedside table. There are some beads in there we made together. Her red shoes are neatly placed together under the white dressing table. My heart feels like it is breaking, but I can't let the tears come yet. Not yet.

I hear voices outside and more laughter. I blink into the sunlight as I strain to see the cars outside. Daniel's is there and a red convertible beside it. That isn't Jem's car. I listen at the door. Daniel is talking, but I can't hear what he is saying. The door opposite opens and shuts. Then I hear footsteps. One set. Going downstairs.

My forehead is damp and my heart pounding. My hand is

on the door handle, but I can't. I can't risk it. What if whoever it was came back? Then the door opens again.

'Dan? Dan. Fetch the hamper as well.'

Footsteps.

'Here.'

Glass clinks and she giggles. Then a muffled noise. I am sick to my stomach. He goes back downstairs.

'Fetch some plates, too.'

I hear Daniel tread the staircase heavily.

'Hungry, baby?'

Baby? I cringe. That's not the Daniel I lived with. And who the hell is she? I absolutely dare not try to escape yet. I sit on the pink bed gently. I open my phone and stare at it. The app is still on there, but deactivated. I scroll and go to my archive. I need to know when it's safe. That's all this is. I just need to know when I can leave.

I check myself. What am I doing? I have broken into my ex's house, and I am hiding in my daughter's bedroom. I hold the nightdress that lies across her pillowcase to my face. It smells of my little Angel. It's clear she is safe here. My heart almost cracks in two as I admit to myself that Jem is fond of Angel. She loves her. The photographs are natural, and Angel and Ben look happy. This isn't what I thought it was. My children are content here. With Jem and their father. Isn't that what I want?

I am shaking. I locate the app and click the icon. It installs and I watch the spinning screen. It tells me it is locating the signal and then the screen starts to open. I am transfixed as the bedroom opposite opens up before me, the fisheye of the camera capturing everything. Daniel is pouring champagne and a thin woman with long dark hair is lying on his bed in purple underwear. His and Jem's bed.

I want to look away, but I can't. He brings the glasses over and sets them on the bedside table next to a vase of pink roses.

Then he sits on the bed and, starting at her chin, traces a line down to her cleavage. I can feel his fingers on my skin as he does it, hardly touching yet velvet soft. I lean forward as he leans forward and kisses her gently while reaching around to unfasten her bra. He gently takes it off and kisses her breasts, first one and then the other.

I can feel it, all right. I can feel it because this is exactly what he did with me. To me. He liked me to lie on the bed so he could see me. In our most intimate moments, he was a man of routine. He wanted me to do the same things in the same order – it turned him on and he told me it was ours. Our thing.

I know what will happen next. He will lean over her and press his body on her, whispering in her ear that this is theirs only, just for her and him. And he does. Right on cue.

But it isn't just hers. It's mine. And it's Jem's. And God knows who else. I am drained. The wafer-thin bottom of my world that was still intact just fell through as I realise Daniel's duplicity. His lies. I was never special. All his words were meaningless. Just a repertoire that he performed over and over.

I feel sick. As if this on its own isn't bad enough, I can see the huge picture of him, Jem and the kids looking down on them. How could he? I hold down the vomit and try to breathe. My fingers automatically turn off the app – I don't need to see any more of this scene; I have seen it repeatedly. It was the one thing that kept me going through all the bad times. The times I hit the depths because his eyes followed another woman across a room as she side glanced him. The times I sat with our children as he went out, night after night. All the times I had to put up with his bloody mother backing him up and mollycoddling him.

He might have been absent quite a lot, but when we were alone, he was always attentive. He was always loving and just the right amount of bad. If I am completely honest, he still thrills me. But now I know a large part of it was because I thought it was ours. Even with two small children, there was still something just for me and him. And as the kids grew, he took more of an interest in them and even when time was short and we were both working or tired, it was still the same.

It was still the same right up to the day before he left. People say that you always know when your bloke is playing around. I didn't. I had suspected, but Daniel was always home at the time he said he would be. And we were still sleeping together. So how could things be so wrong?

The real question is, how could I have got it so wrong? How many women had he had in our bed? Jem is missing, and he is here with someone else. I search my soul for a reason he would do this. A good reason that he would leave our children with his mother and bring another woman here, to his and Jem's bed. I am horrified that I am suddenly siding with her. But I empathise. I really do. Except Jem isn't here to see this, is she? She isn't here to walk in on them.

My lip trembles as tears threaten. The pit of my stomach feels empty, and I need to get out of here. Daniel is a bastard. He has always been a bastard. I roll back a year and wonder what would have happened if I hadn't walked in that day. Would he have stayed and played me? Carried on sleeping with me while he was with Jem. My skin crawls. The reality of it cuts me and the pain is almost unbearable. Almost.

But even now, as I hide in Daniel's home as he makes love to his mistress, I know that deep down this will make it right. I know it's the catalyst I needed to shake myself out of whatever delusion I was under. I can already feel the spark of recognition that there is a way forward.

I check I haven't left anything, and I listen at the door. Daniel's girlfriend is moaning loudly, and I think I can guess where they are up to. I try to laugh, but the pain is too great. But not too great to make a run for it. I open the door and Pepe sits outside wagging his tail. I scoop him up and take him downstairs. The same Mulberry bag I spotted the other day is in the same place on the worktop.

I quickly feed him – that piece of shit won't be thinking about that – and I open the back door. I stand outside for a moment and watch as Pepe runs around in the garden. It's enclosed, so I leave the back door wide open.

He will never suspect it is me. He is too wrapped up in his lies. I hurry to the fence and flip it up and climb through. My stomach wobbles at the thought of that fourth camera, but what is done is done. I can never go back there now. I run along the lane and reach my car. I sit inside and it is only then I can think about what this means.

The shock of it all, the shock of being in my daughter's bedroom that I had never even seen before, and she was too scared to describe to me for fear of hurting my feelings. The shock of seeing, for the second time, my husband with another woman. I grip the steering wheel. I shouldn't have to put up with this. How he makes me feel. What he makes me do. It's only then I realise I'm still wearing her sweater.

I should never have had to endure Daniel's hold over me. It wasn't a tight grip, but it was enough. I had no voice. His calmness was control in itself; he never showed anger, and I always wondered why. Now I know. Because none of it mattered. There was always another woman waiting in the wings. Just in case.

All the times I had that sense of him scanning the room. Looking for his "type" before he could spot them and distracting him by being overattentive and charming. I almost hate myself for it, my simpering and stroking and laughing a little too loud. But not quite. Somewhere in my psyche, I knew I was doing it and reserved a small place of forgiveness – I wanted to keep my husband. I would do anything. Anything.

Now I know it was all in vain. Lulled into a sense of false security by his reliability, I had put up with it all. And when it got too much, he would recruit his mother.

I stare at the house through the wavering shrubs. It's still windy and rain threatens. Nothing is as it seems. But I need to leave it be. I need to find a way to put this behind me and focus on the kids and my work. It's important.

But the issue is inescapable. Daniel isn't stupid. I've seen him weigh up risks and face up to some dodgy situations. Daniel cares about Daniel and he would never put himself in danger. Jem isn't some casual girlfriend; that house has her hallmark all over it. He's let her get close to our children. He's put her before me more than once.

Yet he's still brought someone else into their home. And it's not a one off. I saw them on the footage last time and who knows how many other times she has been there. Some people get off on the thrill of getting caught. The risk and the danger. But I don't think it's that. I don't think Daniel is doing this for kicks. No. He simply doesn't care. I was expendable.

He discarded me almost overnight. No arguments or discussion. No. Daniel gets what Daniel wants. Now, one minute he's on my doorstep crying about Jem and the next in bed with someone else. It doesn't make any sense, but at the same time, one thing is clear. He is super-confident she won't be around. That she's not going to burst in. Champagne and a hamper are not a snap decision. This was planned. Get the kids out of the way so that he can have some "Daniel time".

I can almost hear him say it and the anger rises. I look at the house again. Where is she? Where is Jem?

And what has Daniel done?

CHAPTER FIFTEEN

Back at home, I pull off the sweater and shower. I wash all the delusions and the sadness away. I know it will be replaced by anger, but there are more important things now. I feel stupid. Stupid for letting him do this to me and ashamed that I fell for it, hook, line, and sinker. Oh yes, he had me there, but not anymore.

I phone Ben and Angel. I hear my voice, high and stressed, as Belinda answers the phone with the phone number.

'Hi. It's Lauren. Can I speak to Ben and Angel, please?'

'Lauren, how are you?'

I do not miss a beat.

'I'm fine, thank you, Belinda. How are you?'

I give her a chance to discuss the situation with me. How terrible it is about Jem's disappearance. But she doesn't.

'We're all fine here.' There's a pause. I wonder if she is going to say something, but I hear the landline phone I can picture in her hallway clunk on the retro phone table. She is distant. 'Children! Your mother is on the phone. Come on...'

I hear the TV pause and Angel laughing.

'Mummy! Grandma let us watch *Chitty Chitty Bang Bang*!'

Her excitement is palpable, and I wonder how much sugar she has had. There is a tussle and Ben speaks now.

'Grandma's getting a puppy. A Labrador. We're allowed to go and choose.'

I swallow. I need to be close to them. I need them near me.

'That's lovely. Really lovely. Look, do you two want to come back tonight?'

He pauses. 'But the puppy, Mum. We're going to choose tomorrow.'

I nod into my mobile phone. 'I know, darling. But I could drop you back over tomorrow.' I don't want to do this, but I have to. 'Why don't you ask Daddy what he thinks?'

'He's at work.'

I hurry my words. 'Oh? On Saturday?'

Belinda retrieves the phone.

'Is there a problem, Lauren?'

Straightforward and to the point. As usual. I take a deep breath.

'Not at all. I just wanted to take the kids out for tea. Things have been difficult, haven't they? You know, with Jem? Anyway, put Daniel on, please.'

She laughs. 'He's not here. He's at work. You know, Lauren, you must let Daniel have his time with the children. He doesn't do this on your time, does he?'

Under normal circumstances, I wouldn't dream of arguing with her. It's just not worth it. But today is different.

'No, he doesn't. But this is different. With Jem being missing. I thought he would have stayed with them.'

I can almost hear her seethe.

'Are you suggesting I can't look after them?'

I snort. 'Of course not. I just thought Daniel would want to be with them. I certainly do. You know, to make sure they are okay. We are their parents, Belinda.'

Not you, I think, but I don't say it. She rapidly returns service.

'Well, I don't think you should take them without Daniel knowing. And he's not here.'

My temper rises.

'That's fine. I'll call him. Or go over to the house and ask him.'

She almost barks at me. 'He's at work.'

I draw it out. I stay silent for longer than I need to. Finally, I speak.

'Is he? You'd think he'd be out searching for the woman he loves. Or with his children.' I pause for her reply, but she is silent. 'But I suppose we're all different. At least they know I care. Enjoy the puppy.'

I end the call. Things are going to be different now. I go upstairs and open Angel's bedroom door. It's the opposite of her room at Daniel's. Chaotic. Lived in. Clothes strewn all over the place. I pick them up and put them in the Barbie washing bin. I pull her duvet over and straighten the shoes under her bed.

I run my finger across a picture on her wall. A man with brown hair. Two children, a boy and a girl. And a woman with yellow hair. All holding hands. I wonder if the woman is Jem, or me. Waves of sadness wash over me as I think about how Angel will miss her if... no, I mustn't think like that. I must be positive. She will be found.

I suddenly wonder if she has found out about that woman and left. She could. She had nothing keeping her there. It seems a dramatic way to do it, but Jem is dramatic. Maybe she's too scared to come back now the police... *maybe, maybe, maybe.* I concede that I have no idea what has happened. All I do know is that I hope she is okay.

I go to Ben's bedroom. Neat and tidy. He doesn't say much, but I know when he is hurting. He's sensitive, like my dad. He loves football and all his posters are of Manchester United. I pull back his curtains and that's when I see that someone has trampled my plants. I "meadowed" the back garden under the window with some seeds Lisa bought me as a housewarming present. Easy to maintain and pretty.

Now there is a clear pathway through the garden. Imprints in the lush greenery that turn into trainer prints that give away a trek through the muddy area on the other side of the fence. I hurry downstairs and out into the garden. This place is like Fort Knox. The windows were falling out when we bought it, so it was the first thing that was done before we even moved in.

My heart thumps as I inspect the windows for any sign of a break in, but there are none. Even so, someone has been right outside my kitchen window, peering in. I shiver. What the hell is going on? And then the awful realisation dawns on me. Whoever needed Jem out of the way could also want me gone, too. I cannot bring myself to think that Daniel would do this to the mother of his children. I can't. But I have to.

I turn Bekah Bradley's card over in my hand. I could call her, but what could I tell her? How would I explain I had been in the house when Daniel was there?

I lock all the doors and check all the windows. Then I unlock the back door and hurry up the garden to check the gate. I had long ago wedged down the unsecured fence panels Daniel is so fond of. But the gate is almost the same as the one at The Rosarium. Twisted wrought iron secured with a heavy chain. The chain has been cut, and the gate is slightly open. I feel the chill of fear.

I go back to the house and phone Lisa. I try not to sound panicked. I want to spill it all out to her, but being in that house today will sound too... I search for the word and rest on "criminal". I had broken the law. Up until this moment, I had defended what I had done by telling myself they deserved it for what they had done to me. But now I am sorry. It is incredible to me now that I took this risk. But another part of me knows it is all part of me finding out what has happened.

'Lisa. It's me.'

She laughs. 'You okay, mate?'

I force a laugh. 'Yeah. Listen, what are you up to? Do you want to do something? Or come over here?'

I'm not usually so direct. She is more serious now.

'I can't, I'm in Leicester with Mark. Are you all right?'

I toy with telling her everything. At least someone would know, then. But I can't think how I will explain about Daniel. I still don't have it straight in my head. Just a feeling things aren't right, somehow.

'Yeah, yeah. Fine. Just... bored. You know.'

She sighs. 'No sign of Jem, then?'

'No. Nothing. And the kids are at Daniel's mum's so they don't get upset.'

'Ah. Okay. Well, I'll be back tomorrow. Shall we catch up then?'

'Yeah. Thanks, mate.'

I end the call. I scroll through my contact list. My preoccupation with Daniel coupled with my hatred of Jem has kept me out of contact with friends. All my contacts are work colleagues with the exception of Tim. After the other night, I don't want to call him.

I consider booking into a hotel, but how long for? How long can I keep this up? I'm damned if I do and damned if I don't. The kids will be home on Tuesday and I need to keep them safe.

There has only been one other time in my life like this. Following the visit from the thugs that Belinda scared away, I was followed. At first, I thought I was being paranoid, but I kept seeing the same face as I turned in Tesco with Angel in a baby sling and Ben sitting in the trolley. Someone out of place, out of context.

I would see him on street corners, watching me, and behind me in my rear-view mirror as I drove out of multistorey car parks. I told Daniel, but he said it was "just my imagination", especially when I couldn't ever locate the face when he was around.

It drove me mad for months. Mad with fear and mad with frustration that no one understood. I even tried to talk to Belinda, but she told me to go to the doctors and get some medication. It stopped as instantly as it had started, but the fear lingered. I had the locks changed – we were still in our old house then – and had all the outside gates secured.

I feel it now. That glint of horror in the pit of my stomach. I am alone.

The same alone that drove me to watch Jem take my kids to school. The same alone that made me watch Jem's life from a distance, following her into car parks and watching through windows as she ate lunch. All the crazy things I had done were down to this loneliness and a sense of wanting to get my own back.

No court would ever entertain me lodging a charge on Daniel's heart. It isn't criminal to cheat on someone or to hurt them. But I was hurt so badly that I thought it should be. I am not the only one. In the shadow of crimes of passion, lots of people do uncharacteristic things. Because there is no other way to feel better. No way to prosecute for battered emotions.

I slump in an easy chair in the lounge. I have endured so much and not acted in the right way. I could have moved away. I could have made a new start. But the compulsion to know what happens next in the soap opera of my life was too strong.

I hear a window rattle and I jump up. This is no soap opera now. It's rapidly turning into a horror story that I couldn't understand before. Or am I just jumpy because of what has happened to Jem? Fear rises again, and I grab my phone. I message Tim.

Hi there. Thank you! Want to come over?

I press send, realising how desperate it sounds.

He sends a row of smileys then a message appears.

What for? 😊 And no can do. But not long until our dinner date tomorrow X

I hug myself. Tomorrow is better than nothing. I have to trust that the police will investigate this and come up with the right answer. Quickly. I really don't want to spoil the date with Tim by not being in the right frame of mind. I message Tim again.

All good. Pick me up around three x

Today has been too much. I need to think. I go round the house and check the windows again. Then I set the burglar alarm. I hardly ever set it, but I know it covers all the entrance points downstairs – I will be well warned if someone tries to get in.

I lie in bed, half watching box sets and half wondering where Jem is. I can't get her face out of my mind. The last thing I imagine before I fall asleep is that she is locked away somewhere, screaming, and that is the image that punctuates my dreams.

CHAPTER SIXTEEN

When I wake, I jump up and check all the windows. The rain has washed away the footprints and made the meadow patch look even again. It makes everything seem normal, although I know by the knot in my stomach that it isn't. I think about getting some security cameras installed and then I remember the three cameras in my bag. My heart sinks as I remember the fourth camera. I know I will never, ever return to get that camera. I will never set foot in that house again.

My train of thought wanders to what will happen if Daniel is responsible for Jem's absence. What will happen to the children? All the pain it will cause. As if they aren't worried enough now. And the inevitable arrival at what would happen if I was harmed.

I shudder and open my laptop. I work on next month's client plans. When I am finished, I am pleased with the results. I have to move forward. I can't live like this forever. Bekah Bradley was right. She saw something in me that shouldn't have remained. That closeness to Daniel's life, to his situation, that should have ebbed by now. I pull the picture of him from the fridge and study it.

He's kept me here. He's intentionally done it. It's becoming clearer and clearer now. He's made sure I am engaged in this battle with Jem so that he still has control. All the comments when he drops the kids off. All the phone calls "to talk about the kids" that result in him overexplaining his life with Jem. She is complicit, of course. I stare at his smiling face in the old photograph and wonder if he was really happy back then, when the kids were very small. Or if he was living the same double life.

It jolts me back into reality. I need to break away from this. Disengage. Live my own life. Push the photograph into a drawer. In an ideal world, I could just cut off from him. But he's made sure I still live in our home by providing just enough for me to stay. My God. He's manipulated me to fight for the house by making it the most important thing. That's how he sells expensive cars. By making them a must-have. Working on his clients to make them believe their lives will be incomplete without it.

But things have changed now, since yesterday. I look around at the house. Somehow, it no longer matters. We could live anywhere. Yesterday I was still involved in a property tug of war with my ex. Today I am not.

It's a mausoleum of my sadness. I call the estate agent and ask them to come round and value it next week. Even half-finished, there should be enough equity in it to get me started again. Somewhere smaller where I won't have to rely on Daniel. The arrangement made, I feel a little bit better. Perhaps the footprints were the window cleaner or Bekah Bradley and her sidekick having a look around. Maybe I have this all out of proportion.

Then I remember about Jem. I still can't believe that Daniel has... what? What has he done? I go over the facts in my mind. Her car was left on a bridge, but she is nowhere to be found. She must be somewhere. But wherever she is, the police can't find her. It's been nearly a week. I know from working at the station that the critical time for someone who is missing is forty-eight hours.

I'd googled DS Bradley. Rebekah. I'd looked at all the cases she'd been involved in. Her and her sidekick. I like the police and I loved working there.

When I worked in the support centre, I sometimes worked on missing person cases. I held case conferences with Larry Jenson, the senior missing persons investigator. We'd attend the scene with the press and they would rake over details with anyone who would talk. I loved my job and I struggle to see now why I stopped doing it.

Larry and I were a great team. He had the middle-aged act vibe, and I was the willing young sidekick. I sort through my memories of those cases. We got involved when it came to the attention of the police. Often a body found or some evidence. And sometimes we would have to contact the desperate family. Even in these heady days of social media and going viral, people still trust the police first.

But when I went freelance, it was different. People who have long-standing problems they have not coped with – or only just been strong enough – are the people I work with now. Those people who are on the peripherals of cases and don't qualify for agency help as they are not the official victim. My speciality is to help them to move forward. Like the families of the people who had disappeared. Which makes it all the more laughable that I cannot move forward with my own life.

I think back to the missing person investigations. They were usually reported by a partner or parents. They would have been reported to the police with worried awake-all-night words. The police would ask if it was out of character and determine if there had been any crime committed. They would look at last sightings and if it looked like the missing person had just left, they wouldn't log it as a missing person. It's not a crime to run away. If something isn't right, they will follow up, but they have to prove it.

The relatives, partners or friends are often left with no answers. Their anger builds as they refuse to accept that their relative or friend has walked away. Then they start their own campaigns. And we were there to catch them at the end of that campaign. If their relative is found alive, we would help them work out why this had happened. If time passed and the loved one didn't turn up, we would help them rebuild their lives around the gap they left. And if a body was found, we would instigate grief counselling, which meant that in the cases where it turns out a crime has been committed, we were already involved.

I remember a man I had talked to when his partner disappeared. She had gone out shopping and never come home. Her car was still in a multistorey car park. He'd gone down the police report route, but CCTV had her walking away from a cashpoint, down an alleyway and she was never seen again. Her bank cards were not used, and she did not have her passport with her.

He was completely devastated. I could see both sides. From the police side, she had simply walked away into a new life. She never appeared at the other side of the alleyway and there were no clear images of the people in the cars passing through at that time, or their registration numbers. There was no abduction or struggle. No one had reported seeing a woman being bundled into a vehicle, and there were plenty of people about and no one saw anything unusual.

He was convinced she had been taken. He was in tears when we met at the station and was sure that she could never have left him. He told me that everything was normal, and she kissed him before she left. She took nothing except her handbag and a shopping bag. The only difference was that she was wearing her best coat. He told me through deep sobs that he had asked her why she was wearing it and she had said, 'Why not? You never know what will happen tomorrow.' He stressed she had been smiling through the words and he never imagined that it would be the last time they spoke.

I checked the files later. There was still no trace of her. Nothing at all.

Like Jem. There is no obvious crime. There's an abandoned car. There is nobody. Taking my own emotions out of the situation, I realise that Bekah Bradley's visit was probably a routine "when did you last see her" for the files. Because of the message. It goes round and round, but every time it lands on the message. *Help.*

But the note. I saw it with my own eyes. It was definitely Jem's language and in her handwriting. He didn't look like he was lying when he showed it to me. I snort to myself. What do I know about Daniel lying? I was oblivious, and I probably still am. I turn other explanations over in my mind. Kidnapping and a ransom from rich parents. Yet no appeal for anything. An accident. Yet no investigation. Lisa said it was being treated as a missing person enquiry.

Even if Daniel isn't behind this, he has still brought that woman home and slept with her while Jem is a police matter. He seemed pretty certain she wasn't coming home. I wait for the "benefit of the doubt" feeling to descend on me, as it usually does when I suspect Daniel of something. But it doesn't. And that feels good.

I shower and get ready for my date with Tim. I suddenly feel a little nervous. Like I pushed him to do something he wasn't ready for. But I hear his car and I look out of the window. Too late now. And it might do me good. He's talking on his phone. He is very sexy, I tell myself. This can be a distraction; an opportunity to think. I need the space and I can usually rely on Tim to provide it.

He's out of his car now and leaning over the bonnet, stretching. Looking up at the house and nodding slightly. I watch him and I blink into the daylight. He is very different from Daniel. More indie. More laid-back. He always looks like he might have just finished work.

I pull on my jacket and catch sight of myself in the mirror. I immediately think of Jem. Jem. But I push the thoughts away and hurry downstairs. Tim has walked to the end of the short gravel path.

'Hello!' I call out to him, and he turns and grins.

'Hiya. Wow. You look great.'

For a split second, the world goes into slow motion as our eyes meet. I feel guilty that I am happy in the middle of all this, but today is about escape. About me and Tim. The other night was probably a misunderstanding. A case of me not knowing the rules of dating now I've been out of the game for so long. Today seems different. He is smiling back at me.

'Thanks. So do you.' I look at the floor. 'Thanks for this, Tim, and the flowers.'

He laughs loudly. 'You psychic or something?'

I stare at him. He reaches into the car and pulls out a bouquet of sunflowers and greenery. He hands them to me and I laugh.

'More? Oh, thank you. Shall we take them with us?'

He looks puzzled but nods. 'If you want. I've got some more surprises. Just you wait!'

We laugh and get in the car. I cover his hand with mine.

'Are you sure about this? We can just as easily stay here.'

He smiles at me. 'What, now I've gone to all this trouble? Oh no, you will have dinner. I've got shares in Marks & Spencer after this afternoon.' He looks into my eyes. 'You will stay over, won't you?'

My heart races. I hadn't even thought about it.

'Oh. I didn't bring a bag.'

He laughs. 'Well, still time to get one.'

For the first time in ages, I am excited. I rush into the house and throw some underwear and an animal print negligee into a bag. I already keep a make-up and wash bag ready for our hotel excursions, and this is hardly different. But this is a real step forward for us. Tim is keen and he's made an effort. I catch sight of myself in the mirror and I can't help but smile.

CHAPTER SEVENTEEN

I wind the window down and let the cool breeze hit my face. The radio is on, and Tim is driving fast through town and over the ring road. Yes. This is what I need. Some time away to think. Something different. I watch the trees whiz by, and the red-brick terraced houses turn to the more traditional stone-built cottages as we head to the outskirts of town.

The city is behind us, and I suddenly feel freer. I watch for "for sale" signs and fantasise about coming to live out of town. I can work from anywhere and there is a train line straight through connecting to the city. I smile to myself.

I wasn't sure if we were at the comfortable silence stage, but Tim drives silently until we reach the quieter roads. Then he smiles too.

'Happy?'

I turn to look at him. His eyes match his smile.

'Yes. Yes, I'm happy. Just thinking what it would be like to live out here.'

He nods to himself. 'Nice. Pricey, though. Are you selling up?'

I laugh. 'I won't have much choice, eventually. My ex...'

He holds up his hand. 'Been there, done that. Got the T-shirt. 'Scept we had no kids. Surely you can keep it till–'

I interrupt. 'Yeah, but I can't afford it. And I want a clean break.' I toy with the idea of telling Tim about Jem. No. This is meant to be fun. Not about my problems. 'Anyway, I'm ready to start again now.'

He puts his hand on my leg. 'I thought you had already. We've been seeing each other for a while now.'

I take the prompt. 'Yeah. I am, but I'd like to, well, you know. Make it a thing.'

He moves his hand onto the gearstick, but he's still smiling. My heart is beating really fast, and I feel my face flush. But he doesn't miss a beat.

'Would you? What sort of thing?'

It's playful. He's teasing. I play the game.

'You know, seeing each other. An item.'

He laughs. 'It would be easier if you got your own place, for sure. I always feel... I don't know. The kids. It's like it's their house.'

I want to tell him they will always come first. That it's their home, not their house. But I keep it low.

'Well, maybe when I move it will feel more like ours.'

I know I am pushing this. We've never discussed anything serious, let alone something shared. But he laughs loudly.

'Aw, baby. That's nice. But you'll have to get that front window sorted before it's valued.'

My mood dips. 'What about the front window?' I hear it shoot from my mouth, sharp as a knife and loud.

He winces. 'Jesus, Lauren. All right. I was just saying...'

I am shouting at him. 'The window, Tim. What was wrong with it?'

He slows down on the empty road and turns the radio down.

'It looked like someone had jemmy'd it. Wasn't there the other day. All scratched up. I saw it when I walked up the front. On the gravel.'

I am shaking. I need to go home.

'Stop the car. Why didn't you say this before we left?'

He speeds up.

'It was just some scratches. It'll fix. What the hell...'

He turns the radio up full blast. I feel tears sting. This wasn't a good idea. I need to go home, but he's driving fast now. I turn away from him and we spend the rest of the short journey in silence. By the time we reach some neat apartments beside a stream, I have calmed down a little. He gets out of the car, and I think at first he's going to go in alone, but he comes around and opens the door.

'There you are, milady.'

The smile is back. He sweeps his arm and I get out and smile back. We are here now, and I'll just have to make the most of it. But as I step out of the car and he fumbles for his key card, I can't help but think about the window and the footprints.

Tim goes to the boot and starts to get the bags, and I open my phone. I scroll through my Facebook feed and then I see a message. My phone rings and I turn away from him. It's Lisa. I cancel and I'm halfway to the apartment when a message pings.

Lauren. Answer the phone. It's important.

I touch Tim's arm. 'I need to make a quick call, babe, nothing serious.'

He smiles. 'Inside or...' He gestures around him, the views are breath-taking. I gauge his expression. He is fine. Smiling. Happy. 'You go ahead. It'll give me chance to do a last tidy.'

He's laughing as he goes inside. I call her back. She answers before it's rung properly.

'Mate, I just wanted to tell you they've changed it. The Jem thing. They've changed it to abduction.'

I am silent. I replay the scene in my mind. Jem's car at the bridge. Her not falling over or wandering into the forest. No. In this scene she is dragged from the car and... I blink it away.

'Abduction?'

She is breathless. 'Her parents. They're going to do an appeal. But it doesn't look good.' We are both silent for a long moment. She says exactly what I am feeling. 'I feel so bad. All those jokes. She could be dead, Lauren. Dead.' I nod into my phone. She continues. 'Where are you, anyway?'

My children's faces flash through my mind. They are going to hear about this now. Especially if Jem's parents do a public appeal.

'I'm at Tim's.'

I look at the building behind me. I have no idea where I am, really. I know I am somewhere about ten miles from home. Possibly. There are sheep in the field behind us, and I know the hills in front of us are the Pennines.

She sighs. 'My God. Daniel will be devastated.'

Daniel and the dark-haired woman flash through my mind. His lips on her neck, him whispering to her. Devastated.

'Mmm. Look, I'll be back in the morning. Send me anything you have on this.'

'I will. It's mostly local reporting. I didn't know she was an heiress, did you?'

I pause and check myself. I even doubt Lisa now. Wondering if Bekah Bradley has asked her to find out what I know.

'No. Not really. Daniel said something about her parents being loaded. But no.'

I hear my phone ping multiple times.

'There you go. All the links to the story. I didn't find out much more from my colleagues. But something must have changed.'

'Unless it's pressure from the parents?'

She sighs again. 'I don't know. It feels like it's been ramped up, somehow. I'm really worried. About you too. Are you okay?'

Tears threaten again. I'm not okay. Far from it. It strikes me I am with Tim when I should be at home. He appears behind me. 'Everything okay? Tea or coffee?'

My heart melts. He says it like we are an old married couple. Maybe I should be here. With him. A new life. I smile anyway.

'I'm fine. Lisa, I'll speak to you tomorrow.'

I am itching to read the reports, but I can't. I laugh in all the right places, but the story on Jem is burning into me. I toy again with the idea of telling Tim all about it, but he is standing over two steaks sizzling in a pan telling me about his sister and brother.

He has gone to a lot of trouble. The wine is excellent. His place is really lovely – very man cave. All greys and blacks with a flash of red here and there. Completely at odds with how he dresses. He is a jeans and shirt man.

The table is a complete contrast to the apartment. He's set out a candelabra and he dims the lights and lights the candles. It immediately transforms the clinical apartment into something much more romantic. I relax. This reminds me of an old black-and-white film where dinner for two is elegantly arranged in the couple's home, for the sole purpose of enjoying each other's company. I've been running to catch up with myself for so long I'd forgotten how to relax.

He serves a first course of French onion soup and rustic bread. He rests the steak and we laugh about the barman in the last hotel we stayed at. I sip my wine and I am falling in love with Tim. I suspected it before but now I know.

I know that feeling. I know the fear and the excitement. It feels like an opportunity and a betrayal all at the same time. And the more he smiles and touches my hand, the more sure I am. This is different from the coffee shops and the hotels. Different from my house – and now he's told me why, I understand. This is real. This is us.

He serves the steak with a dressed salad – how I always order it in the hotel. He has paid attention to what I like. He has bought in a particular mustard I like and he fetches more bread.

'Of course, I don't cook like this for myself. So don't get used to it. I'm an egg, chips and beans man.'

I laugh. 'That would have been fine. But this is... wonderful.'

I lean across and kiss him. He returns it and then pulls back.

'I really want this to work, Laur. That's why I was saying about taking it slow. I don't want anything to spoil it.'

I nod and kiss him again. I suddenly get it. What this is. It's not about Daniel or even my children. It's about us. He is interested in me. It's been so long since this happened. So long. I can't remember the last time someone was interested in me, just for myself. It feels unfamiliar and makes me a little self-conscious. But valued.

'Let's take one night at a time, then. Suits me.'

When we get to the bedroom, he pulls me to him and we make love. It's tender and gentle and everything I could ask for. Yet when he is asleep and his breathing is even, I open the bedroom door and pad along the long landing to the bathroom, clutching my phone. I go inside and lock the door.

CHAPTER EIGHTEEN

The light of my phone glows in the darkness, and I open Lisa's messages. I read them one by one until I come to the last one. All the others are breaking news short articles with basic details. But this one is different. I read on.

The article spells out that Jem's parents are rich. She is an only child. There is a photo of her now, one that I recognise from Daniel's lounge with him and the kids snipped out. And there's a photograph of her as a child. It had never struck me she is someone's daughter, a child, like Angel. I suddenly feel a deep grief. Her poor mother. And father.

I read on. Jem has a degree in environmental science. And she worked at the Calais Jungle for two years with refugees, completely against her parents' wishes. I swallow hard. The people she worked with described her as a beautiful person, inside and out. A school friend is quoted as saying that Jem is a very charitable woman who would never harm a hair on anyone's head.

My jealousy reflex screams that she did. She harmed me. She stole my husband. But I wonder now how much stealing there was. What he told her. If he said it was over and we were only married in name. Only living together because of the kids. It would certainly make sense of how she acted that day when I caught them, standing in my kitchen close to my husband.

It is all so sad. The final paragraph pushes me to the limit of my sanity.

> Jem Carter's partner, Daniel Wade, refused to comment. Jem is stepmother to Daniel's children, who live with them. Angel (9) and Ben (11) are thought to be staying with relatives. In a police statement it was announced Daniel Wade is helping police with their enquiries.

I scroll up the message app and look at Jem's text again. What had he done? Why was she asking for help? And where is she now? The questions reel in my brain. I close down the messenger app and dim the light on my phone.

Here in the dark, miles and miles away from home, it feels safe to think about what could have happened. In the middle of my busy life, it's hard to think straight. It's hard to admit to myself that the man who told me he loved me, then told me he loved Jem, is just a lowlife. I sit on the ornate plastic toilet seat and blink into the darkness. It seems impossible that Daniel could have arranged all this single-handedly. But it also seemed impossible that he could be a cheating bastard and have bedded so many women while we were married. And after that too, seemingly.

Even now, I cannot imagine him harming her. I push my imagination to its limits and try to think where he would have taken her. Not their house. No. I try to remember anywhere the kids had mentioned, even the walks we used to go on. None of it means anything because I am starting to realise I never knew

Daniel. I don't know this man who can so easily separate out sections of his life. Who can lie to his children and his mother – even though she will know some of his wrongdoings instinctively, I can tell by her constant defensiveness. But I never knew him.

I do know what "helping with enquiries" means, though. I picture him, sitting in front of Bekah Bradley, his poker face set, and a lie on his lips. They are lining up their evidence and now they have sifted through anyone who knows Jem or might have a motive they are picking off the likely subjects. They wouldn't have taken him in if they didn't have a reason.

I lay awake most of the night and now I'm sitting at Tim's breakfast table. He rose early and set it perfectly. Toast in a rack and a checked tablecloth. The opposite from last night's romance, this is French café chic. Tim certainly knows how to capture a mood.

He is cooking bacon and eggs. He taps his foot to the music on the radio and nods his head to the beat. I press a button on my phone and it springs into life. I turn around and take a selfie – me smiling and the apartment and Tim in the background. I make sure only his profile is visible to protect his feelings. I send it to Lisa with the caption *#timsplace #international-manofmystery*.

Then I scan for news. More reports are online, most of them syndicated from the one I read last night. I scan for any new information and then google Daniel Wade. Nothing except for the derivatives of the article. I am acutely aware it is Monday morning, and I need to get back. I shouldn't really have come; I can see that now the situation has escalated so quickly. But at the same time, I acknowledge I couldn't see past the bleak weekend that seemed so dangerous.

It's so easy to sit here and pretend that this is real life. This is the everyday. If only. Life would be so simple. I smile to myself. Tim turns.

'Won't be a minute.'

I laugh. 'Don't worry. I don't have to be in until later. Kids aren't back until...'

He turns back to the cooker abruptly. I see the muscles in his shoulders tense. He turns back around and places a plate in front of me and a platter of assorted breakfast food on the table. He sits down but doesn't start to eat.

'Look. There's something I need to say.'

I nod. I take a slice of toast and butter it. 'Okay.'

He breathes in deeply. 'Your ex. You seem a bit preoccupied with him. I wanted to check that...'

'We're getting a divorce.' It's true and it should tell him everything he needs to know. 'The children will live with me half time and him half time. Like they do now. That isn't going to change.'

'No, no. It's not your children. It's just... I don't know. I can't put my finger on it. It seems like when we're together it's just us, but other times you're distant.'

I feel a bead of sweat trickle down my back.

'So you know his girlfriend? The one I mentioned? Jem Carter?'

His expression changes and he reddens. 'Yeah. Yeah. I know.'

I continue anyway. 'She's missing. They found her car. And I'm worried for my children. She's been caring for them half the time for months. They'll be upset.' I wipe away a tear. 'I'm upset, Tim. I don't like her. But I wouldn't want anything bad to happen to her.'

He looks away and sniggers. I stare at him. Then he leans towards me.

'I think the best thing would be for you to be as far away from her as possible. And him. Otherwise you'll look like some kind of bunny boiler.'

I feel anger rise.

'Is that how you see me? Is it?'

'No. But you need to keep away from them. I don't know how to put it any differently. But it's me or him.'

I stay calm. He doesn't understand. He doesn't get it.

'That's not why I hate her. It's not him. It's the kids...'

'Well, you won't have to worry about that now, will you?'

I reel. How could he say that? How could he?

'Tim! That's awful.'

He raises his eyebrows and pulls some crispy bacon onto his plate.

'It's just a fact. From someone on the outside. You're too close to see it.' He chews and thinks. I am speechless. But he continues. 'You know, this all seems like a lot of needless drama to me. Not that she's missing. No, that's bad but separate. Their life. And you're still connected to it.'

I push my point home sharply. 'I have children with him. That's my connection.'

He pours coffee for me and I add the milk. Something isn't right. He is cold and calculating about Jem. Or is this how everyone else sees it? As someone else's problem?

'You see, the problem is you're constantly distracted. Always on your phone. Checking–'

I interrupt. 'On my children.'

He nods. 'You have to trust that they are okay. But if you are really concerned, go ahead and involve social services. Family courts. Otherwise you'll never...'

My smart watch buzzes as if to confirm.

'What.' I place my butter knife gently beside my plate. 'Never what?'

He smiles. 'Move on.'

The mood is gone. I decide to not challenge this. I don't have the strength. Tim's got his nice little neat world here and that's good for him. It seems ordered and uncomplicated. Maybe he's right. Maybe that's what I should aim for. But it seems a long way away right now.

He washes the dishes and we chat about his job and my job but I just need to get home.

In half an hour we are pulling onto my drive and it's clear we have both had enough. But he gets out of the car and opens the door for me. I half expect him to apologise, but he doesn't. He holds my shoulders.

'I only said all that for your own good. If we're going to have a future, then Jem needs to be out of the way.'

It hits me like an avalanche.

'What... what? What the hell?'

He looks puzzled. 'I only meant...'

'Out of the way? She could be dead. Who are you, Tim?'

He looks shocked. He steps backwards.

'I meant her and Daniel. You can't expect me to...'

I rally. 'And you can't expect me to cut everything off. Drop everything for you. You have no idea how far I've come. How this has been for me. No idea. Because you never ask. You want it all tied up neatly with a bow. Well life's not like that, Tim. Life's not like that.'

He shakes his head. 'No I guess not. We still okay, though?'

I blink at him. The morning sun is hot on my face and I suddenly feel tearful.

'Yes. Yes, give me a call.'

'Later, then?'

I nod at him as he walks away. I must be a sure bet. My phone pings. It's Lisa.

> Daniel's at the station. They've got him in the interview room.

I don't reply. I go into the house and put my bag on the worktop. I stand with my back to the door. I felt like I was falling in love with Tim but maybe he is right. Maybe this isn't the right time for us. But if he was the right one, he would understand. This isn't some tiny misdemeanour. Jem is missing and my ex is in the police station.

I should never have insisted he take me to his home. Not yet. He is my escape. My salvation. Or so I thought. He was so unfeeling about Jem's disappearance. I feel the tears come. And the anger. It's times like this that I seriously doubt there are any good men. Anyone with the honest loving feelings that I have. Who aren't just in it for themselves.

My dad. He's a good guy. In my eyes, anyway. Him and Mum argued, but he cared. Really cared. Some of the women I have worked with are married to their best friends. There is no tension between them, just an easiness. I let Tim's attitude wash over my mind. Daniel's was perpetually competitive, as to who could get their own way. I thought Tim's was integrity – his understanding and honesty made me think it. But now I wonder if he is just trying to put me in another space specifically created for "Tim's girlfriend".

I shiver. This doesn't bode well. Daniel in the police station and Tim pushing for me to break all ties so he can have me to himself. In between all this are my children. They are the ones who matter. And that's exactly what Tim could not comprehend. It's not Daniel or Jem or even me. I need to keep it all on an even keel for Ben and Angel. A delicate balancing act where we all sacrifice a little of what we would really love to unleash in order to save those two little lives from a moment of grief.

Except Tim, who is more interested in division. It's disappointing because I had expected more. But I need to put all this right to protect my little ones, even if it means losing Tim.

CHAPTER NINETEEN

I shower and change. All the while, I am on red alert, alone here in the house. I hurry downstairs and check the back of the property. The gate is still secured, and no one has trampled through the grass. I walk around the front and see scratches on the window frame. The windows are super-secure and there is little chance of prising them open. Someone would need to smash the glass. Clearly, whoever was trying to get in didn't want to enough to attract attention.

I reason that it could be the same person. It could be totally unconnected with Daniel or Jem. It could be a burglar. Come to think of it, the scratches could have been there for some time. I wouldn't have looked. I fold some of the children's clothes to take my mind off my worry. *Do normal things, Lauren.* Normality is exactly what I crave right now, I realise. But what is normal?

I thought it was Daniel. I craved our life back, but that is gone now. And I wonder with that camera still in his bedroom if anything will be normal again. My heart beats faster at the fear of it being found. But if they find the camera, they will inevitably find evidence of his latest conquest. And if they do forensics, they will find evidence of her. And, I realise, me. I was careful. I wore gloves. But I sat on Angel's bed.

I am sweating. I can barely work out now if I have done something wrong or not. I just wanted my husband back. It's not a crime. My mouth dries as I acknowledge that some of the things I have done are against the law. And I am truly sorry. I wasn't at the time. I was deranged with envy. Hurt. Sadness. And most of all, heartbreak.

You see it all the time. Women who make public declarations of their husband's infidelity. Women who smash windscreens and burn clothes in the street. Who shower the pavements with their lover's belongings in a very public display of ending. I didn't do that. I wanted to keep it quiet. Most of all, I didn't want Jem to see how much she has hurt me. Or Daniel, although he already knew.

I feel a tear trickle down my cheek. Some of the things I did were unbalanced. Jem must have known it was me who cut her roses, but she didn't call the police. Her tolerance of me and my temporary break-up derangement somehow made it worse. I wanted a reaction. I wanted her to be as sad as me. I wanted her to be sorry. If I am honest, I wanted her gone.

But not like this. It's messed up and all I can do is carry on. I pull on my leather jacket and grab my bag. I know I will be safer in town than here worrying over things I cannot change and the realisation hits me like a brick. I'm afraid to be alone because I am afraid of what will happen. How many women live like this? Afraid to walk somewhere alone? Afraid to be in their own homes? Feeling safer outside amongst strangers?

I'd heard other women talk about it but until now I had never been afraid to be alone. Even when the children weren't here, I felt safe. And bored and uncertain and unsettled, but not afraid. Walking the streets in the dark had never fazed me. But this is different. I know it's external, but something has taken root inside me. It's gripped my heart and soul and made them shaky and unsure. Made me look over my shoulder.

I catch myself staring into space now and then, wondering if there is something about all this I have missed. I need to keep moving. Keep finding information. Keep trying to fix things. I know that standing still brings on the thoughts of fear, the *what happens next* and the flutter of anxiety that this could be your last moment. I check myself for unnecessary drama, but this is the real deal. My only comfort is that Daniel is in the police station. Lisa would have messaged me if he wasn't.

In half an hour, I am parked and sitting in Evelyn's Café in the city. My heart has returned to its normal rate, proving my theory that being amongst people is safe. I choose green tea and while I wait for it to arrive, I scroll through further reports of Jem's demise, scouring them for evidence of previous break-ins at The Rosarium. There are no such reports and not much has been added to the articles. I am hungry for more details, so I message Lisa asking her if there is anything else to report.

She rings me immediately. She is whispering. 'I'm in work. I can't talk, really. But he's still here.'

'Are there any developments? I mean, they must have found something?' I hear my own desperation. 'The thing is, Lees, a few strange things have happened.'

Her tone changes. She is gentle now. 'Oh. Are you okay, mate? What's happened? Not the kids?'

'No. He took them to his mum's.' I remind myself not to mention Daniel's woman and the house. 'It might be nothing, but I think someone tried to get in the front window with a crowbar or something. Tim noticed it, and the back gate chain was busted.'

She is panicked now.

'Wait. Back up. Tim? Why was he there? Did he stay over? I hope he's looking after you. Have you reported this?'

Have I reported it? No. No, I haven't. I should have. I suddenly realise that I really should have. What if it's connected to Jem? Clearly, Daniel isn't doing this by himself. He wouldn't have stepped through grass carrying a chain cutter and crowbar. Her question about Tim jolts me into reality. No, he's not looking after me. He's looking after Tim. He saw that window but he just wanted to get to his apartment. No comforting or understanding. I file it for later.

'I was scared. I needed someone there.'

Silence. Then she speaks, again gently. 'Oh my God. I'm so sorry, mate. When you phoned me the other day...'

'Yeah. But it's fine now. I'm in town. Working. Waiting for a client. Don't worry. But let me know when he gets out as soon as you can.'

She sighs. 'I'll try, but he'll probably just be interviewed. I won't necessarily know unless I ask. And, well...'

'It's okay. Thanks, Lisa. Thanks.'

She pauses again.

'Look, are you okay? Things are tough at the moment. Those things that happened, you need to tell Posh 'n' Becks. Today. I can come over Friday night if you want. Bottle of wine? Takeaway?'

I smile into the phone. Lovely Lisa.

'That would be great. Shall we say seven? You can say hello to Angel and Ben. I've got loads to tell you.'

She laughs. 'I bet you have. Great. See you then.'

I go to turn my phone off so I can work and I see a new message from Lisa. It's a picture. A screenshot of a group of men. I zoom in and it's Tim and Pete and some workmates. The caption is #partyatpetesplace and it's from the Instagram account of someone called Brian Jenkins. I read the narrative.

All the window guys got together at Pete's pad to celebrate the big contract.

I stare at my phone screen. I feel like I'm going mad. She's making a point of this now and I feel a little angry. I message her back.

That isn't Pete's place. It's Tim's place. I was there at the weekend.

She responds immediately.

Must have it wrong then. But there's Tim. Kerry Lawson knows him, apparently. From communications. Her hubby works with him. Kerry with the blonde hair. Kids go to your kids' school. Anyway. Phone those things in. Probably nothing but don't be scared x

It had never occurred to me to call in my own issues. How low have I got that I don't matter? It's the first thing that I tell my clients. Focus on you. Extreme self-care.

A lot of people I see are lost. They aren't depressed or anxious, they are just overloaded and tired. Life gets so overwhelming for them they just stop. I studied it in psychology. The saturated self. What happens to us when it all becomes too much. I loved it so much I based my practice on it. I know I need to take my own advice – I promise myself every day that I will when things get easier. But they are just getting harder. Much harder.

I am at a loose end now. My client called to cancel. I had a couple of hours scheduled for this at the surgery but I may as well do it here. I can finally finish the case files I am so behind with and have a fresh start. I open my laptop on the table and finish the case notes and send them over for filing. I order a toasted cheese sandwich. It arrives and I eat it as I send the emails.

When I am done, I feel a surge of accomplishment. In the middle of all this drama and chaos, I have managed to pull together a major piece of work in record time. I know it will take time to set up more meetings with clients but I have done it. I've done my job and not completely crashed. That has to mean I am on the right track. That I am healing.

Back in the car, I find myself driving towards Daniel's house. If I'm honest, I had known this would happen. That I need to fix this before I can move on. I need to talk to Bekah Bradley this afternoon. I know, really, the reason I haven't phoned the recent shocking events in to her is because of that last camera. I think I always knew I would go back there.

I park in the same place and look through the bushes. They are still today in the sunshine, and I can see the house clearly. I get my gloves and the key from my bag. I'm not dressed for this, but it won't take long. I push the car door shut quietly and hurry along the lane. This is the last time. After this I will have no reason to come here.

The gate is still unlocked, the chain hanging loose from the wrought iron. I squeeze through and I am in the garden. I look through the window of the back door. There is no sign of Pepe, and I push the brass key in the lock and turn it. I squeeze my eyes together and wait for the alarm to go off, but it doesn't. The light is still green.

I hurry through the kitchen and up the stairs. The beautiful house is silent, so silent, and the carpet soft under my tread. I try not to look at Jem's beautiful home. It is so compelling to me, so what I wanted. I know I am at the very end of this now and that I must get the camera and go, but something about this makes me want to see what else she has done. It's like a morbid fascination with something I am not supposed to see. My rational mind tells me I am crazy to do this, but I open the door to Ben's room. It's the only room I haven't seen.

I step inside and close the door behind me. Ben. My firstborn. The beautiful child I loved so much the moment I set eyes on him. We understand each other, our mutual silence comfortable. He has sat next to me and hugged me when I was upset, never flinching away from my love. '*It's okay, Mum. It's okay.*' I see a photograph of him smiling out at me from the windowsill. No big show of Jemi-love here. She clearly knows where Ben's line is.

Football posters and Pokémon art. Expensive originals that he had asked me for, but I couldn't afford. A twinge of jealousy reignites and then I remember there is much more at risk here. I open a drawer and Ben's perfectly folded school shirts and trousers lie on the blue drawer linings.

There is nothing more to see here. Our son's bedroom, perfectly created by his stepmother. Step-mum. I had resisted it for so long. I hated the sound of it as I rolled it around my mind. Step. Mother. She was not his mother. Or Angel's. They had me. She had no children. I remember revelling in the fact that she must resent me. My vicarious presence through the kids must rankle her.

But in reality, she was just getting on with it. Creating a home while I was hanging over the ghost of my marriage, wishing ill. I open the door and stand on the landing, hypnotised by the décor. It's only then, in the near distance, I hear a car door slam and voices.

CHAPTER TWENTY

I rush across the landing and into Daniel and Jem's bedroom. My senses take in the perpetual smell of her perfume but there is no time for that now. I grab at the camera that is wedged in the wardrobe, my hands shaking. Panic rises in my throat as I pull it free and push it into my pocket.

I hurl myself over to the window just in time to see Bekah Bradley disappear around the corner. I run back into Ben's bedroom and watch her and DC Sharples stop in the garden and look towards the gate. They walk over and I see them huddled around the broken lock.

Then they look up at the house. Looking for cameras. I hadn't even considered that. The overwhelming joy I felt at getting the fourth camera crashes into a feeling of naivety. What else haven't I considered? I suddenly feel like a sitting duck. They walk towards the back door, and I flash back to my entrance and the fact that I did not lock the door behind me. I feel deep into my pocket. The key. It's still in the door. Shit. Shit. No, it's here. I still have it. But I didn't lock the door.

A trickle of sweat runs down my back as I lean over and try

to see if they have opened the door. I look around for places to hide. There are none in Ben's pristine room. His wardrobe is built into an alcove and narrow. In a sad imitation of every shit film I have ever seen, I place myself behind the door and try to control my breathing.

I realise I am crying. I cannot hear any footsteps or voices, but I am too afraid to even listen at the door. My body is rigid as I try to make myself invisible. The carpets are soft, and I wouldn't hear them pad upstairs and across the landing.

Minutes go by and I hold my breath as much as I can. I berate myself for even considering this, then forgive myself because I have been forced into this position. It's a loop I have endured for too long, and in turn I promise myself that, if I get out of this, I will stop. It will all stop. I hate myself for not just staying home and looking after the kids and myself. For all my thoughts about Jem, and even Daniel.

My heart beats out the seconds, minutes and I wait, wait, wait. Then I see the door handle move. The door opens and I almost collapse with fear. I try to prepare myself for the inevitable and hold in the tears. But they don't come in.

'This must be the boy's room. Same as the others.'

Bekah Bradley's voice is crisp and clear in my muddy senses. I will them not to walk towards the window. Incredibly, they don't. DC Sharples answers.

'Yeah. So, what d'you reckon?'

She is standing right in front of me on the other side of the door. I can almost feel her prickle.

'Well, she's not here. And there are no security cameras. He's giving us nothing, really. And we shouldn't be in here.' She pauses. 'Why would he leave the back door open? Anyway. Let's see if any of the neighbours have dashcam or cameras. It looks to me that it happened away from here. The note. He's slippery for sure, but she left a note. I can't see how we can keep him.'

I exhale slowly as she pulls the door shut. I count invisible footsteps in my head and visualise them walking through the kitchen and going outside. I tiptoe over to the window and peer out just in time to see them standing in the garden again. Bekah looks up suddenly, and I duck back. Did she see me? Did she?

They walk away. Back around to the front of the house. I am exhausted. I want to lie on Ben's bed and go to sleep. I want to sink into it and disappear. This is all too much. But I know I have to carry on. I hear a car engine in the distance, and I dare to cross the landing. They are driving away.

I have new-found strength as I sprint through the house. I reach the back door and step outside. I lock it and hurry to the gate. I look back momentarily. I will never see this place again. I said it before, but I have reversed what I did. I haven't put it right, but I have made sure that I will never be tempted to look at Daniel's life again.

A pink butterfly on a stick whirls in the breeze, a touch of normality. I need more of that. I need to go back to the life I had with my mum and dad. A surety that one paced day will follow the next. A calmness that is missing now. I wait on the pathway under some trees to make sure they have gone before I emerge. Dad would be ashamed of me. Him and Mum were so dignified when they realised they had fallen out of love. There had been a short period of awkwardness in the run up, but the majority of the decisions had been made in late-night murmured conversations in the lounge.

They separated and divorced soon after. Minimum legal input and no shouting or arguing. No recriminations. Certainly no creeping around each other's houses. Shame stabs at me and I pick up my steps. I tell myself that their split was straightforward. No one else involved. But I am blaming someone else. I am blaming Daniel and her, when, if I had just kept my dignity, there would be no need to break into my ex's home.

I tread down the path and stop at the end in case they have spotted my car and are waiting. My life seems to be a series of me pre-empting difficulties. I need some calm. Some positive momentum. I need this to be over.

I drive home in a daze, my body sliding out of the shock of being in that house. I feel at the camera in my pocket and check my phone. No messages. I check my emails and there are some bookings coming through the patient portal and an email from Sarah telling me she has my files and is actioning. It is too soon to think that this is the turning point where everything starts to go right. But I feel a spark of optimism.

Once home, I make coffee. The kids will be out of school soon and I will ring them. My phone buzzes and it's a message from Lisa. It's news I already feel.

They're letting him go.

I type back.

FFS

She responds quickly.

Where is she, though? This is really bad, mate. Hope you are okay.

Am I okay? I still feel in shock. All this introspection has made me forget about Tim. I didn't even think about it when I got home. Or the footprints and the scratches. That I could be in danger. And now Daniel will be around again. On the plus side, the kids will be back tomorrow. My heart wakes up a little from protecting itself and I welcome the thought of routine. The school run and cooking. Washing and tucking them in at bedtime.

They will be full of puppy news, and I cannot wait to hear it. I check the time and dial Belinda's number. It rings out and goes to answerphone. I don't leave a message. I expect they have gone to get Daddy. I wonder if he will take them to his house or if they will all stay at Belinda's. Then I realise I'm doing it again. I'm involving myself in something that has nothing to do with me.

I feel bad about Tim. I tried so hard, but now I realise I shouldn't have needed to. It needed to be easy and relaxed instead of perpetual grand first dates. It could never develop into what I thought me and Daniel had even though that was what I kept trying for. He had some set ideas and I knew that from the start. It's just difficult to know what to do in a new relationship with an old one trailing behind. I don't think it is over. But it will need to be very different if we are going to continue.

I was just trying to compete with the golden couple. Everyone seems to be married and happy or living together and in love. I wanted it too. My childhood was spent wishing for a partner and a wedding and when I met Daniel, I was sure that it would last for a lifetime. It was a big shock to find out I had been kidding myself. And every time I think about it, I go back to asking myself what else he has lied about. Or is lying about.

I call Belinda's house phone again. It goes to answerphone again. I call Daniel's landline and imagine the white vintage dial phone ringing out in the empty house. The echo up the stairwell. My fingers go to my apps and my old habit of watching the house kicks in, but I realise that is over for good. I take the cameras and put them in a plastic bag. They cost a lot of money, and someone could use them again. But for now, I take them upstairs and push them to the back of a drawer in my bedside cabinet.

Back downstairs, I take the rest of the photographs off the front of the fridge. I leave just the pencil drawings from when the kids were little. All my photos are on my phone, but I will have some of them printed. Photos of my children. Not with Daniel. I feel a sense of him ebbing away, an icy coldness replaced by a little warmth.

I eat dinner and watch a little TV. I try Belinda's house phone again, but no response. It's hardly surprising, on reflection. She is hyper-protective of Daniel, but wouldn't I be about my precious Ben? My children are the reason I was worried. I didn't know Jem, and I was worried. Jealous too. But I didn't trust her – or him – with my precious cargo. No doubt Belinda is worried out of her mind about Jem, no matter how calm she sounds.

I take my laptop up to bed. I look at the list of new clients and book a couple and it feels good. Things are nowhere near normal, but I am making a dent in the chaos. Instead of scouring Instagram and the internet in general for Jem and Daniel, I look on Vinted and eBay for clothes. I think about getting my hair cut. A new look.

I know Lisa would call me if there was any news about Jem. I think about Ben and Angel, protected from all the terrible news. Although I don't like Belinda, I know she will wrap them in a cocoon of gentle silence. She will be deftly switching TV channels and turning off radios. Shushing people who talk about it. Belinda gives her full attention to any project she takes on, and her full loyalty. They are safe. But I want them back here. I miss them so much.

I can't sleep. I go down to the kitchen and hear the iron of the gate crashing against the gatepost in the wind. I don't want to go out there because I am scared. But if I don't, I won't be able to sleep.

I wrap a throw around me and unlock the door. As I step outside, the cool air sobers me. Thousands of people all over the world will be outside in their own gardens at night. Completely safe from any harm. I acknowledge I am afraid, which is one thing. I shut the gate and stand in the garden, the wind on my face. It feels like there is something just out of reach, something I don't know.

I think about tomorrow and the kids coming home and warmth floods me. Then a car backfires over on the top road above my house and makes me shudder. I consider a trip away to Dad's. It would do us all good. But it wouldn't seem right with Jem missing. And the kids need to keep to their routine. No matter what happens.

I take my phone from my pocket, and it lights up the garden as I switch it on. For the first time in ages, I check the dashboard attached to my smart watch. My sleep meter. My steps. My heartbeat. Incredibly, they are all normal. I bought it to get back on track after a period of coming home and getting straight back into bed after dropping the kids off at school. One of my clients told me she had one and it has worked for her. Made her accountable.

I went out that lunchtime and spent the remains of my bank account on the best fitness tracker I could find. All whistles and bells. The intention was that I would start running. That would both fill the time the children were away and make me fitter. Healthier. I stare up at the stars. Jem is somewhere under the same sky as me. Somewhere. I make a silent wish that she can be found as soon as possible.

I look at the smart watch app on my phone. Still time for the running plans. Still time to change. Still time. For me and I hope for Jem. I watch the little heart on the app beat and listen to the sound of distant traffic and hope that today I've undone the damage I did. There's still time for a new start.

CHAPTER TWENTY-ONE

Tuesday morning starts with the sound of an engine revving outside. I jump out of bed and run to the window just in time to see the back end of a red car turn the corner and onto the road. Whoever was in the car has turned a wheelie in the gravel. They want to be seen.

I am strangely calm. All I can think about is when Angel and Ben come home. I hurry downstairs and see a folded piece of lined paper on the doormat. I pick it up and open it.

You'll pay for what you've done.

It's handwritten in a scrawl. The letters are uneven and bumpy, as if it's been penned as an afterthought across a dashboard. My heart quickens. This is so far from the covert attempt to prise my window open. I know in my heart that if someone wanted to hurt me, they would. This is a warning.

Maybe it's all a warning. To keep my nose out of Daniel's business. But I won't. He knows some dodgy people but he usually likes to do things face to face. Unless he thinks he's already in enough trouble.

I wrack my brains for anything I would need to pay for. There was an incident with a client once who was unfortunately more unwell than we knew and should have been seen by mental health services. It could be something like that. But I doubt it. I am increasingly worried that all this has something to do with Daniel. First his partner going missing and then his ex-wife receiving notes and being scared to death.

Yes. This has to do with Jem and Daniel. I leave the note on the worktop and sip my coffee. It's an addition to the growing body of evidence that I will present the police with as soon as my children are settled. My anxiety is eased a little with the relief that I got the camera back. I blink into a shaft of sunlight that breaks through the kitchen window. This is a new beginning, I remind myself. It's time to share my worries with someone else.

I shower and dress and clean the floors. Excitement bubbles in my stomach. It feels like the kids have been gone for ages. I make their beds and decide that their bedrooms are just as special as their rooms at Daniel's. I begrudgingly admit that Jem has done a good job. But this is their home. I know I function better with them here. The school run and the baths and bed are things I previously took for granted.

I take some clothes out of the dryer and fold them on the worktop. My mobile lights up. I see the school's office number and my heart skips a beat. There have been four missed calls from them over the past hour while I've been cleaning. My fingers fumble to respond. My children. My children. It rings and I hear a high-pitched voice.

'Broadstead Primary and Secondary College. How may I help?'

I speak quickly. 'It's Lauren Wade. Ben and Angel's mum. I had a missed call. Is everything okay?'

I listen for any panic in her tone, but she is super-chirpy.

'Oh yes, yes. I just wanted to see if Ben and Angel are okay. There's a bad stomach bug going around and as you didn't ring them in absent...'

Blind panic sets in.

'They're not in school? It's Daniel's day today.'

'Oh, I see. We did try Mr Wade but...'

In a flash, I feel the whole situation with Daniel being at the police station leak into our conversation. Of course they would be following it. None of this was private property now. I adopt a business tone.

'Ben and Angel are staying with Daniel's parents while he is busy.'

She is guarded.

'Of course. Mrs Wade is down as an emergency contact, and we did try her in between calling you. But we have you now so as long as you are aware...'

I end the call. The kids aren't in school. To be completely fair to Daniel and Belinda, if there was ever a problem when the children were with either of them, they would ring me. They had never denied that I was their mother. I scroll through my call register, searching for a missed call. Maybe from a new phone number or from Daniel's solicitor.

Nothing. I try Daniel's number and it goes straight to answerphone. Then I try Belinda's mobile. It rings out. Then her house phone. Again, straight to voicemail. I leave a message.

'Belinda. Please can you ring me? The school rang saying Ben and Angel aren't in. Are they okay? Oh, and what time will you be dropping them off as they aren't at school? Or will Daniel? Let me know.'

I stare at my phone. Something isn't right. I know things are not at all right at the moment, but this has never happened before. Belinda is a big believer in stability. She wouldn't keep Ben and Angel out of school unless there was something wrong. Then it hits me. Have they found Jem? I look at the news reports. Nothing. But wouldn't they tell Daniel first?

I need to be with my children. This isn't time for division. No matter what has happened. I need to support them through this. I suddenly realise that the school receptionist was fishing for information. Trying to find out why the children were out of school. Maybe she had heard something.

I grab my keys and my coat, and I am out of the door and into my car. I message Lisa as I fly out of the gate and around the corner onto the road.

Has something happened? With Daniel?

I throw my phone onto the dashboard and head for Belinda's house. It's seven miles away and I put my foot down, weaving in and out of cars on the dual carriageway. I flick on radio for the news, but it's just some guy talking about an airport extension. I try to tear my mind away from Jem. It can't be good news, or it would be on the news straight away. I feel a weight in my chest and realise it is grief.

I don't know this woman really, but I feel like I am inside her. I have been in her home and seen how she has treated my husband and children. How she has drawn a circle around him I am not allowed to cross into. But I have anyway. And if I feel like this, how do my children feel? I have to get to them.

I narrowly avoid hitting a white transit van as I swerve to take the exit I nearly missed because I am distracted. I concurrently pick up my phone. No reply from Lisa. Once on the country lanes, I speed up – the area is flat, and I scan for vehicles. There are none so I fly round bends and brush the hedges. In the distance is the estate where Belinda lives. I focus on it and block any other thoughts. The kids come first. They always have. Even though, in my desperation, I have risked that, I love them more than anything in the world.

I sometimes have to push it to the back of my mind when they are with Daniel, or I would spend all my time pining for them. When we first split up, I watched other single parents carefully. I didn't know what to do with myself when my lovely children were with their father half the week. Add the thought of Jem playing mum, and any ambitions of productivity soon disintegrated into my obsession with Jem and Daniel. But when I remember what it ultimately led to, the bitterness and hatred, I choke up.

I am here. I pull up to the house and I know immediately something is wrong. There are usually two cars parked in the small driveway, but today there are none. The house is usually alive with a TV that is on from first thing in a morning until last thing at night. The kitchen light is always on as Belinda likes to give the impression of a complete domestic goddess, installing an expensive Aga in the small kitchen of the semi-detached.

Yet all is in darkness. I park up and hurry towards the door. I listen. Ben said they were getting a puppy. And Pepe must have been there. I knock lightly. No dogs bark. Pepe would have gone crazy. I walk to the bay window and peer through. There is no movement at all, and the lounge is perfectly tidy. No school bags or shoes or anything else to suggest there has been an emergency. I walk around the back. I try the kitchen door, but it is locked.

As I stand on tiptoe in the stony veg patch to look through the high window, I hear a noise behind me and then a man's voice. It's Jimmy Lowe, their next-door neighbour.

'Can I help you? If you're a journalist...'

I smile. I am family. Ex-family.

'No. I'm Ben and Angel's mum. I was just...'

He nods deeply. 'Oh. Yes. Of course you are. It's just that

I'm used to seeing... anyway. They all left early this morning. Belinda and Tony.'

My chest tightens.

'Was Daniel with them?'

He steps forward. 'Yes. And your children. I expect it's about all that terrible business with that lovely young woman. Very sad.'

I stare at him. 'Why? Has something else happened?'

His expression changes. His willingness turns to a guarded tone. 'Isn't her being missing enough?'

'You have to understand, I'm worried about my children. If something has happened to Jem, it would affect them.'

He smiles a tight smile. 'I'm sure they will be fine with Daniel.'

I can see him adding two and two together and coming up with me, not knowing where my own children are and wondering why.

'Yes. Yes, I'm sure they will. I'll go over there now. If they come back, please could you tell them I've been here?'

His gaze falls to my feet. I'm ankle deep in mud and as I raise my foot to move, there is a deep suction noise.

'Yes. I'll tell them.'

He turns and leaves. I scrape my trainers on the grass. They've left in both cars. Daniel was with them. I try his phone again, but it goes to voicemail. I leave a message.

'Dan, what's happened? Ring me.'

I drive over to The Rosarium. I park up the lane and walk along the front of the road. There are no cars in front of the house. I look up the road. None of the Wade cars are parked up. The house is in darkness. They're not here either. I feel sick.

Where are they? I check my phone. Lisa has read my message and not responded. Anger bites at me, but I must stay calm. I go back to my car and scroll for news of Jem again.

There is nothing new at all. I know how these cases work. Forty-eight hours in is the tipping point. This has been a week now with no developments except Daniel being taken in for questioning.

I can already see new missing person reports of other people who have disappeared into nowhere. Drip-fed by the police looking for any public sightings or discarded clues. But there is a time limit. Eventually, cases are shelved pending further evidence and go cold. That's when relatives come to people like Lisa. I wonder who Daniel will go to. If he will pursue it to make it look like he cares, when in reality he is entertaining his new interest.

My phone rings and I grab it. It's Daniel.

'Oh, Dan. Thank God. I–'

He interrupts. 'Lauren, listen very carefully. I won't be bringing Ben and Angel home today. This has gone too far now, and they will be staying with us.'

There is silence. I wait for him to continue, but he doesn't. Tears come quickly and I speak through them. 'But why, Dan? Why are you doing this to me? Can I speak to them?'

His calm tone fractures. 'To you? To you? After what you've done?'

I start to ask him what I have done, but I suddenly become aware of where I am. Sitting outside his place spying through the trees. Up to my knees in mud because I was peering through someone's window. Even though I said things had changed, I am still here doing the same thing.

'Can I speak to my children, Daniel? Dan?'

He has gone. I start the car and drive slowly home. Whatever has happened, I will find out in good time. In the meantime, I will contact my solicitor and tell him Daniel has broken the family arrangements agreement. And face the consequences of my actions.

I am almost in the driveway before I see them through the blur of tears. Bekah Bradley's car and two marked police cars parked on the gravel outside the front windows. I almost back out of the drive, but it's too late. I don't know what Daniel has told them, but this all seems out of proportion.

I park up and get out of the car. Bekah steps out onto the gravel and stands beside DC Sharples. A uniformed officer approaches me from behind and her gaze is off me for a second. Then she steps forward.

'Lauren Wade, I have a warrant for the search of your property. I am arresting you for the abduction of Jemima Carter. You do not have to say anything, but it may harm your defence if you do not mention when questioned something which you later rely on in court. Anything you do say may be given in evidence.'

CHAPTER TWENTY-TWO

I am in the back of Bekah Bradley's car. I want to scream that none of this is anything to do with me. I let them into the house and gave PC Roland my spare keys to lock up. I watched as they went upstairs and into my lounge, spreading out to get the job done.

She is concentrating on driving. DC Sharples is looking at his phone. The radio plays 'Albuquerque' by Prefab Sprout and his head dips a little on every beat. I am in shock. I feel for my phone and wonder if it's okay to look at it. I already feel imprisoned in the back of the car.

'Can I check my messages?'

Bekah nods. 'Yeah. But we'll need your phone when we get there.'

DC Sharples chips in. 'You can either let us look voluntarily or we can get a warrant. Your choice.'

Bekah catches my eye in the mirror. 'You okay? You look very pale.'

I sigh. We pass through the gates of the station, and I see the gate guards wave at Bekah.

'I'm worried about my children. Did you see them?'

'We'll talk about that later. What's going to happen now is that we will admit you and you'll go to a holding cell. Then we'll ask you some questions.' I search my memory bank for the amount of time they can hold me without charge. Twenty-four hours. Then ask for an extension. She continues. 'You can ring your brief and let someone know you are here.'

She pulls into a parking bay. I can let someone know I am here. I think about my family and friends and I have no one. No one at all. I already know Lisa won't be allowed, and in any case, it wouldn't be fair to ask. Tim isn't an option as he made it clear he is very separate from this situation. Dad's not around, and everyone else I know is connected to Daniel.

I can't believe this is happening. We walk towards a side gate and DC Sharples scans it open. We are suddenly in a holding area, and Bekah takes us through security. I am patted down and at the other end there is a high desk with a low gap in the middle. I peer through the gap and there is a hive of police activity.

A police officer appears and Bekah fake smiles at him.

'Joey, this is Lauren Jane Wade. We've brought her in on suspicion of the abduction of Jemima Carter. Can you do the necessary, please?' She hands him a bundle of paper. 'We've done the paperwork in advance.'

She turns to me. 'Don't be scared, Lauren. We'll see you later in the interview room. We should have the report from the search of your house then.'

I manage to speak. My voice comes out thin and watery. 'I don't understand why I'm here. I haven't done anything. I haven't abducted anyone. And I was with someone when Jem went missing. You can check.'

She stares at me. Hard. She considers me and nods. 'We will. The thing is, I've got a problem here. Over the past week, I've spoken to a lot of people and got a lot of information. And you seem to be the common denominator.' She turns to the side and moves closer. 'My advice at this point would be to tell the truth. This is very serious, Lauren. We'll know if you're lying.'

She walks past me. I smell her perfume. It's Poison. I hear her heels click down the tiles of the corridor. I wonder if I will lose my job. If I will lose the chance to help people. I know these are distractions to take my mind off all the things that loom large in my past that could punctuate my dislike for my husband's new girlfriend.

But I didn't take Jem. And that is the crux of the matter. They can't prove that I did take her because I did not. DC Sharples is chatting to Joey and then he is gone, and Joey takes my phone and asks me to empty my pockets and take off my jewellery. I watch him put everything into a bag.

'We'll need your clothes, love.' He points at a room to the left. 'There's an officer in there and she'll show you what to do.' I look at my muddy trainers and wonder how I will explain being in Belinda's garden. 'Just sign here.'

I take the pen and sign. He passes me a mobile phone.

'You can ring your solicitor and one other person.'

I look at him. Suddenly I am tearful.

'Am I allowed to google him? I don't know the number.'

He sighs gently. 'Who is it? I'll have a look for you. Take a seat. Do you want a brew?'

'Tea, one with a dash of milk, please. It's Mark Smithers. Jenner and Co.'

He nods and smiles at me. Another officer takes his place at the gap. Another pair of officers come in and book in someone who has robbed a shop. They sit in a row of seats opposite and stay with him until he is taken away to a room far left. Joey comes back with the tea.

'Drink this. You look terrible. Here's your brief's number.'

I sip the tea and call Mark Smithers. His secretary takes the call and all the details. She tells me he or someone else will be with me as soon as they can. I want to ask when, but I have no baseline for how long this will take. I have no watch or phone and therefore no idea of the time. I have a feeling this is going to be a very long day.

A female officer calls me from the room on the left. Once inside, she hands me a pile of clothes. Some paper-like underwear and a grey tracksuit. Some blue disposable slippers.

'Just slip those on behind that curtain, please.' She hands me an opaque plastic sack. 'Pop your clothes and shoes in there.' I turn towards the curtain and spot another door. I look back at the officer and she looks away.

I change and hand her the sack. I know the door on the far side of the room leads to the cells. Bile rises in my throat.

'I haven't done anything. I haven't.'

My hands are shaking. Weakness consumes me as she opens the door and gently guides my arm. I know there is no point resisting, but something inside tells me to fight. This is not right. This is not justice.

She leads me to a cell. There are no windows, just a flap in the door. There's a toilet in the corner and a moulded bench I guess is a bed. This one has no mattress. The officer sees me shiver.

'It's just until they call you for questions, love. Try not to get too upset.'

It has the reverse effect, and I am more upset than ever. There is nothing to do here but think about how it has come to this. How my life has descended into sitting in a police cell waiting to be asked questions about something I have no knowledge of. The only good thing about this is that they haven't found Jem dead.

My imagination ran riot earlier, but Bekah Bradley wouldn't have arrested me for abduction if Jem was dead. I think about

Ben and Angel and tears spill. They don't deserve this. If this is Daniel's doing, he's hurting his own children to get his own way. They would be missing me and asking for me.

My heart thumps hard as the minutes tick by and I imagine the worst scenarios. I shut my eyes and try to breathe evenly and slowly. I could never have imagined how difficult it is not to have a point of time reference. I try to count to sixty and count the minutes on my fingers to distract myself but lose count and lie down. I imagine my mum's face when she heard about me being arrested, if she were around now. The shame, on top of the shame of splitting from Daniel. Mum was straight down the line until the day she died. The terrible spell is broken as the cell door opens and the female officer stands outside.

'They're ready for you now. And your solicitor's here. I'll take you to the interview room.'

We retrace our steps to the outer sanctum of the station, and she leads me into a stark, grey room. A man I have never seen before is sitting on the other side of a table. He stands up and holds out his hand. I just stare. He's about forty-five and looks a lot like my usual brief.

'I'm Mark's brother, Sam. He's on another case and I have precedence here.' He looks around and sits. I stand. He continues. 'So, you've been arrested for the abduction of Jem Carter. Right?' I nod as he reads from a sheet. 'Who is your ex-husband's partner? And there's been a search of your property. And car. And you granted access to your phone.'

I sit down. 'This really has nothing to do with me.'

He is reading. He doesn't speak for a while. Then he looks up at me.

'Okay. They've completed a search of your property and removed some items.' I scan my home for anything incriminating. He sighs heavily. 'There's some... graffiti?'

I nod. 'Look, it doesn't matter what they found. I can

explain. But what matters is that I have done nothing to Jem. I was with people when she went missing. And Daniel told me she left a note.'

'Yes. So I see. And there's been no ransom. Who were you with?'

'I phoned my friend Lisa earlier in the day. She works here, at the station. And then Tim. Tim Watson. I was with him all night.'

He writes.

'Good. Have you got contact details? For Tim Watson? So we can confirm?'

I think. I've got his number – oh yes, I've got that all right. I retrace my steps at Tim's apartment. I lower my eyes.

'It's a pretty casual relationship. I've got his number. It's in my phone. And his flat is on Tiverton Street in Holmfirth. Number 5.'

He looks up. 'How long have you known him? Is he a reliable witness?'

I flash back to Tim's intent stare and his unwavering attention. And his reluctance to commit.

'About six months. And yes, he will definitely confirm he was with me. He lives at that apartment now. He lived with his mum before that.'

Sam's eyebrows raise and I can't tell if the fact that Tim lived with his mum makes things better or worse. I have lost my gut feeling because nothing is how it seems to be. He is writing frantically, then he pauses.

'Look, we don't have time to discuss everything, but I'll get the notes from the questions. Just remember you don't have to comment if you don't want to.' I grimly remember every police drama I have ever watched and the endless 'no comments'. He leans forward. 'I believe you when you say you haven't abducted

Jem Carter. I'll defend you as my client. But you need to tell me the truth because some of this looks tricky.'

My stomach lurches. 'Tricky?'

'Yes. They're saying they have some compelling evidence. I was wondering why they had brought you in when you had witnesses to say you were with them when this lady went missing. But let's see what they have to say. Just ask me if you are confused about anything.'

I can hardly breathe. What compelling evidence?

'How can they have compelling evidence if I didn't do it? I don't understand.'

He pauses and thinks. 'They build a case. They use all kinds of evidence to build a picture around the crime scene. They are testing it by asking you questions. If you can disprove the evidence, all well and good. But if not...'

I stare at him. 'What?'

'Well, if they charge you, it will be up to a jury to decide.'

The reality hits me square in the face. This isn't just a questioning session. This is the beginning of trying to frame me for a crime I have not committed. I feel vomit rise and I rush towards a wastepaper basket in the corner of the room just in time to see Bekah Bradley and DC Sharples enter.

CHAPTER TWENTY-THREE

I don't vomit. I grip the bin to my chest, but Bekah takes it from me. I panic again.

'I feel sick.'

She reaches into her bag and hands me an air-sickness bag.

DC Sharples laughs. 'Ready for anything. That bag's like Mary Poppins's.'

I stare at Bekah. She is the least Mary-Poppins-like woman I have ever met. Her features are soft, but she is pale and her auburn hair makes it more pronounced. Her lips are almost purple against her blue-white skin. DC Sharples is tanned in comparison. She waves us to our seats as a uniformed officer arrives with a large cardboard box. She smiles at us.

'Here's another bag of tricks.' She clicks on a recorder. 'For the purpose of the recording, the interview has begun at four forty-five on sixteenth October. DS Bradley and DC Sharples are interviewing Lauren Wade who is represented by...'

She turns her attention to Sam. I realise that they have never met before and wonder how experienced he is.

'Sam Smithers. Jenner and Co.'

She smiles at us. 'Okay. Let us begin. Lauren, we have

reason to believe you have abducted Jem Carter. We have already established in a previous informal interview your relationship with Ms Carter and Mr Wade.' She pushes some papers across the table. 'I'm going to ask you up front, Lauren. Did you see Jem Carter on the 5th October or the 6th October?'

I shake my head. 'No. I was with Tim Watson. We went back to mine after spending the weekend at a hotel and he left before the kids were dropped off. I didn't see her at all, but I did get a message from her.'

'So, what is your relationship to Mr Watson?'

'He's my boyfriend.'

'How long for? How often do you see him? You say he lives in Holmfirth?'

I sigh. I suddenly feel ashamed. It creeps through me as I imagine the police knocking on Tim's door and explaining what has happened. It will be the last straw.

'Six months or so. He stays over when Daniel has our children. I stayed at his Sunday.'

Bekah taps the pen on the desk. She reads some notes Sam has passed to her.

'You told Mr Smithers it was casual. That doesn't sound casual. To be clear, I'm asking because we need a full picture. We'll check with him, of course.'

'It's casual in the sense that we have our own lives. We don't live in each other's pockets or live together. That's what I meant.'

'But he can confirm where you were on certain dates?'

'If he was there, yes. And we exchange messages and speak on the phone.'

She looks at my mobile encased in a plastic evidence bag.

'Yes, and if necessary we'll have a look at that too. So you received a message from Jemima Carter? And the message read: *Lauren. You've got to help me. Please.*'

'Yes. I phoned it in.'

'So I see. Days later. After you'd checked with your ex-husband Daniel what he thought had happened to Jem?'

I feel a sharp sting of danger. Is that what he said? Is it?

'No. I told him about the message. He showed me the note. He told me not to worry. Then when her car was found he came over to mine all angry.'

'So, you went over to Daniel's home?' She reaches into the box and brings out the brass key in a polythene bag. 'When were you last at Daniel's house, Lauren?'

I look at Sam. He nods.

'I... I...'

She presses on. She reaches into the box again and brings out something pink. Oh my God. It's Jem's jumper. They must have found it in my bedroom.

'I can explain...'

She's in the box again. She brings out a photograph and lays it out in front of me. It's the paint daubed on the bedroom wall. I can almost smell the turps mixed with Jem's expensive perfume. I am horrified as she produces an evidence bag with hair in it.

'We found some debris in your bed. Obviously, it hasn't been analysed yet, but this isn't your hair, is it?'

I look at the long blonde hair in the evidence bag. I flashback to Jem on top of my Daniel. 'Sweet Home Alabama'. Her laughing.

'She was there. With him. In our bed. I haven't been in there since–'

DC Sharples interrupts. He holds up the photo of my terrible artwork. 'The paint was still wet.'

'I was trying to wash it off.'

I realise I am sobbing. Sam holds up his hand.

'Can we take a pause?'

He hands me a bottle of water and I swig at it. One eye is on the items on the table, and I wonder what else she has in her box. They wait patiently until I control the tears. I still feel deep sobs, but I try to breathe normally. Then Bekah goes again.

'DC Sharples and I were at The Rosarium the other day. The back door was open, which was unusual. We alerted Mr Wade, and he went straight over. The door was locked when he arrived.' She waits for me to say something. When I don't, she leans forward. 'Lauren, Daniel has told us all about your behaviour towards him and Jem. He's been worried about your mental health. He believes you were in the house that day. That you had a key.' She picks up the evidence bag with the key in it. 'And you do have a key.' She puts it down. 'Lauren, were you in the house when we were there the other day?'

I stare at her. I suddenly feel very cold. I cannot move. I know what is happening now. I know where this is going. She waits, then speaks again.

'Okay, Lauren. Were you in Daniel's house the day Jem Carter went missing?'

I answer quickly. 'No, I was not.'

They both nod. DC Carter makes a note. Bekah produces a writing pad. I feel weak. It's my jotter. She opens it. I'm faced with the picture of stick men and women with all our names on them. And Jem and Daniel crossed out. My God. This does not look good.

'Anything to say about this, then?'

I feel tears in my throat. 'I was drawing some boundaries. That's all. Just some boundaries. I do that in my job. I needed to keep away from them. To move on. Daniel was trying to blame me. Please. This is nothing to do with me.'

Bekah produces my phone. 'You see, the problem I have is that you have messages on your phone from a woman who has gone missing.' She reaches into the evidence box again. She pulls out the note from earlier, again in a plastic evidence bag.

'And another note from someone telling you that you will pay for what you have done. You can see how that looks?'

I snort. 'To you, maybe. But Jem was asking for help...'

She shakes her head. 'Not just to me. There are two ways to see Jem's message. I gave you the benefit of the doubt when I saw you the other day. But if you had kidnapped her and taken her somewhere that message is asking you to help her.' She holds up a photograph of the message. '*You've got to help me. Please.* And when I heard about your former behaviour from Mr Wade, how you'd harassed them...'

I finally blow. 'Well, he would say that, wouldn't he? He wants rid of me and if I'd taken Jem somewhere, she'd hardly have her phone, would she?' I hear myself shouting, disconnected. 'He's with someone else already, you know. She's not been gone two minutes, and he's already sleeping with someone else in their bed.' My voice bounces off the wall. There is complete silence. They all stare at me. Then Bekah speaks.

'How do you know that, Lauren? That's very specific. Almost as if you were in the house.'

My breathing is heavy. I am almost blind with rage. But Sam's warning look stops me from answering. She continues.

'We've also had a report that you were at Daniel's parents' house this morning trying doors. And we looked at CCTV around The Rosarium and we saw you driving away not long before we picked you up. What were you doing, Lauren?'

'I was looking for my children. They should have been in school today. But they didn't take them. They should have been back home with me. Why don't you ask him about that? Keeping my children from me? Eh? He's taken my children.'

I am crying again. I can't stop. She sighs again.

'He's their father. And that's not our job. We're not here to referee in your marriage, Lauren. We're here to solve crimes. What I am wondering here is if you've got the two mixed up.

More specifically, if you've decided to take matters into you own hands and remove Jem from the equation?'

I feel hysteria rising. I am standing and Sam is trying to pull me back into my seat.

'I haven't. I haven't done anything to her. I have no idea what has happened to Jem. You're right. We weren't best friends, but I would never hurt her. Never.'

DC Sharples nods deeply. 'Except that time in the nightclub.'

I slump in my seat. 'I told you. I didn't do that either. Daniel's setting me up. It's him you need to speak to. He needed Jem out of the way so he could move her replacement in. Like he did with me. Now he wants me out of the way.' I wipe my eyes. 'Ask Tim. I was with him when Jem disappeared, and he knows someone tried to break in.'

DC Sharples returns service. 'Yet you didn't report it?'

'No because I thought it was something to do with Daniel and–'

Bekah chimes in quickly. 'You were scared you might get caught for what you have done.'

I am suddenly calm.

'No. No. Look, I have nothing to do with Jem's disappearance. I haven't done any of the things you are accusing me of. All this has done is make Daniel think I have done something to Jem and now he's taken my children somewhere.'

She studies me. She is tapping her pen on her lips. Bekah is super intense. I can sense her thinking and working things out. Finally, she speaks.

'And you think your ex-husband is implicated?'

'That's my theory. Based only on the fact that he's got a new girlfriend already.' I admit to myself that in all probability, that could also be because he is a complete bastard. But I don't say that.

'Is that what you're doing with Daniel? Getting even? Bringing justice for what he did to you when he cheated on you with Jem?'

I blink at them. Sam butts in. 'You don't have to answer that, Lauren.'

But I answer. I dredge up the strength from somewhere inside and blast out my words. 'No. It isn't. Daniel was cheating in a marriage. But no, I am not after justice for me because, well, them's the breaks, right? I might have resented Jem and Daniel, but I certainly wouldn't harm either of them. I *haven't* harmed either of them. All these things Daniel has told you I did? Most of them are an exaggeration or engineered by Jem. But yes, I was upset. He's telling you about them now, but if I am such a bad person, why didn't he report them before?' I lean forward. 'The same reason I didn't report the note, or the scratched window frame or my broken gate lock or the footprints in my garden. Because they amounted to nothing. No one was hurt.' I pause. 'Now poor Jem is in danger, it's all spilled out of his mouth. And you're adding two and two together and getting fifty. Daniel will get his justice in time. People will see through him, eventually. See him for what he is. A shallow mess. A liar.' I stare at them. Then I shake my head. 'And if you think it's me who has hurt Jem, tell me this. How would I send myself a message from her? And why would I call Dave to report it?'

They are all staring at me. I see Bekah's mouth turn up a little at the edge. I swear she is forcing back a smile. She writes some notes, pushes some papers at Sam, then stands.

'Right. Sam, these are the rest of the evidence sheets. There are still some interviews in progress. We'll reconvene in the morning and see where we are then. Sharpy, box.'

DC Sharples throws the evidence back in the box, picks it up and follows her out. Sam exhales heavily. I look at him.

'Have you done this before?'

He shakes his head. 'A couple of times.'

I sigh. 'Perfect. Bloody perfect.'

'The good news is that they don't have enough. For the abduction, anyway. Are you sure Tim Watson will confirm your whereabouts?' I nod. He'd better. Sam continues. 'Problem is the rest of it. If they do charge you and you go to court, the other business won't look good. Is there anything else you want to tell me before we go any further?'

I think back over the past, the cameras, my sobbing outside the window at family scenes. Following Jem to school. The sarcasm and the sadness. The sneaking around with the big brass key. And finally, reclaiming the cameras. I want to tell him. I want to tell someone. It is seeping out of my pores and now is the time to come clean. But I can't. Even now, when I am on the precipice of being found out, I am too ashamed. I am too afraid of them taking Ben and Angel forever if I tell them what I have done.

'No. No. Nothing else.'

CHAPTER TWENTY-FOUR

My night in the cell was unbearable. The noise of drunks and criminals in adjoining cells was almost as sharp as the pain I felt missing Ben and Angel. Wondering what Daniel had told them. Going over and over the case Bekah Bradley was building against me. How I hadn't helped myself. Regretting all the mistakes I have made and hoping Jem was okay.

Sam Smithers was right. If I am fitted up for abducting Jem, my erratic behaviour will seal my fate. My body is sore from turning on the barely there mattress that appeared on the hard slab while I was being interviewed. I am desperate. I turn Bekah Bradley's words over and over in my mind and arrive back at Daniel.

Belinda has never liked me. She would see this as an opportunity to consolidate her 'bad mother' narrative. She has occasionally dropped the kids off when Daniel has been busy, and I saw her eyes wander to my unkempt lawn and unwashed windows. I can only do so much. But Belinda could never see past the fact she had never worked and had devoted all her time to raising Daniel and his sisters.

None of this is her fault, but she would relish the

opportunity to take Ben and Angel away from me. When Daniel left with Jem, she encouraged him to take up shared parenting when he had originally offered to have them every other weekend. She pushed and pushed and eventually he agreed. Her rationale was that she would get to see more of them that way. That she was a stabilising influence. In reality, they were spoilt and pandered to. I saw it creep through into their behaviour when they came home.

But she is their grandmother, and my mother is dead, so I put up with it. They spent more and more time with her as Daniel and Jem began work on the house, then suddenly, when their bedrooms were ready, they came home with excited stories about how Jemi had let them order their own toys and posters for their rooms online. How they were going to stay at The Rosarium half the week and how Jemi would make pudding after every meal – they even had an ice-cream maker.

My blood boiled. First Belinda and now Jem Carter. Both children would repeat what they had said about me, the barbed comments about the house and my cooking. I know only too well that women can be bitches, but I was in no state after the shock of Daniel leaving to deal with it. Fast forward to today, sitting in a cold cell in a police station. I only wish I had dealt with it better.

The cell door opens, jolting me from my regret. Bekah Bradley appears and I wait for DC Sharples to follow her, but he doesn't appear. She closes the door gently and sits down beside me.

'So, Tim Watson has verified that he was with you when you said he was.'

I stare straight ahead. 'Aren't I supposed to have my brief here?'

She nods deeply. I look at her boots. Shiny and new. She smells of pressed linen.

'I just wanted to let you know that you'll be free to leave soon. When the paperwork is done. But...' She sighs. I see her hands clutching the edge of the mattress, her knuckles white. She reaches into her suit pocket and pulls out an evidence bag. My heart thumps. She holds it up in front of me. 'These.'

She holds up the bag. It's the cameras. I feel fire inside me. But I blink at her.

'Okay.'

'So, what are these?'

I breathe in. This is my opportunity to come clean. I could bare my soul here. Tell her everything. I try it out in theory and feel the relief ebb through me. But the consequences loom and I falter.

'Cameras. I was going to use them to CCTV my home.' I turn to look at her. 'You know, after someone tried to break in.'

She nods and places the bag between us. 'Yeah. Tim mentioned the window and the gate. But I was wondering if you'd already used them, say, to watch someone?'

She stares at her feet. I am too scared to speak in case the truth spills out. The words push in my chest. But she fills in for me.

'Look, Jem Carter is obviously in danger. If there is anything you can help us with, then we could come to some arrangement. I'll spell it out. I know you've been in her house. I can't prove it at this point. I also have a feeling you've been watching your ex. Again, I can't prove it. But I'll have these cameras checked and it would be better if you told me now...'

I feel a tear escape and wipe it away. When my voice does appear, it is choked.

'Have you ever caught someone you loved with someone else? In your bed?' She doesn't look at me. But she shakes her head. 'I was in shock. Deep shock. Everyone was telling me it happens to dozens of women every day. That half of all marriages end in divorce. But I thought he loved me.'

Even as I say it, I know it sounds pathetic. Weak. Desperate. And I was. I continue.

'I was left with two children who I would move mountains for but somehow I was incapable of doing anything. All my strength was gone. Everything was gone.' I turn to look at her and our eyes meet. 'I had to get my strength back somehow. I had to know what was happening to my children. You have to understand that I was in a battle.'

Her pale cheeks are a little flushed. It occurs to me that perhaps Bekah isn't used to people baring their souls. Perhaps she is used to cold, hard facts. She'd said as much yesterday.

'You told me yesterday that you weren't social services. That you were investigating a crime. I didn't do anything to Jem. I was worried about my children. That he would find a way to take them away. He knew what that would do to me. He knew. And now he has.'

She pulls in her lips. 'What would it do to you?'

I stare at her. 'It would lessen me. What he did already weakened me, but he wanted more. I thought I was imagining it. He did everything he could to make sure I was least able to function. He hardly paid maintenance. He taunted me with her. Bit by bit I was less and less. He pushed and pushed, but it was only when Jem's car was found that I put it together. He wanted me to fail. He wanted me on my knees. I was an inconvenience. And now, Jem is too. She's gone, and I'm here. I can't prove this, either, but I feel it. I feel it inside.'

She looks at me. Her eyes soften. She clasps her hands in front of her.

'There's something else, Lauren–'

I interrupt. 'Jem's dog. She would never leave that dog. And

Daniel did seem genuinely upset when he came over to mine. But that woman... did he...?'

She shakes her head. 'Mr Wade stuck to the facts. He didn't make a complaint against you. The things I said yesterday were my theories. He hasn't put it together. But I have. You in the house. Recently. For whatever reason. You knew a lot about his movements with this woman. The cameras hidden in your home.'

Her breathing is shallow and quick. Her exterior is cool, but I can tell she is panicking. I think about Jem and her smirk. Her holding Angel's hand as she walked her into school and side glancing my car where I sat weeping. Her kissing them and waving as they ran into their classrooms. The pink, pink room, and the roses. The understated gold-edged life she led compared with my lead-weighted existence.

Whatever has happened to her, I know she doesn't deserve it. I desperately hope that she is found and returned to Daniel as soon as possible. I feel for her parents, having barely put Angel in her place for a second and experienced the pain of empathy. She asked me for help. And I would have if I had known how.

But this. This. Admitting to my episodes of deep jealousy is sacrificing myself. Being jealous is one thing, but playing it out is another. I would never, ever be able to explain what I had done adequately. I don't even know what the consequences would be. My mind reels over stalking and harassment, and potential charges as I weigh up my options.

I can't. I can't sacrifice myself for Daniel. Or Jem. I can't lose my children. Chances are she will find out anyway, but hopefully Jem will be found before that. I thought I would be free once I got the cameras back, but in reality, I am more trapped than ever. Just waiting around for Bekah Bradley to find out I was watching my ex. I rub my arms and tell myself I am sorry. Sorry for doing it. Sorry for ever thinking it was the right thing. I suddenly blurt out my feelings.

'Where's the line? Where is it?'

'I'm not with you? Line?'

'Yeah. He hurt me. Badly. I thought I wouldn't recover. Yet there was no one to tell. Lisa, yeah, she listened. But her answer was to have a good time. Like in Sinead O'Connor's "Nothing Compares 2 U". You know?' She nods. I spew out more. 'My mum's dead and my dad's in Spain. I have no one else. I had to provide for my kids and keep a roof over my head. All the time I felt like I was dying. But I couldn't report a crime. When does it become a crime? Where's the line?'

She thinks and then speaks. 'I was going to say when it harms someone. But no. It's not that. It's when something happens to break the law. Criminal law. So, I'm thinking more Alanis Morrissette. "Your House". Problem is, life isn't forgiving, is it?' I shake my head. Her eyes are shining, and I see a glint of empathy. She continues. 'And it's one thing thinking those thoughts or writing a song about them. But it's another thing following through. I guess that's where the line is. It might not seem fair, but that's where it is.'

I nod. My throat tightens to suppress the truth. *I was in a bad place* won't cut it here. I can't ask her what the consequences will be if I tell her what I did. She already knows what Daniel has told her and no charges have been brought for that. But I know if he found out I have been in his home – I shiver – his and Jem's home and spied on them, he would make me pay. I shudder when I think of the camera in their bedroom. How would I explain it? How would I tell them I never watched them? I only watched him the other day because I needed to escape undetected.

No. I can't. I can't tell her. The silence in the cell is deafening.

Then she touches my arm. It's the light touch of someone who is going to tell you something bad. I panic.

'No. No. They haven't... she isn't...'

She shakes her head. 'No. Jem Carter is still missing. But I have to ask you some more questions.' Her eyes say 'off the record' and I nod. 'Did you receive some flowers at your place of work?'

'Yeah. From Tim. Just Tim and a kiss.'

She takes a deep breath. 'They were ordered on Jem Carter's credit card. We went to the address you gave us and I can confirm that the property belongs to Peter Jakeson who lives there. We checked the electoral register and one Timothy Watson who works with Peter Jakeson lives at 23 Dobson Street, Manchester.' She looks me straight in the eyes. 'With his wife and two children.'

I gasp. 'No, he... he...'

She continues. 'We obtained a warrant and searched his house and found Jem Carter's credit card in his possession. His wife said he worked away at weekends and could not provide an alibi for the 6th and 7th October.'

I am silent with shock. Tim is not who I thought he was. Lisa was right. My God. Bekah presses on.

'Lauren, I want you to think back to that weekend. Was there any time that he left or could have left?'

'No. We went to a hotel. We were together the whole time on the 5th. Then on the 6th he left just before Dan turned up. She wasn't with Dan and I wondered where she was.' My lip trembles but I am too shocked to cry. 'They were inseparable. She was always in the car.' I want to mention the woman I saw the other day but I don't. This isn't the time. Tim. Tim. Married. With kids. 'The only time he could have gone anywhere was when I was asleep.'

'We've checked with the hotel. His car didn't move from the

car park. They checked the CCTV and neither of you left the whole time.'

I reel even more. She thinks we were in it together. None of it makes sense to me or her.

'But we only stayed one night. We came home at lunchtime on Monday.' I think. He did pop into work. I can hardly bear it. The reality that he could be the one who has Jem hits me. I blurt it out. 'He did leave for a while. Just after we got back at around one. He said he was going into work. He was a couple of hours.'

She is alert. 'Anything else?'

'Yeah. I thought it was strange. I was talking to him about it on Sunday and he was clinical. Cold. All "now she's out of the way". Have you arrested him? Is he here?'

She nods. 'Yes. We have.' She pulls her lips in. 'Look, you can go for now. But we'll need you back in with your solicitor to answer some more questions about Mr Watson. Did you know he was married?'

'No! I'd never do anything like that. I thought he lived at that apartment. He never had any trouble getting away...'

Which was, on reflection, not true. The messages. The awkwardness. The abrupt 'no's to invites. The scrupulously arranged plans that could not be broken. The out-of-town hotels. I am so, so stupid. Again.

'If there is anything at all...' I shake my head. I need to get all this straight in my mind. 'You'll get your personals back when you leave. But please think about it. Her life might be in danger.'

Bekah sighs. Eventually she stands. She hands me another business card. I take it and try to smile at her.

'I will call you the moment I have anything. Please find her. Please.'

She smiles and knocks on the cell door. The lock clicks and she opens it.

'Okay. Look, don't go anywhere. We'll still need to talk to you. But I'll send someone down to fetch you.'

She leaves and I am wracked with a guilt that I have brought this on Jem. I might not have taken her, but this is all because of me.

CHAPTER TWENTY-FIVE

By 9am I am on my way home. My clothes and personal possessions were returned and in minutes I was back at the desk signing for them. I read and signed a statement which more or less repeated what I had said in the interview, and another that detailed what I had told Bekah at the house. It was almost as if the past eighteen hours had never happened. But it had. And I was much clearer about what had preceded them.

I asked about Jem and the desk sergeant just shook his head. 'No news.'

I switched my mobile phone on. There were seventeen missed calls from Tim and two from Lisa. None from Daniel or Belinda. One from Sam Smithers. Thirty-three messages. My knees buckled from tiredness and hunger, and I resolved to wait until I got home to read them. My memory argued, *look what happened last time you didn't read a message immediately* but my body was weak. I needed time.

I wanted to google Jem and see if any more details were online. I wanted to phone Daniel and tell him to bring my children home. That I had been released without charge and he was wrong.

But all that would have to wait until there was a space in my life to sit down and make a plan. This couldn't go on. I'd made some bad decisions, but that didn't mean that I had to keep making them. I need to think. About Tim and how this had happened. About the danger I had been in too.

I ordered an Uber and waited outside the police station until it arrived. Now, as it turns the corner up to my home, I see a Blue Renault parked beside my car. As the Uber grinds to a halt on the gravel, a woman gets out of the blue car. Her tracksuit bottoms and blue hoodie tell me she is not the police. She stands, arms folded, until I get out of the car. Then she steps forward.

Her eyes are angry, and her brow creased with a frown. Her bottom lip trembles and I momentarily wonder if she is related to Jem. She doesn't look like her at all. Completely different. Her hair is a dark sharp bob, and she is much shorter than Jem's model height. I wait for her to make the announcement, but she doesn't. She just stares at me, tears welling.

I step forward and, quick as a flash, she slaps my face hard. The sting takes me by complete surprise and I stumble backwards onto the bumpy gravel. In that moment a baby starts to cry. She hurries to the car and opens the door. The crying is louder, and I hear a child's voice.

'Mummy's sad. Sad, Mummy?'

She's suddenly comforting and soft. 'It's okay, Jenny. You look after Dane. Mummy's not sad. Mummy just needs a moment with the lady.'

She shuts the car door as I rise. I stand in front of her.

'What the actual...? Why did you do that?'

My face stings and I veer away as she moves towards me again. Then I see what is wrong. Her eyes are crazed, and her face is a question without a certain answer. Her shoulders slump and she holds her arms across her. I recognise the madness of seeing someone you had only imagined in your worst nightmare for the first time. The shock of the fall. I try to explain.

'Look, if it's Tim, I know. I know what he's done.' I glance at the car and the horror sinks in. 'Are they...?'

His children. Are they Tim's secret children? We consider each other, our anger approaching an equal level. But her face is contorted with confusion.

'Know what?'

I snap back. 'Look, let's not play games. You obviously know what he's done, or you wouldn't be here assaulting me.'

She steps back and glances at the car. The mention of assault appears to have made her think of her kids and I rue the day I didn't think about mine when I crossed the line. She blows air out and runs her hands through her hair.

'Are you Lauren?'

'Yes. Lauren Wade. And you?'

She paces up and down. She's skinny and pale, like she's been worried for some time. Like she's been wondering where this guy who says he loves her is. Oh yes. I know it well. She's wondering how this all fits together and how she can get him back. And hurt me at the same time. Because it's this kind of madness that being on the hurting end of lies and deceit brings. A searing drive to *get to the bottom of it* and to *get some justice* that takes someone to another person's home, to their personal space, to dole out whatever they can to set the record straight.

When she doesn't speak, I fill in. 'Look, I know what Tim's done. You must know about Jem. It's all over the news. Is that why you're here?' I snort and shake my head. 'I swear I knew nothing about you and your children. He's a liar.'

My face stings and I step backwards as she walks towards me. But she stops and calms a little. Then she speaks.

'Oh yes. I bloody know who you are.' She is pointing and I

can feel droplets of spittle hit my smarting face. Her children are crying, and I can see she is conflicted. She looks at the car and looks at me. Then she begins to walk away down the drive.

I hurry after her. 'Wait. What are you doing? Your kids...'

She spins to face me. 'You want him? You get them as well. I'm done. Done.'

She starts to walk again, and I panic. I grab her arm firmly.

'You can't leave them. Tim's not here. He doesn't live here. He's been staying at his mate's flat in Holmfirth. He's not here. I live here alone. With my children.'

She shrugs my hand from her arm and stares at me, confused. 'Tim's children? Timothy Watson. And I'm Tracey Watson. And they are our children.'

Her eyes brim over. She shakes her head and looks around. But I am a step ahead.

'No. My children from a previous marriage. I've only known Tim for a few months. It wasn't even serious.'

She is in my face. She is shouting at me and I back away.

'Oh. A bit of fun, was it? A bit of fun? You've no idea, have you? No idea what's going on.'

It's all starting to make sense. The children are still crying, and I look at the car.

'Yes, I do. I do now.' I can feel the little strength I had drain out of me. 'Look. You'd better come inside. We can talk there. Bring your little ones.'

I walk towards the house. She is unsure. I can sense the crazed anguish as I hear her footsteps behind me on the gravel. I walk towards the car, and she follows me, sobbing. She hurries forward and opens the door. Jenny jumps out and holds her arms out to me as Tracey unclips and lifts out a baby carrier. I look at her and Jenny, and she nods. I pick her up and she is light as a feather.

We walk slowly round the side of the house to the back door, and I open it. I hadn't realised that when the police search your house they do not tidy up after themselves. Papers are strewn across the sofa and cushions upturned. Contents of drawers are on the kitchen worktops. I dread to think what the bedrooms are like. Jenny is into everything, and I scoop up the debris and fling it back into drawers.

'Mummy, I need the toilet.'

I look at Tracey. 'Leave him here, it's just upstairs. Sorry about the mess. Police search.'

She nods. I put the kettle on. The baby has Tim's eyes. He sucks his fist and smiles at me. I try to smile back and somehow manage it. He lets out a little giggle and I feel a sob in my chest. How has it come to this?

Tracey returns. She gives Jenny her phone to play with and she and the baby are distracted. I can barely look at her.

'Tea or coffee?'

She shrugs. 'Tea. No sugar. A dash of milk.'

Like Tim, I want to say. But I don't. I look around the kitchen. 'They were searching my house as my ex's partner is missing. They thought I might have... but obviously I...' I dig the hole for myself, and she falls into it.

'... obviously you couldn't have as it was him. They came round. Asked him where he was. If he was with you.' Her voice trembles. She looks around. 'And they found things. Her things.'

I want to ask her what. What things? What happened? What did he do? But I can't

'Look, I had no idea at all about–'

'Me. And the kids? I find that hard to believe.'

'He told me he lived in an apartment. We went there.'

She stares at me. 'So, where did you go when he said he was away with work?' I'm horrified. I flash back to the loved-up

Sundays and Mondays and the overnight stays. The nights away and the romance. She makes a hollow laugh. 'We've been together for ten years. Married eight. These two came along and he took up longer hours and shifts. I thought we were forever. Then this. It's made me...' She thinks deeply for a while. I hear the kitchen clock tick in the background. 'Hollow. Empty.'

I know that feeling. I know it. I want to rush to hold her and tell her how sorry I am. But she is spiky and hurting. So I sip my tea.

'I honestly had no idea.'

She nods through her tears. 'How long?'

I count back in my mind. It's been a while. 'Months.'

Pain sears across her face and rebounds around the kitchen. She winces. 'There must have been another one, then. Before you. Did you... sleep together?'

Oh my God. She still doesn't see fully. She can't understand through the block of despair. No. That comes later. That clarity when the veil of lies blows away. I stare at the stone worktop.

'I'm not going to lie. Yes. And he never promised me anything. We weren't officially a couple.'

I'm not sure if I'm making it better or worse. She blows her nose on a tissue.

'Right. Was it here? Did he come here?'

I am under pressure. *Tell the truth, Lauren, tell the truth.* Lies have got me into this mess. I try to speak calmly. 'I met him in a café. I went there to get out of the house after my separation. Tim and I...' I see the pain again, a dent in her armour as I line myself up with what is hers. '...we went away a couple of times. And yes. He's stayed over here. But not when my kids were here. My ex has them half the week.'

Her eyes go to the freezer. 'That's them, isn't it?'

'Yes.'

She swallows hard. 'We live in a scruffy little terraced house. We've bought it. Saved every penny for five whole years. Had a new kitchen. It's yours and Tim's, Tracey, I told myself. That's all that matters, I told myself.' Her gaze traces the underlit cupboard and the beautiful linear worktops. I see my own face when I first saw how Jem had decorated The Rosarium. Bitterness mixed with pain. 'Nothing like this. Nothing so posh. Just some chipboard B&Q cupboards. But it was ours. But this.' She whistles and looks around. 'I can see why he was attracted to you. You're so pretty. And clearly loaded.' She snorts. 'So don't be under any illusions that he loves you. Tim only loves himself. Still, you seem to have slipped nicely into my husband's life. I hope you enjoyed it, I really do.'

She goes to pick up the baby carrier. I can barely stand as the shock waves hit me so hard. I turn to her as she passes me.

'Slipped into your husband's life? What do you mean by that?'

But I already know before she speaks. I have already been in this particular scenario. Except I was playing a different part. Could Jem have felt like this? Could she have not known the full story about me and Daniel? I cast my mind back to that day. She certainly seemed to think we were already over. Had he told her we were living together in name only. Or separated?

Tracey turns to me. She is very close. Right in my face.

'Life with kids is hard. Especially when you like your posh meals and hotels. He's found another me. Someone who isn't constantly knackered and smelling of cooking and baby sick. Someone with a posh house he can doss about at. A convenient shag.' She starts to laugh through her tears. 'I knew. Oh yes, I knew. But I couldn't accept it. I told myself you were a work colleague. Or a friend. Because Tim loves me.' She fake laughs, but her expression is not amused. Their baby laughs at her feet, a hysterical giggle, as their daughter tickles him. She looks at them.

'I've watched you through your windows. I put a note through your door. *You're going to pay.*' It all makes sense now. The trampled grass. The window. It was her. 'But you're not, are you? You're not going to pay. It used to be me. Now it's you.' She turns around and throws her tea over a pencil sketch of me hanging on the wall. She reaches into her handbag and fetches out a bundle of bank statements and credit card bills. She rips them and throws them into the air. They scatter like confetti over the stone floor and worktops. 'Enjoy.'

She is gone. She is out of the door and I hear her car start. She is turning out of the drive and out of my life before I can move.

And all I can think of is Jem. I have obsessed about her and hated her. I have punished her and made her life difficult. All the while, I had resented her wriggling into Daniels' heart and bed – into my place.

I stand at the lounge window and look out over the gravel drive. Lots of tyre treads from police vehicles and Tim's car. I have judged Jem and other women harshly for stealing married men. My own standards deigned anyone who had an affair downright evil. It is slowly occurring to me I might not always know the full story.

I certainly don't in this case. Suddenly I am the other woman; I am the person causing distress and desperation. Unintentionally, but I reluctantly admit that the red flags were there. Tim would never commit. He never took me to his place. He never let me see his phone. He always had to leave suddenly. He was unavailable for long stretches.

I am an idiot. I am the woman who he used. He was slowly getting his feet under my table. Getting me to chase him. Trying to separate me from my life. Getting a bit too comfortable with his bossiness. He'd quizzed me on my job and income, jokingly but thoroughly.

He'd suggested taking it to the next level. That was staying over more often. Yes. Tracey is right. I am mortified. I am the new woman. I am the fun. I am the sex. I am Jem.

I am the replacement.

CHAPTER TWENTY-SIX

I look around my beautiful home. The police made a messy dent in a few rooms that were reasonably okay. Now, it's littered with a layer of white shreds. I am in shock. The past twenty-four hours have driven home just how desperate I have been. Lying to the police and stealing someone's husband. Is that who I am? Who I have become? My God. Is that how people see me?

I slump onto the kitchen stool. I automatically reach into the space beneath the stone worktop where I keep my laptop. It's a gap for storing chopping boards and the like, but also an ideal place to hide it from Angel and Ben so they can't commandeer it for games. Pushing it under there has become second nature, and I feel shock that it is gone.

There is nothing on that laptop that they can't see on my phone in any case, as they are linked. If anything, my phone offers more insight into my life through my almost constant messaging. I open my phone instead. My email account springs onto the screen, and I can see a message from Linda Tomson, the practice manager at the surgery. I click open the email.

Hi Lauren,

I'd like to meet with you as soon as possible just to find out what is going on. As you know, the police came to the practice yesterday and took away some things from your office.

Please don't worry, we will support you any way that we can long term, but I'd like to discuss short-term options.

Let me know when you are free and I will make some space for that discussion.

Best,

Linda

I read it again. I'm not even an employee but I am contracted. I try to decipher if she's evicting me or just asking me to come in and chat. It's still important to me. Things have been so mixed up recently. My horrendous, desperate decision-making. My unknowingly becoming the person I have been persecuting. But one thing that reassures me and, in this moment, feels like a glimmer of warmth is that I put my work before it and completed the case notes.

It's at times like this that I appreciate my work. This is a huge crisis and there have been others. Difficulties coping with a newborn and a toddler. My separation from Daniel. Any time I felt less than a good mother or a not good enough wife. My work was reassurance that I am not completely useless.

I know that I never took a job to match my qualification. I was encouraged to carry on and study for a doctorate, but I wanted to get on with helping people. And I know I have. With the police and with the surgery. There are so many people suffering. The people I see are either recovering from a mental health problem or were clawing their way out of a huge life event. People for whom medication is not the answer. "They need someone to talk to" is a huge oversimplification but that relationship they form with me – holding the problem between us – is the first step on their recovery journey.

I think about getting therapy. I should have before. I had mentioned my issues with Daniel to my supervisor, but never my issues with Jem. It seemed disloyal to talk about another woman like that. Weak, somehow.

I email her back and tell her I will be at the surgery at 10am tomorrow morning. I completely understand that police traipsing through their workplace is not ideal, and I can't promise it won't happen again. I revisit the spectre of the worst possible scenario and shiver. But I do know that whatever happens I will be fine. Me and the kids will be fine. I know this is playing out now and it's inevitable my past actions will surface. But I didn't do this to Jem. I can't think about Tim yet. No. I can't conceive that he has done something like that.

I take my own advice. The advice I could have taken sooner, but I didn't. The advice I give to all my clients. To those people who are desperately looking back and punishing themselves, or in pain from past hurt. To those people who are predicting the future based on the past in the worst possible way. I stand in the warmth of a streak of sunlight streaming through the window. In this moment all is fine for me. And it will be again.

The light doesn't last for long. I look around me and consider clearing up the mess. Things need to change. I can't carry on like this. I sweep all the papers into a neat pile and push it into a bin bag. The obsessive side of me wants to pick up the statements and letters and see what Tim has been spending his money on. But deep down I already know. Hotels. Those two tiny children aren't enough for him. Tim wants the thrill of the chase.

He's suddenly no longer a distraction. The other night, right here in the kitchen, was bordering on his two worlds meeting. Made worse now by my knowledge of Tracey. His phone beep, beep, beeping while he stood there awkwardly. His breath on my face while she messaged him asking where he was.

I doubt I will ever see him again and relief surprises me.

What I want now is my children. I tidy up the mess that the police have left and push the sofa cushions back into place. It's time to face Daniel and Belinda. I call them both, but it goes to answerphone. So, I message Daniel.

> Daniel. I would like the children back, please. As you know, Jem's disappearance has nothing to do with me. I would like to come and collect the children. If you haven't replied by 5pm, I will ring my solicitor.

I hope Bekah Bradley is monitoring my phone. I hope she sees that my biggest concern is getting my children back where they belong. Despite feeling like I have committed the biggest crime ever known to man, I have nothing to hide now. Everything will be straight down the line from now on.

Of course I care about Jem. A little part of my heart wobbles every time I think she is in danger, or worse. Despite my utter dislike of her and what she did to my family, I can't bring myself to even think that she deserves whatever has happened to her. The likelihood of her having walked away is narrow now, and even Bekah Bradley admitted she wasn't optimistic.

Daniel hasn't taken Jem, but I can't shake the image of him in bed with another woman while the police search for his partner. That he is not the person I thought he was slowly permeates my soul. I'm in the awful position of knowing this, but still having to deal with him as we share two beautiful children. The knowledge that he will play on the fact I won't want to upset them so he can continue his behaviour unchecked stings me.

But, along with millions of other wronged partners, I will have to put up with it. That is behind the line, where all the domestic wrongdoings can never be brought to justice. I seethe at the injustice of it all and how emotional hurt and torture go completely unpunished, even though it's often the lever for revenge. My revenge.

That was the huge elephant in the prison cell. Bekah had those cameras. She's smart. I knew I'd said too much in temper in the interview, and she went away looking for how I knew so much about Daniel's life. In detail. Not watching from a car.

She put it together and asked me for help. I pace around, asking myself what I should do. I've been in situations when I've walked into a crowded restaurant and seen two people I know on the other side of the room. Usually seated in a shadowy corner for privacy. Two people who are married to two other people I know. Heads too close. Hands entwined. They don't see me because they are completely involved in each other, oblivious to the world.

But all the while, it turns over and over in my soul. Do I tell their partners or not? Do I tell the truth and cause pain, or take part in lying by omission and hope it's just a flash in the pan?

I'd even spoken to Daniel about it. He'd looked at me earnestly. 'Just leave it. Someone else will tell them.'

I'd wanted to point out that my job was to ease that sort of pain. Salve the distorted world of people who are hurt into something more liveable. That it was part of me. But I didn't tell them. He must have been laughing inside. Congratulating himself that he was getting away with it.

It occurs to me now that he has been tying himself in knots with lies all this time. Instances of his philandering had floated in my consciousness for a long time, but he was always able to explain. He was pristine in his explanations, even providing a 'and if you don't believe me, ask' or 'you can check the restaurant reservations'. He made *me* feel guilty for asking. Just like he made me feel guilty about going over to his house to tell him about Jem's message.

I know I have to take responsibility for my actions, and no one made me sit in the darkness of Daniel and Jem's garden watching them feed my children stir fry and home-made pink candy floss. No one made me snap and break into his house and plant those cameras.

The house is completely still. The chaos has closed in until it is almost pressing against me. The landscape of my home is littered with the mess of people who have become involved stepping ever closer. I can hear my breath and I silently ask myself why I did it. Why did I do all those things?

I have numbed the pain down. Taken every blow of my separation. The punches were not to my body, but to my mind. The perfection of Daniel and Jem's life. The success they made of quickly erecting a beautiful, functioning existence against the backdrop of my half-built chaos. I did all those things because I loved my family. I loved Daniel and Ben and Angel and me. The completeness of it.

When it broke, so did I. My knees buckle at the thought of it. The knowledge that we will never sit on the sofa cuddled together again or laugh together. We will never watch our children open Christmas presents together. It all seems sentimental against the possibility that Jem is dead, but it fits together in a way I haven't worked out yet. Jem is nothing to do with me, a stranger who barged into my life. Yet she has never been more important.

My phone beeps and jolts me out of the silence. It's Daniel. I scramble to read it.

> We're just coming back from Chester this evening. We took the children away to Dorothy's while you were indisposed. As my solicitor tells me you were released without charge and normal access must resume, you can collect them from my house tomorrow at 3pm. But I don't want any contact with you so please restrict any further contact to important issues about the children.

My thumbs are ready to tell him I want them now. I want to come and get them and hold them close. I want to face him and tell him I know what he is doing. I've always known, really. I know he has replaced Jem already. Then I remember Tracey's hurt. Her admission of staring through my windows and dropping anonymous notes. Her haunted eyes as she looked at me.

No. I won't do that anymore. I won't be in the game. I will fight for my children, but I won't fight for my marriage anymore. He will expect some smart remark about my solicitor and my access and my innocence. Something to keep this drama going and suddenly, my senses fix on something. Drama. Quiet, unassuming Daniel. His calmness and his straightforward talk, always designed to hit right at the bullseye of the matter and state his unmovable case. All the while, he is either stirring something up or hiding it.

His position statements, telling me what will happen; they are the curtains behind which he lived his duplicity. I expect doom to set in, but I feel pure joy. My realisation frees me. Daniel wants drama. I gave it to him in spades. But not anymore.

I respond to the message with one word. He has stated what

he wants me to do. I shake my head. These things take time. This has been a long, long journey to understanding what has happened. But I can finally see the light at the end of the tunnel. I tap send and Daniel hasn't got what he wants this time.

Fine.

CHAPTER TWENTY-SEVEN

I tidied up last night. All the debris of the past few days into black bin bags and put out for the binmen. I stood in the back garden, the long meadow grass bathed in moonlight, in the surety that there was no bogeyman coming to get me. The footsteps were Tracey. She had been the big bad wolf in my mind. I'd got carried away because I was worried about what had happened to Jem. Relief mixed with regret hit me, but there was no time for that.

I'd looked up at the stars and sworn to myself that tomorrow would be the start of a new life. I had to move forward. I went inside and made a list, a real list: handwriting on paper rather than a hastily put together to-do app prompting me for more and more tasks to complete. It is that list that greets me as I make coffee this morning.

It's seven fifteen, and I have made some decisions. I will agree to sell the house and move into a smaller place. I don't need all this space and this is where the ghosts of my marriage live. I tell myself I love the house, but now I realise I love the idea of it, waiting here for Daniel with all our things in it. And Tim. Bringing him here was just another shot at revenge for what Daniel did to me. I shock myself in admitting that I had used him for this – as well as fun. I need to own my sense of fun again.

Yes, I will sell up. That will free me from future Daniel – all that will be left is our divorce and co-parenting. I know his no-contact statement was to gain superiority and to bait me, but he is right. I was still running to him whenever something went wrong. Lisa saw it, and he used it. I was in his harem of women who need Daniel for something.

If I lose my space at the surgery, there won't be enough cash to keep me going, but it will allow me to make some changes. I check to see if the booking for my service has been paused and it hasn't. None of this is about money, really. It's about freedom. It's about not being reeled in by my ex. I feel anger bubble as I think about him portraying himself as the anxious partner to a missing woman while all the while he is with someone else.

This is what I must pull myself back from. That focus on Daniel's life at the expense and detriment of my own. There will be no more revenge escapades or weekend trips to posh hotels. No more going out with Tim or sitting in the dark at weekends. Even the thought of leaving that darkness that I was so fond of pulls me back in, but I will resist. I know I have said this a million times, but now I mean it. I have to.

And I will be honest. I will tell the truth and face the consequences. This is the scariest part of all because it means facing what I have done and never, ever doing it again. I'd often wondered what it meant when someone said another person was brave. It was often a comment on something that seemed so ordinary, but none of us know where another person has climbed from to reach that point.

Some of my clients are brave. Quietly stating their private anguish, often without a context. By the time we do dig deep and uncover the things they have been through, it is obvious that they have swum up from the depths already to face the problem they are suffering through. I hear *but other people can cope* so often, but those people may have a solitary problem and not legions of pain trailing them.

I grab my car keys from the worktop and push the list into my bag. I scan the house again for any sign that the police have been here. Or Tracey. I want Ben and Angel to feel that everything is the same. Stability. This is what I want for them. Finally, I push the laptop back into the space under the unit. A wave of excitement sears through me as I lock the door behind me. The children are coming home. Finally.

I sit in my car on the drive. First, I must do the right thing. I must do it before my meeting with Linda Tomson and before I pick up our children. I don't know the consequences, but whatever happens I will have done what I have to do. I will have shared any information I had and stepped out of the game I had been taking part in with Daniel. The behind-the-scenes competition for who could get away with most – and carry on hurting each other.

I take Bekah Bradley's card out of my bag. I don't want to speak to her because I will stumble over my words. And whatever happens next, this way I will get to spend time with the children before the next load of trouble rains down on me. But this time it will be trouble I have caused for myself. And I will accept that and take whatever is coming my way. I can only pray with all my heart that I type a text message to her mobile number that people understand.

> Hi. It's Lauren Wade. About the cameras. You can find what you are looking for in this app. The username is LWade pw gfhadurygh45. Goes back about a year. I hope it helps. Sorry and I do regret it. I can explain.

I reread it. It sounds desperate because it is. I have tried to pre-empt what will happen when she logs into the app and sees the footage from the four cameras. I know that in major enquiries the police overlook minor misdemeanours if there has been no complaint, and it helps move the enquiry on, as long as it isn't ongoing. This clearly isn't. But I am still worried. Daniel would definitely make a complaint. Or would he? Bekah told me he thought I had been in the house, yet he didn't make a statement.

He will definitely know the details of my arrest and the evidence produced – his solicitor would have asked. Jem's jumper. The key. Yet he hasn't made a complaint. I waver a little. But then I realise that admitting everything and taking the consequences cancels out the possibility that he can use all this as a lever against me.

I press send. She knows everything else because Daniel would have gone into great detail about how twisted I was after the separation. He exaggerated about the night at the party with Jem, making me look like a violent thug. He was determined to sully my name. Yet, I realise now, it would be difficult for him to take action because it was all on the emotional crime side of the line.

This isn't, but I am prepared. I own it. I did it. Even if it was a temporary madness, I did much, much more than I ever meant to do. I am sorry. So sorry. And now I've told someone it doesn't feel so heavy.

I drive. It's a beautiful day and white fluffy clouds puff above the hills in the distance. I put on the radio and nod my head to a Taylor Swift song. My phone pings and I pick it up from the passenger seat. It's eight forty-five and I am right on time. I see a response from Bekah. I tap on it and it's a single word.

Thanks.

No clues whether it will have consequences or any questions. I run the scenario through my mind. Her logging into the footage and watching it. They aren't recording all the time. I set them to only respond to movement. The guy I bought them from told me that this is how the battery is preserved. It charts the journey of my madness from when I installed the cameras to when I removed the last one. I gasp as I realise I will be on the last part of the footage, creeping through The Rosarium.

But she will most probably just pinpoint the day of Jem's disappearance. See what she was doing before she set off. What she was wearing. Jem writing a note to Daniel. Kissing Pepe. Ben and Angel told me she carried him everywhere and kissed him a lot. None of it makes sense, but I hope this helps. And I hope she sees Daniel sleeping with someone else days after and who knows what else he's been up to.

I message Lisa. She has been a good friend. I know it will be okay to speak to her again now and I can't wait. Tonight, I will have the kids tucked up in bed and she will come over. It will be like old times. Coffee and chat.

Still on for tonight? I could do with a shoulder 😊

She replies immediately.

Yep. Is 7 too early? X

I need more time with the kids.

Would 8 be okay, not getting the kids back until 5?

She responds with a thumbs up. That's everyone who matters contacted. I throw my phone onto the passenger seat. Que sera, sera. It will all be out in the open and I can make a new start. Eventually. I drive. I take my usual route to work but I am early. I can use this time to plan what I am going to say to Linda. I am five minutes from the surgery when my phone rings. It's an unknown number. I pull over and answer. It could be the police.

'Hello? Is that Lauren?'

I know instantly it is Tracey. She sounds more upbeat today. I can hear a radio in the background.

'Yes. Is everything okay?'

There is a pause. I wonder what this could be about. I thought we had said everything we needed to yesterday. Eventually she speaks.

'I just wondered... well, I wondered if you would talk to me about what happened. I know it's a lot to ask, but there's no point us hating each other.'

I stare through my windscreen as a car whizzes past me. If only I had done this with Jem. She's calling a truce.

'What did you have in mind?'

She laughs. 'Oh, thank goodness. I thought you might think I was a bit mad. After yesterday. I just wanted to meet up and show you something. And talk. We're in the same boat, me and you, aren't we? Both been duped by Tim.' Silence. Then she speaks again. 'I suppose I wanted to help as well. Help find that woman.'

I jolt. Jem. She wants to help find Jem.

'Why, do you know something?'

She sighs. 'I don't know. I just have a feeling... he's–'

I interrupt. 'Are you free for lunch? I need to do something before and I'm busy after two but...'

'Yes. Yes, brilliant. Where shall I pick you up? I know a nice little place just outside Greenfield.'

'No need to pick me up. I can meet you there.'

It's inconvenient and I don't know if I would make it in good time. I weigh it up carefully. She might be a bit bonkers but what's the harm? Especially if she has a theory about Jem. But she agrees.

'No, no, fine if you want to meet me. Look, why don't we meet in Uppermill and I can show you what I wanted to, then we can have lunch? Up near the entrance to the old school?'

She sounds needy. I can hear a desperation in her voice that reminds me of the times I would call Daniel's home on his days and demand that I speak to my children. Who can blame her? I'm surprised she has even surfaced yet after what she found out about her husband and me. And what he did.

'It's just something he said.'

I think.

'Did you tell the police about this?'

She laughs. 'No. No I didn't. It sounds a bit crazy, but you'll see what I mean.' Her voice trembles. 'And you know him, so I wanted your opinion before I tell them.'

'Okay. I'll meet you in the layby opposite the old school.'

It sounds like she is going to cry.

'Thank you. Thanks. I don't see the point in being bitter. If we can make a difference, then it makes us better than him, doesn't it?'

I nod to myself. Yes, it does. And if only I had taken this approach to my own bitterness, none of this would have happened.

CHAPTER TWENTY-EIGHT

I drive to the surgery and meet with Linda. She is both upset and sorry that the police arrived and took my things and happy to keep the space open for me. She stressed that asking me to not attend was a short-term arrangement and in no way placed any suspicion on me, rather protected patients from what she called "press intrusion".

Linda told me that the staff were horrified that the flowers were sent by Jem's abductor and wished me and my family well, and that Jem was found safe. I blinked at her and told her I did too. I didn't mention Tim by name but her face pleaded for a morsel of gossip that would allow her insider knowledge.

I obliged. 'They have the person who took Jem. It's just a matter of time before they find her now.'

She cocked her head sideways. 'And how does that make you feel given you dated him? Must have been a shock.'

It was the first time I had considered it, really. How much danger I had been in. All the times I had been alone with someone who could abduct a woman he barely knew. How he had been in my home. How much he knew about me. I form an answer quickly.

'It was a shock. And thank you, I am really grateful to you for being so understanding about the time I will need away from the surgery to get over it.'

I knew full well that wasn't her intention, but the tape recorder she had pointed to and asked my permission to record the interview has captured it for posterity. I had a contract, and I would not let her break it. She said her goodbyes and bustled off to the staffroom.

It was a shorter meeting than I intended and now I am standing by my car in the layby in Uppermill. I know this area. It's a favourite for tourists, and Daniel and I used to bring the kids here to collect conkers from the trees near the garden centre.

I wait and eventually see her blue Escort zooming up the road. Tracey pulls in behind me and waves. She looks incredibly chirpy compared with yesterday; I expect she has had time to think. She gets out. She's wearing a black Adidas tracksuit and her hair is freshly washed. She is pretty and I wonder what went so wrong between her and Tim. She smiles at me.

'Hello. Thank you for this. It's a bit weird, I know, but if it helps that poor woman.'

I don't tell her *that poor woman* played my part in a different break-up. I push my hands into my pockets.

'It certainly is weird. And please believe me, I never meant all this to happen. I had no idea.'

She is nodding and stamping on the ground. 'Mmm. Well, let's put that behind us for now. This is much more important. I was thinking about what he could have done with that woman. Jem, is it?'

'It is, but don't you think the police...?'

She laughs. 'Yes, of course. But let me explain. Tim liked walking. He liked traipsing over the tops and country pathways. He had his favourite spots and that's what I'm thinking. We could map them. Work out where he...' We are both silent. She stares at the ground. I blurt out what I've been wondering since I found out it was Tim.

'But why? Why would he do it?'

She shrugs. 'Why would he do any of it?' She looks directly at me and I see her eyes are pools of vivid blue. 'You weren't the first, you know. Not that I can prove it. But before you he used to go away for weeks at a time.'

I have my theories but I can't tell Tracey. I can't tell Tracey that her husband did this despicable thing because he wanted Jem out of the way so we could be together more. He more or less said so at the apartment. There isn't another reason. Unless Jem isn't the first. I shiver.

'Oh my God. What if he's done it before?'

She frowns. Deep lines appear on her forehead. 'Anything's possible. Before the kids I used to work nights. I never knew where he was.' She smiles. 'I'm a nurse. At the general. I still do part-time bank nursing. But his job always...' She waves a hand in front of her face. 'Sorry, sorry. You don't need to hear this.'

I shake my head. I do need to hear it. 'No, I'm sorry. Honestly. Before we go any further, I need to say something. I never, ever meant this to happen. Never. I didn't know about you. Or that he had kids.'

She nods. She is cool and composed. 'Would you have still done it if there were no children? Just a wife?'

My turn to frown. Somehow, I feel angry with her. Angry for making me the bad person. And for accusing me.

'No. Of course not. Look, this is his fault. He told me he was single.'

I think carefully. Did he ever actually say he was single? He told me he had a failed relationship. But I never asked. Not that day in the café. Not on any of our romantic weekends when

Tracey was slaving away in a hospital. Or caring for their children. She is nodding and smiling.

'Anyway, that's not the point, is it? We need to put this behind us and focus. On where your friend is.'

'She's not my friend. She's my ex's partner.'

'Well, whoever she is, we've got something in common. Tim. We both know him and we know how he thinks. We need to think of everything. I've got a pen and pad ready. Shall we go to the garden centre and get some tea?'

I shake my head. 'I don't know, Tracey. I think we should tell Bekah Bradley.'

'Oh, come on. We can do this. I want to be sure before we go to the police. I don't want him getting out of this. Bloody hell, it's the least you can do after...' Her lip trembles. 'I just want to talk. Please. I need someone to talk to.'

My heart flutters. I've been where she is now. Alone. Needing the truth. What harm can a cup of tea do? And Tim. Yes. She might know something. She might know what he has done with Jem.

'Okay, okay. But I need to go and get my kids at three.'

She turns and cuts through a gap in the wall. The garden centre is a short walk away through the field and along the canal. She smiles.

'Tea and scone on me. No point driving. We'll be back in no time...' I slip through the gap and she puts her hand on my arm. 'And thank you. I know you don't need to do this. I really appreciate it.'

The field is wet from a recent shower and I take care not to trample the daisies. She checks her phone and pushes it back into her bag.

'I've known him all my adult life. Been together on and off.'

'Same with Daniel. We've got two kids as well. Makes me

wonder if there are any good men. But I know there are. My dad. Even Daniel's dad. He's had a lot to put up with.'

She laughs. 'Yeah. To be fair, my mate's husband is a gem. Lovely bloke. And my uncle Si. Him too. There are good people around.'

We reach the stile over the tall wall. She jumps over and holds her hand up to help me. Her hands are small and cold. She is shaking.

'Are you okay?'

She nods. 'Yeah. Just a bit cold. It's all been a shock. One minute you think you are happily married and the next minute, well. I'm lucky, though. I've got my mum. She'd do anything for me. She's got the kids now. She watched them when he was away and I was working. She'd do anything for me and my children.'

I think about her angry in my kitchen. But not as angry as I was. She's taking this very well, really. People have very different ways of coping with things. In the days after Daniel left, I felt like I was on autopilot. I wanted to cry but it wouldn't come. Instead it seeped out in bitterness and, eventually, vitriol. I never spoke to anyone. Not even Lisa. It took me weeks to even speak about what had happened. I shocked myself. I never told anyone. I waited for them to find out Daniel had left me.

Lisa was first. She saw the emotion in me and broached it. 'What's he done, mate?'

I'd run out of the café, the same café I met Tim in months later, crying and sobbing. She ran after me and held me on the street corner, hugging me tightly as I cried my heart out. The dam broke and I couldn't stop.

I look at Tracey. No red eyes, yet. No tears for Tim. Not yet. But the simmering anger is there. The hand tremble and the gritted teeth. Her hands are fists and the frown is permanent. We are well along the canal now and I can see the huge conker trees towering over the low bridge in front of us. Branches laden with memories of me and Daniel and our tiny children giggling as he threw sticks up and the conkers rained down. I cheer a little.

'Lovely cakes here. Do you come here a lot?'

'We did. Me and Tim. Before the kids. We bought a lot of plants. We were happy once.'

She hurries. I speed up behind her as we pass under the bridge. The footpath narrows and she stops suddenly and I almost bump into her. She pulls at her shoe and I bend slightly to help her.

'Are you okay? Can I...'

She stands up straight and tall. Her face is taut and dark with hatred.

'I'm fine.'

In a split second she has grabbed my bag. Her arm loops mine and she swings me round. She kicks at a wooden doorway and it flings open. She has me in a bear hug. She is strong. I can feel every sinew in her body tense against me. I can feel her breath on my face. She smells of a mix of vomit and perfume.

I scream as I fall. Ten feet or so into the darkness and I feel my arm dead underneath me as I land, pain shooting into my shoulder. A streak of half-light shows me the space, damp and dark. I pull myself to my feet. The walls are smooth stone. The shaft of light flickers and I know she is still there.

'Tracey! Tracey! Don't do this. Don't. You'll get into trouble.' My mind is racing. How had she duped me so easily? How? How had I been so stupid? I can hear her above me, struggling to shut the door as the light disappears. I feel in my pocket for my phone but it's in my bag. Gradually, the realisation I am trapped sinks in. Once again, a victim of my own good nature; believing the best of people. Benefit of the doubt.

I am terrified. I hear myself screaming but the door is shut now and it is almost completely dark.

'Tracey! Come back! It wasn't my fault. I swear I never knew. He's tricked me too. Please.'

My arm begins to hurt. A lot. It feels swollen and I check for blood. There is none. My face is scraped and I wipe it with my sleeve. But most of all I am rigid with fear.

'Tracey! Don't do this. Come back. My kids. I need to get my kids.' As those words escape, I hear myself groan – an animal noise, deep and visceral. My children. My children. I need to get Ben and Angel. The next words are a whimper.

'Tracey. Please. Come back. When are you coming back? Please.'

I hear a rustle behind me. I turn quickly. A shape is huddled in the corner of the space.

'She said she's not coming back. Not once she's found you.'

CHAPTER TWENTY-NINE

It's her. Jem. Of course it is. My eyes adjust to the barely there light and I see her. She looks small and childlike huddled against a wall. But as she stands, I recognise her shape. Her long limbs and her blonde hair. It's light enough to just see her, but I can't make out her features.

I turn to look at the space. My survival instinct kicks in and I feel the walls all the way round. She comments.

'You're wasting your time. There's no way out.'

But I have to see for myself. I have to feel every inch of that wall to get my bearings. The walls are wet and the floor is damp soil. The ceiling slopes from high to low and I try to visualise how this fits into the canal bridge wall. Why it's here. What it is. I can't look at her.

'There has to be. She can't do this.'

I feel the length of the wall up to the door. There are some metal bumps and it's clear there was a ladder here once. She's crying. It's one extreme to another as my fire melts to concern.

'Are you okay? Did you hurt yourself when you fell? Everyone's been out looking for you.'

She wipes her eyes. 'Yes. I think I'm okay. Is Pepe okay? Did you see him? I was badly bruised down one side, and my shoulder hurt. Bit better now. Just very cold. She's brought me food. And some water.' I peer into the darkness and can just make out a pile of rubbish in the corner. And a bucket. 'So that's something. But she keeps saying...'

She collapses into sobs and I rush to her. I hold her. This woman who has been the centre of my hate for so long. She is sobbing in my arms and no wonder. It's been almost two weeks in this dank, dark room. If you can call it that. I listen as her sobs subside. All I can hear is water. No cars. No footsteps. Just the flow of water.

I know we are near a lock. I try to picture it but my heart won't go past the conker trees and Angel and Ben. Their hands warm in mine. Mittens and the smell of their hair. I have to get out of here. I hold her in front of me.

'Your dog is fine. Right, tell me everything. All I know is you left a note for Daniel. And you sent me a message. They found your car up Lees Valley on the bridge. I don't get it. I don't understand.'

I look at her in the half-light. She is bedraggled and her face thinner than before. Her eyes are pleading with me.

'She... she... she was at the school. When I dropped Ben and Angel off last week. She started talking to me. We made friends.' She starts to cry again. 'I'm stupid. I'm so bloody gullible. I thought I'd finally fitted in with the school mums. They wouldn't speak to me. She said she had kids in the year below Angel. We went for coffee. She invited me to the garden centre. I left a note for him.'

I hug her again. I can't believe I thought all the mothers of Ben and Angel's friends had taken to Jem. In my imagination they had been inviting her to coffee mornings and bring and buy bake-offs.

'It's okay. Tell me. We can make sense of it. But on the note you said you were going away for days?'

She continues. 'I was. I needed some time to think. But Tracey... she... she... we drove to the road at the top, just by the school. She told me her and her husband used to come here a lot. Then we cut through. Then she grabbed me. I think she had a knife. She took my phone and my bag and I just thought she was going to rob me. She's completely mad.'

Mad. Like I was. I know that madness. Mad like when someone takes what is part of you.

'But the message?'

She freezes. 'I didn't send a message. How could I have? She thought I was you. She must have been watching the kids. She's been back a few times, rambling on about someone called Tim. How one of her mates had seen you.' Her sobs have stopped and she snorts. 'Anyway, I wouldn't have messaged you, would I?'

She pushes me away. No. She wouldn't have messaged me. My instincts were right and the small moment of triumph makes me laugh.

'No. To be fair, you wouldn't. So she must have sent it.'

Jem shakes her head. 'You know her, don't you? This has something to do with you, doesn't it? I knew it.'

Even now we are arguing about Daniel. He is at the root of all this. I promised myself I would tell the truth and I will.

'I didn't know her until yesterday. She arrived at my house with her kids. The thing is, I've been... seeing her husband.'

She makes a weak laugh. 'You couldn't make it up. After everything you said about me, you were seeing someone who was married? Saint Lauren?'

'No. It's different. I didn't know he was married. But you knew about me. You knew all about me and you still did it.'

She goes to the corner and sits back down. We listen to the sound of drip, drip, dripping for a long moment. Then she speaks. 'I wish I'd never met him. I wish I'd never moved in with him. I really love Ben and Angel but they're not my kids. All he wanted was a babysitter.'

I blink at her. I run my mind over the idyllic scenes on her Instagram account and what I saw through the window in those early days.

'But you seemed so happy.' It sounds petty and insincere. 'From what I could see.'

She makes a pained noise. 'I guess we were at first. I loved the nights out and the people he knew. It all seemed so grown up and so... Dan. But I didn't sign up to be a... housekeeper.'

I think about what the kids said about her cooking and the crying. I hadn't been able to put my finger on a particular strand of my unhappiness but, it was the same. The same Daniel-curated box. The same compartment. Cook, clean, kids. I am more stressed than I have ever been in this moment but I suddenly have a calmness. An epiphany. Belinda. That's what he wanted. A series of Belindas while he replaced the good-time girls he'd chosen to start with. She's still talking.

'...and don't bother telling me about Amber. I bloody know already. Amber this, Amber that...'

I visualise the Mulberry handbag and the picnic hamper.

'...taking her to "business meetings"...' I see her make quotes in the air with her fingers, 'while I'm babysitting his kids. That's what I was thinking about. That and–'

I interrupt. 'Jem, listen. We need to find a way to get out of here. She's got this stitched up. Daniel was questioned, then I was arrested. Then they let me go and Tim was arrested. They've charged him, I think. She must have used your credit card to order some flowers on his laptop and then planted the card on him. God knows what else.'

She is silent. She's been here ten days and I guess she's thought of every possible way to get out. I wrack my brains. My phone. If Bekah was watching my phone, she would have seen it nearby. I trace my footsteps, but then realise that to anyone watching it would just look like my phone was in my pocket as I walked along the canal. Tracey wouldn't be stupid enough to keep it.

She would have driven Jem's car to the bridge after she messaged me. It's all becoming clear. She sent the message to me to try to snare me. She thought Jem was me. She befriended Jem at the school gates thinking she was me. I think back to the million times she could have been watching me over the past weeks. The times she sat planning to get me here, in this hole.

I need to be ready when she comes back. I need to have all this straight in my head. Bekah isn't going to be able to find me by tracing my phone – she will probably find it in my car. I wouldn't be surprised if Tracey had gone on to the garden centre and sat and had tea and cake. Just to make sure it fitted with a story I hadn't even told anyone. The truth is, no one knew I was meeting her. And no one knows I am here.

I look around. This prison is inescapable. Even if I lifted Jem onto my shoulders, the door is too high above us to reach. I rub my arm. My wrist is badly swollen and the pain comes in waves. I go and sit next to her. She doesn't move away and that's a step forward.

'If you were so unhappy, why didn't you leave?'

She snorts. 'Oh, you'd love that, wouldn't you? If I left. Then you could have him back.'

I have been at this junction so many times in my mind. A place where Daniel is available again and I am faced with this question. Lisa swears I would just blindly go back in, but now I know I wouldn't. Isn't that the reason for all this pain? This period of madness and grieving after a break-up? A reminder of how bad things can get. How devastating. How deep.

I saw the temporary madness in Tracey's eyes. Earlier, when

I mentioned Tim and she faced me. I felt bad. Bad that I'd made her feel upset. But upset is an understatement. She wasn't upset. I know that feeling. She is destroyed. Everything she thought was real has disintegrated and she wants payment in full.

I have been there. Myself tangled in Daniel so tightly that when this woman ripped us apart the roots of our relationship bled. The anger and the harsh reality that, after all, you are not part of each other. That everything you whispered on those hot summer nights was now redundant. That someone else was busy making a secure connection to a place where you still have scars. And more, a determination that overshadows everything else in your world that you will get even. You will somehow make this right. You will pour oil onto this fire until it feels as good as that moment of ecstasy that you just know she is getting with your man.

I realise I had underestimated Tracey just as I had underestimated the strength of my own envy and jealousy and sense of getting my own back. Making them suffer just like I was suffering. I didn't plan. Oh no. I sneaked around. Breaking in and hiding. She is much cleverer than me. But didn't she say I wasn't the first?

My blood runs cold. How many more women has she done this to? Tim went to a lot of trouble to keep our rendezvous out of town. Is it a game between them? Am I the loser? I know what she is feeling. An unrealistic justification that anything she does now is deserved. That *what Tim has done* mitigates all her behaviour in the aftermath. Beyonce's 'Irreplaceable' won't cut it this time. No. She is on fire with fury and hate. She is burning up with determination to get her own back.

Yes, she is better than me. Or is it worse? My fear-ridden brain cannot decide. She isn't just watching. She's acting. She's removing everything from her world that spoils her reality. Me and Tim. Jem is just an inconvenience. She will build a case against Tim to prove he did this. Whatever this is.

My mind won't go there. It won't push to the edge of this. I can't lose hope. Someone will hear us. But no one heard Jem. I am delirious with pain and fear but I must focus. All I can hear is the drip, drip, drip of the water and my own heart beating fast. Jem's breathing and her warmth.

'I don't want him back.' I swallow hard. 'Look, I'm sorry for what I did. All of it. I was in a bad place. It doesn't excuse it, but I want you to know I'm sorry.'

She sighs. 'I'm not going to say it's all right. I'm sorry I met Daniel. I'm sorry I ever set eyes on him. Or you.'

It's not an apology but I'll take it. I nod. 'Yeah. Well. When we get out of here, you'll never have to see either of us again.'

She starts to cry again. She slips her arm through mine and squeezes it. She is shaking.

'I will. That's the thing. That's why I was going away. I needed time to think. I needed to know I was doing the right thing. I had a bag in the car and it could have gone either way.'

She is sobbing her heart out. Her words are stilted and her chest heaves. I try to calm her.

'There's nothing here that we can't fix. Tracey won't want to get in trouble. She'll let us go. And then you can sort things out with–'

She pulls away. 'No. You don't understand. This isn't about me and Dan. Or you. Or her. It's about me. I need to do what's best for me.' She moves very close to me. Her voice is suddenly soft. 'I know this is the last thing you want to hear. I know how you will feel. And I'm a little bit scared of you if I'm honest. But I need to tell someone. I've kept it to myself.' She rests her head against mine. So close that I can smell the last hint of her Peonia perfume in her dirty hair. 'The thing is, I'm pregnant.'

CHAPTER THIRTY

My first instinct is to hug her and she lets me.

'Are you okay? Is everything...?'

She nods into my shoulder. 'I think so.'

'Have you told her. Tracey?'

'No. No, I haven't. I'm too scared of what she will do.'

It isn't until more than a minute has passed that the pain descends. Somehow this makes it all more real, and I feel a wave of anger. They weren't playing at house. They weren't temporary. Daniel got her pregnant. Until now I have felt that I have the higher ground simply because I am the mother of his children. The thought shocks me. I'm not like that. But I am. I have used that arms-folded haughtiness to take the moral peak.

My husband, father of Ben and Angel, has got this woman pregnant. They will be a family. Another family that includes Daniel but is not mine. The wave ebbs and I remember this child will be Ben and Angel's sibling.

'How long? How long have you known?'

'Ten weeks. I was shocked. I'm on the pill, obviously, but I'm allergic to a whole range of things that make me throw up.

He kept saying I was being silly and making the allergies up for attention.'

It sounds familiar. Belinda does not believe in morning sickness therefore Daniel does not either. Belinda definitely does not believe in allergies. She is a right-down-the-line meat and two veg person who bakes her own bread. No gluten-free for Belinda.

'So I was being sick because someone had replaced my special pasta that I was having at lunchtime with ordinary pasta. I swapped it back and then I still felt a bit queasy. I went to the doctors and the first thing they did was a pregnancy test. I went for a scan last week. And there it was.'

I can imagine Daniel's face when he found out he would have another responsibility. He faked pleasure when I told him about Angel. He loves her, I am sure about that, but he was not pleased.

'What did Daniel say?'

'I haven't told him. His mother made a few comments about me being pregnant next, as if I had to trap him into staying with me somehow, when it was him who had begged me.'

It's almost too much. The wave washes over me again and even numbs the pain in my arm. I see red and flinch against her. Yet I'd seen it before. Here in the darkness I allow the past to light up my memory. Julia. A sales rep from one of the bigger car companies. There had been many mentions of her in the run up. Over dinner, in the mornings when I asked him who he was working with.

I hadn't fully understood what was going on until one night when we had found ourselves in a nightclub with another couple, Lianne and Dave Barber. Nightclubs were not my scene and hardly Daniel's; I found myself yawning and sipping my cocktail. We'd been to a boozy dinner which had gone well – we'd danced and laughed and I suppose we wanted to prolong the evening before we fell back into the barbed stand-off that our marriage was rapidly becoming.

I'd watched his eyes drift to a woman standing by the dance floor with her friend. She was wearing an industrial style jumpsuit, something that I would never have chosen for a night out. But she could get away with it. She was quirky, all fluffy hair and earrings. The music changed and she was suddenly dancing to Bon Jovi. I swear Daniel licked his lips.

'There she is! Julia Sinclair. I told you about her. Proper little firefly.'

He dragged me onto the dancefloor and it was obvious that he was manoeuvring us towards her. I can't remember if it crossed my mind to question it. Probably not. I knew he wouldn't do anything in front of me. But when we were near her, I could see her glimpsing and smiling and sashaying and wiggling. All their secrets between them.

Like all the other times, I told myself it was just my imagination. Jealousy. They were in the same business and if he was being this friendly in front of me, there was bound to be nothing in it. Yet only weeks later I saw a photograph online and Julia was in the background. It was a works dinner with no partners. She worked there, so nothing unusual about her being there. But she was completely overdressed. A long Japanese dress which looked like pure silk. High boots and a little hat that sat on top of her hair. Copious amounts of eyeliner. And she was staring right at Daniel and he was smiling at her.

It was hardly evidence, but I knew. I made sure I was at the next company night out. She looked disappointed to see me but, again, I was used to it. I just stared and smiled and blinked at her until she raced to the toilets in tears. I followed and faux comforted. Whatever was wrong? Why are you crying?

These are the games women play with each other. We are desperate to be on the same side but we rarely are when men are concerned. We are each other's competition. Tracey understood this, which underlines my suspicion that she has played this game before. She enticed me into the false security that we were going to solve this together. She fooled Jem that the school-gate brigade had forgiven her man-stealing ways and were willing to take her into their confidence. When all the while she was plotting and planning. Just as I was and just as Jem will be when her baby is born and she wants precedence over Ben and Angel.

Julia knew it too. She was hypnotised by Daniel and his easy sleaziness. She loved the nightlife and the parties and the fun. She sat on the toilet and told me he had begged her to come tonight.

'He told me he needed me there. Here. He said I was essential to him.'

Essential. And so she, or someone else was, it seemed. Someone other than his stand-in Belinda. Of course, when we went back out together into the party and she faced him he dodged the bullet.

'Yes, it's all true. You are essential.' He'd looked at me. 'And I did beg her to come here tonight. I wanted her here. She's my partner in crime.' He kissed my hand. 'But you, my darling, are my partner in life.'

He completely made out that she'd got the wrong end of the stick. And, pushed to confirm it in front of everyone, he trampled on her. I understand better now how he was able to do that. It was because he knew there would always be another Julia. Disposable girlfriend. Replaceable. He divided us and he ruled us. And now Jem was about to fall off the end of the Daniel-operated conveyor belt.

But don't get me wrong. Not for one minute. Even though I know all this and I am learning more by the second, it still hurts like hell. The image of Daniel begging Jem to sleep with him pierces my soul as it has for over a year. After all, I saw it. I saw them. I watched as she edged herself into my husband's heart and bed and, finally, extracted him from my life and into hers.

'What are you going to do? About the baby?'

She shakes her head. 'I can't think about it. Not now. I need to stay calm. I'm really hungry and it can't be good for me or the baby.'

I pull her towards me. It is very cold and at least together we can share each other's body heat. I feel sleepy. My arm hurts a lot but I have a fuzzy feeling that permeates my whole body. Jem is leaning against me. I feel myself dozing on and off for a long, long time. I keep my eyes shut and think about my mum and dad and when I was a child to keep my mind off my own children.

When I look up towards the door, the chink of light has gone. It's dark outside. Would anyone have missed me? Daniel would have. He would have called my phone or messaged me and God only knows what Tracey would have responded. My children would think I wasn't coming for them. I feel the tears on my face.

Jem stirs. 'Was Daniel upset? When they realised what had happened? You said everyone was looking for me?'

I nod. 'He was. He came over to my house. Crying and carrying on. Accusing me. Told the police about that night when... well, they believed him and they arrested me.' She laughs a little. 'They had a pretty good case built.' I wonder whether I should go full truth and tell her about the cameras. No. No. She's upset enough. 'It's a full-scale police operation. They've been on TV.'

'My parents. Oh...'

'They are looking. They will be looking for both of us. I've met the woman in charge. Bekah Bradley. She'll take no shit.

She'll be all over this. I absolutely believe that she'll get to the bottom of it.'

She shivers. 'So why didn't she find me then? If she's so good?'

'They didn't think you were missing for days. Because of the note. It was only when your car was found they started to look. That was on the Thursday. It's been a week. And they've made headway.' Not the right headway, I want to add, but I don't. 'I'm pretty sure Bekah will put two and two together and get Tracey. She's switched on.'

'Really?'

'Really. The thing is, with both of us missing they will focus again. Not that they were...'

She laughs and coughs. 'I know. The forty-eight hours.'

'Yeah. But now they'll reset the clock.'

She pauses. 'I suppose it depends when they think you are missing. I mean, you have been a bit erratic. I can't imagine Daniel thinking someone has taken you too. More like you've fled or something. And who else is there?'

Yes. Who else is there? Who would miss me? Work? No. I am on garden leave and they won't contact me unless they need to. Even then they would leave a message. Lisa? She is due round tonight. She'll see my car gone and message me. Again, Tracey can string this out as long as she wants to as she has my phone. Then I remember it's locked.

'Jem, was your phone locked?'

She used Jem's phone to message me.

'Yes. Yes, it was.'

Shit. She must be able to unlock them. Needs must, I guess, after all I managed to plant four surveillance cameras. She could have answered Daniel's and Lisa's messages, telling them I was going away for a while.

'Yes, you're right. There's no one. You're right. Just my ex who hates me and my friend who will be duped by Tracey. Except Bekah Bradley. She'll be looking. I can't imagine she will give up until she has found us.'

I sound defiant but I realise there is very little to go on. And she might message me too and Tracey might placate her. Jem sighs.

'My parents would move heaven and earth to find me. They'll have everyone out there. But who would look here? Who even knows this is here?'

There is hysteria in her voice. She must be more hungry and weaker than I am; I know she is chilled to the bone. I am thirsty. I search the wall for the drip of water – it is in the low corner and I re-orientate myself and realise that this chamber would be underneath the bridge wall and the outside section would be under the field. My brain is too addled to think about digging out; in any case it is deep and risky.

Jem is suddenly on her feet. I hear a scraping noise and then a rush of fresh air. Two bottles of water drop onto the floor and I scramble for them. The flash of a torch and the sound of a voice.

'I'm back, ladies.'

CHAPTER THIRTY-ONE

She's standing on the ledge in front of the wooden door. She reaches into a bag and throws down two sandwiches.

'They're both the same so it doesn't matter which one you choose.'

Jem scrambles for a sandwich and tears the wrapper open. She takes it over to the corner, chewing fast. I leave mine on the ground.

'You've got this all wrong, Tracey. She's done nothing. Let her go. And we should talk. This isn't my fault. I'm going to be honest here, no one forced Tim to hook up with me. And he told me he was single. A whole story. This is on him, not me.'

She's eating a sandwich too. She's put the torch down and she's chewing, considering.

'True. True. But you must have wondered. He was at home with me most of the time. Didn't seem to be paying much attention to his phone. Seemed to be planning all those work trips with Pete – I read his messages. Obviously they were manufactured and Pete's a liar too, but we'll get to that in a bit. So, bloody riddle me this, where did you think he was when he wasn't with you?'

I am silent. I want to argue but she is right. I can't tell her that right at the beginning I was too busy ruining Jem's life to be worried about Tim. But yes, she is right. As time went on, there was a niggle of suspicion.

Lisa's badgering about his absence from social media annoyed me. I searched for him. I constantly looked at his work website and googled his name. But I stopped myself because he told me he just wanted to take it slowly. Even when I asked about his place and the hotels, and why he didn't come over to mine in the evening, I swallowed it whole.

I blamed it on the kids. It's too soon. It's not good for them. What would Daniel think? In reality it was because he wasn't available, except when he wanted to be. I told myself I was being needy in the direct wake of my own marriage shitstorm. But I wasn't needy. I was shafted.

I can't say this to her. I need to give her the answer that will cause least annoyance.

'He told me he was working.'

Same as her. Same. Maybe she will see that he duped us both.

'Right. And you believed him?'

'I had no reason not to. And we weren't serious. I was just seeing him.'

Even in the half-darkness I see her face cloud with teary sadness.

'So you weren't... you didn't even love him? All this. My kids suffering. All for a quick jump?' Her voice has raised octaves.

I am trapped. Damned if I do and dammed if I don't. Jem is gulping water and coughing. I speak quietly and calmly. 'No. Look. I had no idea. None.'

She thinks.

'You and her. You're the same. You even look the same.

You're that woman who turns men's heads. You've both got form. She might not have gone after Tim but she went after your bloke, didn't she? All over the papers, it is.'

Jem is beside me. Her voice is gravelly when she speaks. 'Yes I did. But Lauren and I were civilised about it.'

Tracey laughs. A theatrical, crass laugh that I have heard inside my own head at my lowest points. 'So why was she arrested then?'

Jem almost whispers. 'There were some instances at the beginning. But it's an upsetting time. I never meant to upset anyone and neither did Lauren.'

I chip in. 'Just let us go. We won't say anything. We understand what you're going through.' I reach backwards and find Jem's hand and hold it tight. I see her shake her head out of the corner of my eye. 'And my children. Please. They're called Angel and Ben.' Jem starts to sob. 'She's their step-mum. You're hurting them too. Please, Tracey, just think about it. There's still time to put this right.'

She is silent. Staring at us. I hear the drip, drip, drip and Jem is trembling. I try again. I have to. 'They'll find out it's you. They can trace your phone.' She snorts and rolls her eyes. Oh yes. She's too clever for that. 'And Tim. He was arrested for abducting Jem. He was at the station. How could he have taken me as well?'

She laughs manically. 'Oh my God. You kill me. Haven't you realised yet? He's a serial liar. Pathological. He'll do anything to get out of the shit. They let him go. He was bailed. And my best bet is that he told them you were in it together. You made him do it.' She laughs again. 'They think you've skipped the country or something.'

I feel like I am falling. My head spins and I feel like I am doomed. Even if we do escape, even if there is a way out and we dig and dig and dig, I will still be guilty. But then I remember Jem. She is a witness to this. Tracey continues.

'So no appeals for you. No parents crying on TV. No partner with tears in their eyes. In fact, your ex has made a statement.' She reads from her phone. 'Don't worry, ladies. This is a burner.' My heart sinks. She's got it all worked out. 'My ex-wife has a history of erratic behaviour directed at myself and Miss Carter. I would like some privacy at this time to protect our children.' She shakes her head. 'Well, he's a prize, isn't he? Runs off with Barbie, then blames you when it all goes tits up?'

She laughs at her own joke. She is almost hysterical. She screws up the Tesco bag she brought the sandwiches in and forces it into her pocket.

'Me and Tim used to come here. It was where they stored the coal at one time. Had a ladder. And some wooden shelving. We used to hide here when we were courting. Laughing and kissing and one night we even fell asleep in here. We both lived up here then. Both went to the school. Happy days. Then when we got married, we tried for kids and we found out I had something wrong. A blockage in one fallopian tube. I waited ages and finally the op was done. But it failed and I still only had one ovary working. Tim was great. Never bothered. But I caught with Jen. It was the best day of my life.'

She falls silent. Then she sobs.

'But that's when it all went wrong. Changed overnight. He didn't really want kids. Not really. Doesn't like mess. But he stayed. Which is something. Then we had our little boy last year. It would have been around the time he started with you.'

I feel a sense of dread. I knew it. I knew there was more to this. There always is. My clients come to me with one thing but there is always a trailing backstory. Something that has triggered it, and usually not something obvious. But this is clear. The more Tracey tried to make a family, the more absent Tim was.

This was a long-term thing. Not an overnight fancy. Not him falling in love with someone else. This is intentional.

While I was going through the throes of early romance and hotel dates, Tracey was pregnant, then had a small baby. It's starting to make sense. His "early starts back to beat the traffic" and "I keep my phone off to give you my full attention".

'Your children are beautiful. I'm sorry this happened. I honestly didn't know. But let's think of them. Our children. Please, Tracey, I'm begging you. Please.'

She stands up straight. 'Begging? Like I begged Tim to get a job that kept him home more. Like I begged him to take us all out for day trips at weekends? He told me he was building his business. Making us secure for the future. But all he was doing was getting his feet under your table. In that posh house you live in. Being with your kids instead of his own. Gradually phasing me and our kids out and replacing us with an upgraded model.'

I gasp. This is exactly what I thought Daniel was doing with Jem. Replacing me. Jem moves forward. She shakes free of my hand.

'Oh, come on. Both of you are going on like these two are the loves of your lives. Like you've lost something precious. But you're just scared of losing. You're scared of being the loser in a game that means nothing anyway.'

Tracey shakes her head. 'No. You're–'

But Jem continues. Loudly and with surety. 'Going on about love and who owns who. You're pathetic. Weak and pathetic. Pretending you're caught in some bosom-heaving, sentimental bullshit about love when really, they're pitting us against each other.' She turns to me. 'And you? The best you could do was chop the heads off some flowers and do some silent calls.'

I can't help it. I rise to it. 'That's what you think. You don't know the half of it.'

She laughs. 'Oh. Go on then. Tell me.'

'I was watching you. I put cameras in your house.' Tracey whistles. 'I broke in and then I broke in again when all this happened to get them back. I'm sorry I even bothered now.'

Jem laughs again. 'See? We're all at each other's throats. That's what they want. It's almost bred into us. Part of what they think we are. Us arguing over them when we should be pulling together. Making us crazy and loading us with "shoulds" so they can go and shag someone else. And it all seems all right because we're all mad, aren't we? Get rid of the crazy ex and get a new one.' She puts her arm around me. She is taller and leaner than me. 'And what did you see, Lauren? What did you see? All you saw was me trying to be you. Trying to fit into a Lauren-shaped hole in Dan-Dan's life while he went on the hunt again for the next Jem-Jem. Not very exciting, was it?'

She wipes her eyes. I can't look at her.

'And believe me, I would have gone. I would have left. In fact, I was on my way. But I don't have those little chess pieces you two are using to hold on to someone who doesn't even want you. Or them. I don't have kids. I don't have that little piece of DNA that binds you together forever and stops you just picking up your belongings and walking out. Not yet.' She snorts. 'And the stupid thing is you could manage perfectly well on your own. Better. Every woman today must know that if they have kids, there's a strong possibility they'll be bringing them up alone. But you two, you're stuck on a never-ending loop of "The One". As if those two losers are the only men on earth.'

She stares up at Tracey. 'And you. You should be ashamed of yourself. You're a nurse. You take care of people. What about us? And Lauren's kids?'

Tracey is silent for a moment. Then she nods. 'You're right. You're completely right. But here's the thing. I don't care about any of that. She's pushed me too far.' She points at me. 'Her and him. Lording it round posh hotels. I found the receipts. I honestly thought he'd stopped. But he hadn't.' She pulls a face. 'Pull together. All girls together. Yeah, you're right. But I can tell you that the minute we stepped outside of here and the police arrived, you'd both be pointing at me. You'd forget all that.'

Jem shakes her head. 'Try me. Go on, try me.'

Tracey laughs. 'No, no. And I'm not going to hurt you.' She pulls the door open and fresh air rushes in. 'In fact, I'm not going to do anything. Nothing at all.'

She is gone. We stand gazing at the door and seconds later we hear a bang, bang, bang as she nails it shut.

CHAPTER THIRTY-TWO

We stare at the door for a long time. I know I should be thinking about what happens next, but all I can think about is how my children will remember me. I try to imagine them happy with Daniel and Belinda. I doubt they will know yet. Belinda will have insisted on taking over and shielding them and, for once, I am grateful. They will play with that puppy and talk to Granddad and then they will have to go to school.

Eventually, some well-meaning person will mention me and tell them what happened and they will ask Daniel and Belinda, and no doubt after much deliberating they will tell them the truth. Their slant on it, anyway. They'll think I ran away. They'll think I am guilty. They'll think I was complicit in Jem's demise.

I know what this means. I know. I know she has left us for... I can't even think it. I can't say it. But Jem has been here longer. I can feel her desperation and hear it in every word she speaks. I can't look at her. All the blame runs through my head. It's my fault. It's my fault for meeting Tim, for not heeding the flags. For pushing my own agenda; I'm not even sure now that it wasn't all about Daniel.

It's my fault for trusting Tracey. But, like everything I tell myself after I've been trampled on, I am a nice person. I always think the best of people. Good old benefit of the doubt. I strain to think why I do that. Why I even did that with a woman I hardly knew. Because I felt bad? Because I felt sorry for her?

The truth is I still believe good things will happen. I look at my children – oh, my children, my beautiful children – and I still know that goodness and innocence is around. It's still around even though I have been consumed by bad at times, almost completely.

As always, even here in the dank darkness, I berate myself for what I should have done. How I have failed. I should have just walked away. Sold the house and gone to live far away. Took my time. It's strange the things you remember when your life is on the line. When stress reaches its highest level ever. I remember watching a film with Sandra Bullock. She was an alcoholic and she was talking to someone about starting a relationship after a break-up. The other person told her that if she could keep a houseplant alive for a year, then get a pet. If you can care for a pet for a year, then maybe, just maybe, it's time to start a new relationship.

I'd told myself I wasn't an addict. I wasn't addicted to alcohol or drugs. But now I know I *was* an addict. Not the old *I'm addicted to love* cliché. No. Worse than that. Because that wouldn't be as harmful. No. I was addicted to Daniel. I had to know what he was doing and how that related to me. I simply had not admitted that our relationship was over.

I should have got a plant. A cactus. Something easy to look after. Dating Tim was just another way to place myself strategically in a position where I could show the world I was okay, while still torturing myself with my ex.

Jem sniffs. I still can't look at her. But I need to tell her something.

'Don't give up on love. What you said earlier.'

She snorts and laughs. 'Are you kidding me? Really? We're trapped in a hole with no way out and you are telling me to not give up?'

'Yep. The thing is, if this is it, we need to know that everyone we love is in good hands. That they will be fine.'

She sighs and sits down. 'But they won't, will they? My parents. They won't be fine. And your–'

I finish it for her. 'Ben and Angel. No, they won't but they will have Daniel.'

She faux laughs. 'Oh, what a prize. Sorry.'

I laugh too. It feels wrong, dangerous, but also a little hysterical. 'Well, if we do get out of here, you've got him for life too.'

I sit down beside her. The drip, drip, drip has become heavier and the ground is wet. I realise what this place is. It's an overflow. The tiny chink of light at the low end is where the water would come in if the canal overflows and floods the field. It's damp from the last time it happened, which probably wasn't so long ago in the storms. I try to see a water mark on the walls. A level. But there is no line. Presumably it would just fill up and then drain through the earth and through the gaps in the stone over time.

I've always wondered what it was like just before you die. How people who were terminally ill coped with the knowledge that they wouldn't be here for much longer. My mum told me she had thought about it a lot, but she never shared her conclusion. Like I don't want to talk to Jem about it because I don't want to burden her, Mum just brushed it away as if it was something insignificant.

I suppose everyone has regrets. I certainly do. I wish I hadn't done all those things to Daniel and Jem and simply moved on, but it goes deeper than that. Much deeper. I wish I had told the truth. Told people how I feel. I was acting out all my hurt, all the desperation, and all the lack of control. Because I couldn't tell anyone. I couldn't even tell Lisa how bad I felt. So it came out another way.

I know a lot of people bargain with themselves and their god. In my training I worked with people who were undergoing chemotherapy. They would make all sorts of agreements to stay alive. All kinds of trade-offs to banish cancer from their lives. I know what my bargain is. If I get out of here, I will tell the truth in future. To myself and to everyone else. And I will avoid Daniel as much as possible. If I get out of here, I will never look back at the past again.

Jem finally says it. 'Do you think she's coming back?'

I shake my head. 'I don't think she is. Or maybe she's just trying to scare us.'

Which I doubt very much. But I say it anyway. She is silent for a while and I feel her rocking backwards and forwards beside me. Then she speaks again.

'I haven't given up on love, you know. But it's not the same kind of love you mean. It's not love for some guy. It's love for me.' She laughs. 'I know what you thought of me. Full of myself. Up myself. But it's confidence. I've always been confident. But he's started to destroy it. Like that was his aim in life, to make sure I wasn't too sure of myself. To criticise and make me doubt myself. That's not love.'

I smile. She's younger than me. By about eight years. But much wiser than I thought. 'Yes. I know you're right. But I was made to believe that loving yourself is selfish. Conceited. I only just caught the end of the self-help brigade.'

She laughs loudly. 'Yeah, whereas I'm knee deep in it. But we're both in the same business, really. You fix people's minds and I fix their perspective. I admired you, you know. I was a little bit jealous of your training. But it's not selfish to like yourself. Or love yourself.'

I think about what Lisa said about her. How unkind we were. It feels so wrong now. A lot of things seem so wrong now.

'I guess I've just been held under for too long. I was like you once. I took no shit.'

'You've always seemed pretty tough to me. And a little bit scary. But what are you scared of? Why can't you just be you? Are you scared of letting Mrs Wade go?'

Am I? I told myself I wasn't, but was I just sitting in my marital home waiting for the marriage to resume. I am horrified.

'Maybe. But I am sorry. Really sorry for what I did to you. And the cameras...'

She flinches. 'I could have you done for that.'

I sharpen. 'Like I would have Tracey done for this.'

She sighs. 'You wouldn't though, would you? Because I promised her we wouldn't. If she let us out. I promised her.'

I don't want to remind her that there is little chance of us getting out of here. But she has rankled me. 'She would have to pay for what she has done. She should.'

I feel Jem move closer to me. I feel her warmth.

'Well, if we do get out, either everyone pays, or no one pays. I will keep my word.'

I rise to it. 'So you'd let her get away with this?'

She fake laughs. 'It's no worse than what you did. You made my life a living misery. That's without knowing about the cameras. It was harassment.'

'Why didn't you report me then?'

'I felt sorry for you. I thought you were unstable. But I didn't do it for you. I did it for Ben and Angel.' She hesitates and I marvel at how, even in this situation, she makes herself seem selfless. But then she continues. 'But mostly I did it for me. If I had kicked off, Dan would have started going on about full custody and you know what that made me? Full-time step-mum. I didn't sign up for that. So I just tolerated it. You.'

It hurts. Just as I knew it would. The lack of response, no acknowledgement of my actions that I knew full well she was aware of hurt at the time. But this. This is what I was afraid of. More than getting caught. The fear that no matter what I did, I was invisible to her. To them.

'And you think, hypothetically, that if we get out of here, we shouldn't tell the police Tracey did this?'

She nods. 'Well, it's going to be pretty hard to do that, because they'd have to have followed her or something. But I wouldn't be pressing charges. On you or her.'

I blow. It's been a long time coming but the pent-up tension erupts. 'Really, Jem? Really? She's left us to die and nailed the door shut and you're saying she doesn't mean it? She knows exactly what she's done. And she doesn't care.'

She is in my face.

'Did you care? Did you? Did you care when you were stalking me around Sainsbury's? Spreading lies about me to the other mums? Putting glue in my car door locks? Spying on me in my own home? Did you?'

I think. Not at the time. But afterwards.

'I do now. At the time I was–'

'Mad with passion. Crimes of passion. And who made you like that? Him. Like Tim or whoever he is. She's not in her right mind. I'm not saying she should get away with it, but it needs to be taken into account.'

I am seething. I try to hold it in, but I can't. 'The thing is, you've painted me bad in all this. Just me and Daniel. But what about you? You barefaced took him without caring about me or the kids, and now you're pregnant with my husband's baby.'

She is silent and I wonder if I've gone too far. If she caught the echoes of Tracey's accusations earlier. But she speaks calmly and gently.

'Ex. Ex-husband's, Lauren. Ex.'

CHAPTER THIRTY-THREE

She is right. I hate to admit it. This is possibly the end for us and it is becoming increasingly clear that I have been fooling myself. That I was still in some kind of messed up relationship with Daniel. No one could tell me. Not Lisa. Not Daniel. Not Tim. Not anyone.

I sift through everything that happened and try to ignore the impact it had on others. Somehow, I had blocked it out, but now it looms over every single action. There must be something in there. Something that saved me. Something that kept me sane. Something that protected me.

I let my consciousness wash over the events of the past year – easier in the dark as they play out before my eyes. But this time I am not inside my own head. No. I am watching. I am watching myself hide in rose bushes and creep behind supermarket shelves. I see myself crouched in my car, watching and waiting outside school. Creeping behind The Rosarium, telling myself that I am only here to check my children are safe, but carrying some garden shears with me to chop, chop, chop at Jem's flowers.

All the while I am quiet and calm. These insane acts are

happening mainly inside my head. It may look extreme from the outside, but I actually carried out very few of my plans on impulse. I watch myself execute the plan to plant the cameras with precision. Every step is measured. Even my worry afterwards is composed and invisible to the outside world.

And that is my strength. Staying calm while the storm rages. I almost laugh at the cliché of it and think Jem would be proud of me. I imagine her making an Instagram post. But it is true. I didn't stay completely calm because I know that inside of me, a place just below the surface and between asleep and awake, was chaotic with grief. But I didn't want to upset anyone. Even Jem and Daniel. Otherwise, I would have just rocked up and shouted my feelings.

Apart from that one time at the party I never, ever did that. I guess somehow I knew it would fade. I knew it was temporary, and I wish Tracey knew that too before she nailed that door shut. No. I was cool and calm. And I can be now.

The chink of light is gone. It must be night. I listen to the flow of the water and move my legs to keep warm. I alternate between *what's the point* and *keep going*. Jem is silent and I wonder if she is going back over everything and telling herself how things will be different when we get out. I can't see her but I can feel her against me. I sense her long legs stretched out in front of her, crossed at the ankles.

I don't hate her anymore. She's okay. I smile at myself. Just okay. I still can't bring myself to say that I like her, even here. Tracey thought we were alike. Not just in looks but in nature. Both sleeping with married men. Both replacements. Both, it turns out, replaced. I wonder how Jem would have reacted if this had played out. If she would have lost her shit at Amber when Daniel finally came clean. Used her pregnancy as her ace card.

She was quick to judge me and Tracy for our reaction, but I

have a feeling she has never been in love. Or betrayed. There was a hint of anger in her faux boredom when she mentioned Amber. No. Daniel was a distraction. She told me she was going away to think.

It all brings me back to the very place I don't want to be. I don't want to think about people searching for me anymore. Tracey's words about Daniel's rage and Tim's blame stab at me. I wonder, if she had been checking my phone, where my car is? Had she driven it somewhere and hidden it? Surely when she switched the phone on they could trace the location? But I suspect Tracey is too clever for that.

My only hope is Bekah and DC Sharples. They are on the ball. I feel my eyelids drop but I must stay awake. I nudge Jem and she groans. Then I wonder if it's best that I just fall asleep. I've heard about it. The slow slip from consciousness into a deep, deep sleep that ends in...

There is a sudden rush of water. It pushes underneath us and Jem screams and jumps up.

'My God! What's happening, Lauren? Lauren? What's going to happen?'

She is hysterical. I grab her and hold her tight. The water washes around our ankles and swirls. I look around but I can't see how fast it is coming in, only feel the slow creep. My feet are cold and wet and I know how this could end. Jem is shrieking and crying. I hold her shoulders.

'Right, Jem, listen. Listen. If the water rises we have to float up with it. Keep treading water. Because if it rises it won't go past that ledge.' She looks up. And is quiet. 'If we can get near we can grab on to the ledge and pull ourselves up. The water won't rise above that.'

Her teeth are already chattering. 'We're going to drown, aren't we?'

I shake her gently. 'No. Listen, we're not going to drown.

We're not.' The water is round our knees now. I feel the weight of it dragging down my jeans. 'Take your leggings off.' I struggle out of my jeans and tie them around my neck. Jem does the same with her leggings. I take off my jacket and discard it. The water is rising and I feel my heart beating in my ears. Jem is sobbing gently. 'Stay calm. We'll be up there in no time.'

She wipes her nose on her arm. I hold her to me. 'I'm going to have to let go of you while we do this. But I'm here. Do you remember when you were a little girl, at the swimming baths? When you first learned to swim?'

She is still crying. 'Yes. Yes. My mum took me. I had lessons.'

'Right. Do you remember the panic when you went under, but it was okay because as soon as you relaxed, you could float? This is the same. If you panic and flap you will sink. If you relax and tread water, you can float and keep your head above. Yes?'

'Yes.'

The water is around our waists. I don't know if this will work. I pray that this is not the end. I want to see my beautiful children again. I want to hold them. I want to see my dad. I want to tell Daniel how much I loved him but I know it is over now. I want to see Jem's baby and to see her safe.

'Okay, Jem, listen. When the water reaches our chins, we need to get ready. It will take a while to fill up high enough to lift us to the ledge.'

'What about when we get up there? What then?'

'I don't know. But we'll be at the door. We can hammer on it. Someone under the bridge will hear us.'

She is nodding. The water is rising slowly. It seems an age and at one point I think it has stopped. But it hasn't. It's silently creeping around my heart and I know that this is it. This is it.

I automatically lift my arm out of the water and, with my coat gone, I see a glow. My smart watch. I see the time. It's three thirty-five in the morning. Everyone will be asleep. The battery indicator tells me it is nearly dead, but the heart is beat, beat, beating. It gives me the hope I need to kick my feet as the water laps my neck. I let go of Jem and she goes limp.

At first, I think she has sunk into the cold water, but then I hear a splash and feel a kick beside mine. My feet leave the safety of the ground – they have to. I am suspended in the water, my legs kicking in time with my arms. Jem is coughing and I touch her.

'I'm okay. I'm okay. But I'm weak, Lauren. I'm weak.'

I know what she is saying. She is telling me she doesn't know how long she can keep this up. And I too am unsure. The water is still rising, but I don't know where the spill point is – or if there is one. All I know is as soon as the ledge is within arm's length, I must grab it and let the water help me.

It strikes me suddenly that whatever should happen will happen. I am not religious but I feel a sudden calm and fear at the same time. I had always imagined people die either quietly and naturally surrounded by family, or in violent noisy accidents. This is neither. It's a slow, silent slip into what seems inevitable.

I am keeping my head above the water. This is taking time and Jem is coughing. The water is freezing and I can hardly feel my hands. When I think about it, I am surprised neither of us was more badly hurt in the fall. I suspect I may have fractured my arm; it still hurts like hell but I can move it. Jem was badly bruised and I am increasingly worried about her baby. I look up into the darkness. There is still some way to go.

Suddenly, Jem slips under. I hear her splutter, then she is gone. I feel around for her and kick out. I make contact with her and lean to pull her. She is fighting to the top and she breaks the surface, spluttering. She can't catch her breath. I manoeuvre her into a lifesaving position.

'Jem, can you hear me?'

'Yes. Sorry. I must have... it felt like I was falling asleep.'

She's fading. I knew she would.

'Right. Remember earlier when I said to relax and just float? Well, you have to do that now. You have to. I'll be here, supporting you. We're more than halfway now.'

She stops kicking and stretches her legs in front of her. She waves her arms gently to buoy herself. The water rises and I am struggling to feel my legs. But I keep going. I have to.

'Perfect. You're doing well.'

She whispers in the darkness. 'I'd be dead if it wasn't for you.'

I want to tell her she still might be. But I stay calm. Somewhere inside is a small chink of hope that if we get onto that ledge we can get out of that door. Wood is weaker than stone and there are people on the other side. Then, in a second, I spot it. A huge rusty nail sticking out of the wall. Where the ladder would have been.

'Jem, I need to let you go for a moment. Just float. Can you do that?'

'Yes, I think so.'

I untie my jeans from around my neck. I need to hook them onto the nail. Then, if it's strong enough, we can hang on to the material to save energy. Everything is a fine balance of energy saved against energy expanded. I hurl the jeans at the nail and it misses. It misses another ten times before I get a grip.

It's tempting to pull myself up on it and try to get to the ledge. But I stick to my plan. Calm. Patient. I hang on to the jeans and stop treading water. I grab Jem again and she is very still.

'Are you okay?'

'I am but I don't feel very well. I feel very weak.'

'Lean on me. Hold on to me. Keep floating if you can. I've got something to hold on to. We just have to wait now.'

She murmurs into the dark. 'I'm sorry if I can't. I'm sorry.'

My heart is breaking. I can feel her body weakening in my arms. Her muscles going softer. Her arms stop wafting the water and I am holding her head above the water.

'Jem. Jem. Come on. Don't give up now. Come on.'

My voice echoes around the room. It seems a little lighter and I think dawn has broken outside. The water is like a mirror, and I can see Jem's ashen face. I can suddenly hear the rain beating against the wooden door. The water is rising fast now. Then I realise I would never be able to lift myself and Jem onto the ledge if she is unconscious or worse. But I couldn't let her go either.

I reach up with my free hand and feel the ledge. It's now or never. But the awful truth is that to save myself I will have to let go of Jem.

CHAPTER THIRTY-FOUR

She is so cold. Deathly cold. Her body is floppy and I think about tying her to my jeans while I hoist myself up. But what then? What then? I can't reach the nail from the ledge. I think about all the times I had wished her gone. All the terrible things I had wished on her. How I wanted her to cry and feel how I did.

Now all I want her to do is live. To wake up and struggle onto the ledge. I shake her hard but she doesn't wake. I want to see her wonky smile and hear the disapproval of me in her voice. I want her to take Angel to school and ruffle Ben's hair.

What I do not want to do is let go of her and let her fall into that icy water. Or to wait here until the rain subsides and the water level eventually falls and my last chance is gone. I listen and the rain is still beating on the door. I could take a chance and wait to see if the water rises even higher. But for all I know, it could be escaping already somewhere below, and as soon as the storm stops it will start to drain faster.

I don't know where the water line is. I scour the wall for any sign of a tide mark where the water has regularly levelled off. I don't know where the line is. But I never did. I shout it into the room.

'I never did!'

Someone has to hear me before I make this impossible decision. I scream it into the water.

'I never knew where the line was. I do now, though. I do.'

It's here, where I am now. Calm returns and I weigh up the situation. I can't let her go. I will have to tie her to the jeans and hope she floats. But if the water subsides quickly, she will be left hanging there. I feel the panic rise. I try to breathe deeply and calm myself but I am breathing quickly.

She slips a little from my grasp and I feel her move. I feel her back arch and her attempt a cough.

'Jem! Come on. We're near the top.'

I hear her breath, shallow. 'Go without me.'

I shake my head. 'No. No, I won't. We're in this together.'

She coughs again. 'I'm too weak. I can hardly move.' She whimpers. 'Look, if you do get out will you tell my mum and dad–'

I interrupt. 'No! No! Don't do this. Don't. They'll find us. They will.'

She gives a weak laugh. 'I don't know. How? They would have come by now. Someone must have seen me with Tracey. Someone must have put two and two together. If they had, they'd have followed her and she would never have got you.'

I think. The water is still rising.

'It all takes time, I guess. They would have to find out where my phone has been.' I know deep inside that Tracey has thought this through. She has burner phones. She would have made it look like I went back to my car. 'She came back. Maybe she'll come back again.'

I can't lose hope. I can't. It's so easy to lose faith in others, but I know Bekah Bradley will have been following every possible lead. She left no stone unturned when she looked into what I had done. She is sharp as a pin.

'Bekah. She had Tim. She would have been aware of Tracey.'

'Yeah. But before you came here she was going on about how she put them off the trail and onto him. How they would never find me.'

Suddenly the rain stops. The drops no longer hammer against the door and all is quiet. I swear I hear a bird call.

'Jem. We have to do this now. Can you hang on to the material? I can't tie it to you because...'

'The water will go down. Yes. I can right now but...'

'Good. I'll climb up and see if I can get out of the door and go for help. How does that sound?'

I can just about see her face. She tilts her head and blinks at me. 'I'm really scared.'

'Me too. But it's the only way.'

She nods. I hoist her up and tie the jeans to her wrist. It's the only way, despite the danger. Then I let go. The tension rips the material on the nail for a while, but the seam holds. I exhale. She is dangling in the water with it helping to support her, but as it falls, she may too.

I grab the ledge. I'm not athletic. I'm not a gym bunny. Pulling myself up is not going to be easy. I ease myself along to the part of the wall where the steps had been and manage to get a grip with my feet. It takes several attempts and most of my little remaining strength to pull myself out of the water but eventually I am on the ledge.

I turn to see Jem looking up at me, her head barely out of the water. I feel the door. It's solid and my heart falls. For the first time I feel like crying. But I don't. As the rain starts again, I hammer on the door and scream. I tell myself that I will do this until I can't anymore. It's all I have left. This really is it. The door does not budge but my determination does. I am close and I will do it.

I press my ear against the door and I bang with my fist for what seems like hours. When I look again Jem's eyes are closed. But I don't go to her. I can't. We made a deal. She will stay there and I will get us out of here. I listen at the door. I can't hear anything except the rain. It's early morning and people will be walking their dogs.

I bang and bang and then my hand is bleeding and I am crying. I am so close. I am inches away from the outside. Then I hear it. A tapping. Then a banging. Then a creak as someone prises the door open. Then someone shouts *stand back* and I edge away from the door and then it opens. Two policemen stand in the doorway.

'Jem Carter?'

I shake my head. 'Lauren Wade. Jem's in there.'

They move inside and look over the edge. Then it is action stations. A woman wraps me in a foil sheet and pulls me out of the darkness and into the tunnel. It is so bright in comparison to the room that my eyes hurt. I blink at the doorway over my shoulder and the woman tries to lead me away.

'No. I need to see she is okay.'

We stand on the canal bank at the tunnel entrance. I am so focused on Jem that I hardly notice Bekah Bradley and DC Sharples appear beside me. I don't look at her.

'Will you tell my children I am safe, please?'

She touches my arm. 'You need to come to the station. You both do.'

I try to laugh but it won't come. 'The only place she's going is hospital. That's if she...'

There's a sudden flurry of activity and a policeman is carrying Jem along the bank in the opposite direction. He lays her down and gives her mouth to mouth. He pumps at her chest and I hear someone screaming. It's me. Bekah's arms are around me and I sob into her shoulder. Her body is tense and her breath fast. Then she relaxes.

'She's alive. She's moving.'

I break away from them and rush towards her. The policeman holds me a short distance away but I manage to see her face. Ashen and taut, her lips curve into a smile when she sees me. 'We did it. We only bloody did it.'

Bekah leads me away and in all this mess I half expect her to arrest me. But she doesn't. She sits me in the back of her car. It's parked opposite the school.

'My car. It was here.'

'We found it at the station. Parked up in the big car park behind. We all thought you'd done one.'

I can hardly ask her the next question. There is time, I need to recover, but I need to know. 'How did you find us?'

I need to know if Tracey relented. All I can think about is Jem making me promise not to blame Tracey. I know my brain is addled, but somewhere deep inside I know I must honour what we agreed. But I need to know if she had second thoughts. If, eventually, she realised that what she had done was wrong. No, not wrong, insane. Bekah nods.

'Someone walking their dog in the tunnel this morning called 999. He heard crying and banging.'

I look out of the car window. A man with a black Labrador is standing by the opening to the tunnel. He's talking to a man with a notebook and I smile at how quaint that is in these days of new technology.

'We were in water. It was rising.'

'What happened?'

I face her. 'I need a bit of time to recover.' I can't. But I have to. I have to tell the truth. I promised myself I would. I look around at the trees and the sky. I could have died in there. 'Look, about the cameras.'

I see a look of irritation cross her face. 'Someone has to make a complaint and they haven't. This is much more serious.'

'The thing is, Jem thinks that the person who did this is... unbalanced. In the same way I was when I... did all those things. She feels they need help rather than be punished. And she said If I send them down the punishment route, then she will make a complaint about me.'

Bekah turns her head so I can't see her face. She thinks for a while. Then she faces me. 'You have to understand that I'm here to do my job. I didn't cut you a break. I still followed the rules. The fact is no one has made a police complaint about the things you allegedly did. Or really produced any evidence. Anyone can say anything, but I have to act on evidence. Which is why we brought you in. We had a lot of evidence of something, it turned out it wasn't about the thing we were investigating. This, on the other hand, is different. We have two sets of complaints.'

I raise my eyebrows.

'Jem's missing person report was filed by both Daniel Wade and her parents. Yours was filed by Lisa Burton and Belinda Wade. So two missing person reports we had to act on.'

I blink at her. I want to ask her if she is sure Belinda made a missing person report about me. But she wouldn't have got it wrong. But maybe I had.

'I'll level with you, we thought it was Tim at first. But not later. We never bought anyone's suggestion that it was you. Or that you had run.'

'Even though it must have looked like it?'

She laughs. 'No. Obviously, that's where it pointed, but no. He was just trying to save his own skin. But we also didn't think he did it. Not after interviewing him. And we had him under surveillance when he was released so it didn't add up.' She licks her lips. 'So this is different. I can't promise that this person will get the help they need. But I can make it easier for you.' Her voice lowers to an even whisper. 'No one needs to know you told me. I will say I worked it out.'

I stare at her. She stares back. Then she speaks again. 'You don't even have to say yes or no. Just nod or shake your head.'

She knows. She knows but she hasn't been able to prove it yet.

'It's Tim's wife, isn't it? Maria.'

I frown. Not Maria. Tracey. But she holds up a picture of Tracey and I nod almost violently. I feel the tears come, finally. 'Her children?'

She puts her hand gently on my arm. 'Lauren, you really need to let all this go now. Make a new start. Don't worry about her children. Or her. Or even Jem. Worry about you. And yours.' It's the same thing Jem told me. Think about yourself. I am shivering. 'But think. Please think if there is anything at all in that room that can tell us she was ever there. Because I have nothing at all to go on if you two won't ID her.'

I go over every inch of the room in my mind's eye. The sandwich wrappers. But they would have been in water for hours. Our clothes were wringing wet. I go over the walls, the door. Was she wearing gloves? No. No she wasn't. She was so sure no one would find us. The ledge. She leaned against the wall. She had a bottle of water.

'There's a water bottle on the ledge. It's in a corner by the door.'

She steps out of the car and hurries around to my side. She opens the door. 'Come on. We need to get you to hospital for a check over.'

I step out of the car and my legs wobble. 'Oh, I need to tell you that Jem's pregnant. In case she's...'

She smiles and herds me to a paramedic. It's all blue lights and stop signs on the road. And that's what it has to be for me. An abrupt halt and time to recover. She leans over and whispers in my ear. 'I'm going to have to ask both of you to identify your abductor. We'll need a statement. But I will make sure she gets assessed. I'll make sure Jem knows. Okay?'

I nod and she leaves. She signals to DC Sharples and they speed away. He's driving and she's talking on her phone and I see two officers hurry towards the bridge with evidence bags. The paramedic wraps me in a warm blanket and gives me water to sip.

'We're going to take you to hospital, just to be on the safe side.'

I nod. I feel very, very tired. 'Jem? Where's Jem?'

She smiles at me. 'Conscious. And already on her way.'

CHAPTER THIRTY-FIVE

I wake before I open my eyes and all I can think about is her. Jem. How much I hated her. Why was that? Why? We probably wouldn't have been friends if we had met socially, but she was okay. I check myself. Better than okay. She was a nice person. Even now, it seems wrong to admit it after what she did with Daniel.

But I know now that was why I hated her. It wasn't something about her. I hardly knew her, really. It was the story Daniel wove between us. I feel a tear escape from the corner of my eye and trickle down the side of my face. There was so much time to say so many things in that room. Why didn't we say them? The fear and terror brought us together, but we still weren't able to discuss the depth of things.

No. It remained buried. We didn't discuss him. We talked around it and plucked the issues that floated to the top. Those immediate, jarring things we had to say to each other to spell out that nothing could get in the way of supporting each other. If I am honest, her just being there made all the difference. A face I knew. Someone else to focus on so that I wasn't constantly thinking about the horrors of what would happen next. It saved me.

I think about Tracey. Or Maria. Or whoever she is. She shouldn't get away with this, and I don't think she will. But then again, is it really her fault? Was she driven to it? That won't stand up in a court of law. She had a choice. A clear choice of whether to act or not. It was all premeditated. Not a few angry posts on social media. No. Solid acts. Ending with the intention to let us die.

It hits me like a ton of bricks. We came so close. She knew that place. She knew full well what could – probably would – happen. She nailed the door shut. We are all free to make those decisions, me included. And in the end, she got to choose and made the wrong choice.

I'm disappointed that she didn't relent. Realise that she could never get away with it. That she shouldn't. I'm beginning to realise it's a journey from that first hint of hate to the decision to put things right, and some people never reach the end of that journey. Some people don't fight that feeling, they defend it to the very, very end. Whereas I chose to fight and now I am free.

I open my eyes and Bekah Bradley is sitting at the side of my hospital bed.

'You've been asleep for a while.'

She smiles at me. Her teeth are stark white. She looks tired. My arm hurts. It's bandaged and my cut hand is dressed.

'Yes. It was a hard day.'

She fake sniggers and hands me a glass of water. 'Here.' I remember the dirty water all around me and the exhaustion. My head is banging, and my stomach does a backflip as the water goes down. 'Are you up to talking?'

I'm barely okay, but I need to get this done. 'Yes. But I have a few questions.'

'Okay. Fire away. Then I'll get DC Sharples in, and we'll ask ours if that's okay?'

Her voice is soft, and I wonder if this is off-duty Bekah. I sort the things I need to know into priorities and start with the first one.

'Have you told my children I am okay?'

She smiles. 'Yes. I spoke to your ex-husband, and he has told them. They can't wait to see you. You just need checking over now you're awake, then you can go home to them.'

I want to ask if she has proof that he told them. If she knows for sure. But then I remember that all this has nothing to do with Daniel. I feel my breath quicken and I sit up. She moves forward to help me.

'Did you...?' I stop short so as to not compromise our agreement.

'Yes. And thank you for sending that camera link. We were pretty sure that Jem had been taken from her car. Then when someone reported your car abandoned, we were even more sure. But that note didn't make sense and something you said told me to check. Check that day on your camera.'

I remember Jem's hands wringing and rubbing together when she told me about Tracey befriending her and coming to The Rosarium, how she wrote the note and added her own lie. She continues.

'We were able to ID the abductor, but that didn't give us any clues where you were. We've been monitoring Jem's phone constantly, and we put an international mobile subscriber identity and covert communications data capture on your phone. She was reported missing, and her parents gave permission. You gave us permission when we brought you in. Both were switched off, so we had nothing to go on. Yours was still in your bag in your car.' She makes a little sound. 'We don't need the camera footage. It proves nothing except Jem knew Maria.'

I feel a weight lift from my body. I need to understand what will happen now. There is so much I need to say. I have her here and I need to tell her more. I rush at it full force.

'But you will be able to prove she did it?' I swallow. My mouth is dry, and my lips cracked. 'She was so careful. She said she had burner phones and... you've got her, though?'

She shakes her head. 'Nothing can go wrong. She hasn't admitted it fully. She's said that she was just trying to teach you a lesson. That she always intended to come back. But we have enough. And I've told Jem that Maria was a suspect, which is true, we had her in our sights, and that we're formalising it with forensics.'

'I'll put everything in my statement. Are you going to charge her? Are you?'

I hear myself, calm and confident. She is silent. She looks away. I see her pull her lips in and when she turns back, she is blinking away tears. She momentarily holds her head in her hands, then smooths her hair.

'It's complex. But I will charge her. And what you have told me will make it easier. What you have to understand is the evidence. I have very little to go on. She has no record. A few people we have spoken to, family, friends, have said she was increasingly volatile. But this...' She looks out of the window. We can see the tops of trees silhouetted against the sky. 'This is major. She nailed the door shut. So it might look like nothing is going on, like we can't prove it, but in reality...' She stops to control her anger. Her voice is breaking as she continues. 'In reality, I am spending every waking moment working towards that goal.'

She stands and walks to the other side of the room. Her hands dig deep into her tailored black trousers. She is shaking her head and fuming. 'She wanted to kill you. That was her intention. I just have to prove it.'

I feel tears threaten again.

'I know.' I look at the door. I can see DC Sharples outside talking to someone. She nods almost imperceptibly to signal it's okay to go further without him hearing. 'I know it sounds stupid but I've been there. Not nailing a door shut, but I did make someone's life a misery. It's like a temporary insanity driven by something I don't quite understand. I have years of training in dealing with people in difficult situations. But this...'

I sip some water and wonder if I'm going too far. But it's important she knows. 'It's like it's driven from outside ourselves. Like a strong urge to protect ourselves from those who have hurt us. Like an anger that can't be expressed any other way. When everyone else is carrying on as normal but your whole world had disintegrated around you.'

She cocks her head to one side. 'I know. I've seen it a million times. But the truth is, if you do something that's against the law, you will be punished. If you break the law, you should be. Love isn't fair and lots of people feel like they aren't listened to. But it's not illegal to break up with someone. It's not illegal to think you want revenge. But it is illegal to stalk and harass someone. To kidnap them and lock them in a room you know will fill up with water. I know you feel sorry for her, and I've yet to talk to Jem about it, but Maria must face what she did.'

I shake my head. I open my mouth to speak, but nothing comes out. She is right, Tracey, or Maria, must pay for what she has done. Bekah nods at me.

'A touch of Stockholm syndrome? Identifying with your captor?' She leans forward. 'I'll stick to our agreement but she will be charged. Whether Miss Carter likes it or not.'

Jem. She was my next question. Jem and her baby. Daniel's baby. I test it out on my nerves. Nothing. Not the slightest hint of jealousy or hate. I think about when I was hiding in her beautiful home in the lovely bedroom she made for my daughter. The photographs of her with Angel and Ben. How she told me that all the while she knew Daniel was using her as an unpaid babysitter while he slept with other women. But she still did that for the kids, purely because they were innocent in all this.

How she didn't call the police when she knew I was following her. Calling her from a long-gone burner phone in the middle of the night and not speaking. She knew her place in it, too. How our silent battle of looks and secrets played out. Her dignity in the face of all that I did to her.

Her parents and her friends. Everyone who knew her. The way she held her arm over her stomach to protect her unborn child. What she went through to get those bruises – both mental and physical. And the way she said, 'Go without me' the last time I saw her. I can't bear it. I can't.

'About Jem. It was my fault. All of it. She wouldn't have been taken if it wasn't for me. I blamed him and her because I hated them. A stupid, petty reason compared with all this. Maria just thought she was me. So if Daniel or her family wants to press charges about the cameras and any of the other stuff, well, I'm your woman.'

She frowns at me. 'Daniel? I don't think...'

I snort. 'No, maybe not. But her parents. They'll want answers.'

'I'm not with you. I think they have all the answers they need. Jem has already spoken to them about what happened. She discharged herself from hospital. Her parents have booked her a private room at a clinic.' She rolls her eyes. 'She's already spoken to reporters.'

Bekah pushes her phone screen in my face. It's footage of Jem. She is propped up in bed and surrounded by pink roses and balloons. Her face is bruised and her eyes dark, but her hair is styled, and she is smiling.

'...of course, the real hero of the day is Lauren Wade. She's the one who kept the hope alive. And I hope I can see her soon to thank her for her support.' She smiles directly into the camera. It's a fake smile and her eyes are still dull. But behind her is a pink balloon that says 'Mummy-to-be'. I look at Bekah.

'My God. She's still pregnant. Thank goodness. All that and she's still pregnant. I thought...'

What I am thinking is that I am not a hero. No. Somewhere inside, I acknowledge my desperate actions embedded in the bigger picture. Jem and I both know what happened. And Bekah. But Jem's story is hers. It's how she copes. If I have learned anything, it's that all of us have our own narrative push us through the separation we feel, however big or small. Bekah smiles.

'Well, it looks like she'll be well looked after now. Do you think you can convince her to work with us rather than make any more announcements?'

I nod. Yes. I can. I think she will listen to me after this. I think Jem and I will have a lot to talk about in the future. And none of it will be Daniel.

CHAPTER THIRTY-SIX

I am home. I stand in my kitchen with Lisa. She collected me from the hospital and drove me home silently. She puts the kettle on, and I look around. It's only been a couple of days, but everything is different now. Lisa chatters in the background.

'Course, I was a shit friend. If I had been there for you, none of this would have happened.'

I smile and put my hands around the warm cup she places in front of me. 'No, not at all. Not one little bit. You've listened to my endless moaning over the years. That's got to stop now.'

She pulls in her lips. 'Yeah. He'll be here in a minute. Do you want me to...?'

'No. No, I have to face this.'

She wipes down the kitchen and starts to mop the floor. I am still exhausted and all my bones ache from holding myself still for a long time. Lisa's going to stay here with me for a couple of weeks. Until I find my feet. We talked about some counselling, and she will arrange it.

I reach underneath the worktop and pull out my laptop that Bekah returned to me. Logging into my emails, I am almost afraid to check. It's only been a few days but it seems like much,

much longer since I last checked. But I need to reconnect with my job. I need to face what has happened, and with Lisa's help, I need to address it.

I gave Bekah a full statement. I haven't spoken to Jem. From what I can see on her social media and the reports of her on the local news she seems to be recovering. But I haven't phoned her and she hasn't phoned me. I know that call will need to happen eventually, but for now, I need time to think. Not about the past. No. About the future and everything it holds for me and my children.

I have been inundated with opportunities to appear on news interviews and to give statements to the press. But I am not interested in that. I've watched Jem sidestep the elephant in the room and that is enough for me. When the reporters ask her what she has to say to her abductor, she grips her mother's hand and tells them, 'I feel sorry for them. They must have been suffering to do such a thing.'

In every interview she looks straight at the camera and says: 'If it wasn't for the quick-thinking and bravery of Lauren Wade, I would be dead.'

I am still trying to understand what people have perceived when my life was hurled up in the air and the pieces landed, rearranged. Was I a victim? Did that make me look weak? Or had Jem's statement helped me soar above that as a hero? I wonder if Jem's earnest statement to the camera is really an attempt to goad Daniel; although she never told me, they must have discussed my past actions. This would be a clear signal that she has changed sides. The fragments of suspicion that are left floating around my heart allow me to think this for a moment. But I know deeper in my soul that it no longer matters what is going on between those two. They have their own path to walk now.

I look at Lisa, sweeping my kitchen floor. My long-time best mate turned live-in therapist. My friend. Bekah's tears and frustration at how much she couldn't do, but a willingness to try. Her humanity as she tried to understand the reasons for my actions, and her flexibility to make sure everyone gave her the information she needed. And Jem. After all I did to her, she just waved it away.

We hold each other up. We raise each other above the victim status the world wants to pin on us to make us invisible. To make us a statistic.

I hear Daniel's car on the gravel and rush to the lounge window. My heart leaps with love as Angel and Ben climb out and rush around to the side door. I sprint to meet them as they burst in.

'Mummy!'

My babies. Angel hugs me tightly and Ben smiles widely behind her. He hands me a picture. 'We did this for you.'

I hold it up in front of me. It has a tall woman with yellow hair holding hands with a boy and a girl. Behind them is a house with a huge door. I feel tears form, but this time, tears of joy. My God. I might never have seen them again. I stick the picture to the front of the fridge, covering old memories. This is a new start.

They are chattering away now about Belinda's puppy and Daddy and going back to school. Ben approaches the critical subject carefully. 'Can we watch TV? Granny doesn't like us watching TV, and we wanted to catch up.'

I laugh and nod. They run into the lounge and settle on the sofa, and all is well in their world. I turn to see Daniel loitering outside the back door.

'Can I have a word?'

He's awkward and his face tells me that this is not going to be a welcome home. But I am ready for him. I step outside and pull the door to. He digs his hands into the pockets of his oversized, clearly very expensive overcoat. He looks sullen and aggrieved. I fold my arms.

'What do you want, Dan?'

He shakes his head. 'You never give up do you?'

I smile. Just as I thought. He's actually on the attack. 'Give up what?'

He snorts. 'Do you know I've had the police all over my house? And whose fault is that? And poor Jem. You do know she's pregnant, don't you? With my child? And all that she went through was because of you.' He steps closer. I feel heat surge through me, but I don't back away.

'Okay. Okay, Dan, this is what's going to happen. After today and what I've got to say, I don't want to speak to you again. So yes, I do give up. Then I am selling this place and petitioning for divorce.'

'Oh, I see. More ways to punish me.'

Bile rises, but I push it down. 'Not at all. I want my freedom. And that way, you will be free too. Second, none of this was entirely my fault. I admit my behaviour around you and Jem was not exemplary. I own it. But you drove me to it. You. By treating me badly. And believe me, if you decide to carry this on, I will say my piece in court, because that is where it will be heard. Not here. Not between me and you where you can bully me, but in a very expensive exchange between solicitors.'

He laughs dramatically. 'You've got nothing on me. Jem and I–'

'I'm not talking about Jem. I'm talking about everyone you slept with when you were with me.' My voice is calm and low. Convincing. 'And Amber. The woman you were with in Jem's bed while she was missing.' I step closer to him. 'You never give up, do you, Daniel?'

He is silent. He is thinking. He has another attempt. 'You

can't prove that. And anyway, it's not illegal. Or dangerous. Not like what you did.'

He stares at me. I wonder what he is going to say. If he knows about the cameras. If he is going to make a complaint. Bekah said he didn't know. But Jem could have told him. She must have told him about the baby. I raise my eyebrows.

'Illegal? *And* dangerous?'

He flushes red. This is a side to Daniel that is reserved for special occasions. Calm but angry Daniel. 'You put my unborn child in danger. You. If it wasn't for you and your boyfriend, Jem would still be–'

'Doing your washing? Cleaning your house? While you screwed Amber? Is that what you mean, Dan? How much this has inconvenienced you?'

He steps back. I continue. 'What happened to me, and Jem, was not our fault. We were kidnapped. We were abused. You have no idea what we went through and the damage that woman has caused. And it's always the abuser's fault. Always. Are you saying I asked for it because I had a relationship? Because I tried to move on?'

'No, but...' He is thinking. 'You caused Jem to be hurt. If you hadn't–'

'Oh, I see. In fact, we could take this a step further with your reasoning. If you hadn't had an affair, she would never have become involved with us, so isn't it your fault? Isn't it, Dan?' I step close to him. 'No. I didn't think so. Because nothing is Dan's fault, is it?'

I think about Belinda, standing in front of him when it gets difficult. Making everything go away. He looks up at the house.

'I want half.'

I smile widely. He's like a petulant child. When he doesn't get one thing, grasping at another.

'You can have the lot, mate. After what I've just been

through, hanging on to some half-finished pile of rubble is the least of my worries. But I expect our solicitors will thrash that out. What you can't have is me. It's over.'

We stand in the morning sunshine on the crunchy gravel pathway that we laid ourselves in what seems like another lifetime. He starts to walk away, then turns back.

'I want you to keep away from Jem.'

I shake my head. 'That's for her to decide. And that child will be Ben and Angel's brother or sister.'

He rubs his hands over his face and points at me. 'That is my business. I'll handle it. Nothing to do with you.'

He would like that. He would like to keep building his little kingdom of secrets. He would like the control. But I know in my heart that it won't happen.

'Again, that's for me and Jem to decide. I guess you will have access to the child as you do to Ben and Angel.'

'Shared custody. But under the circumstances I might go for full custody. Of all of them.'

Only a fortnight ago, this statement would have sent me over the edge. Had me googling and worrying and losing sleep. Now, I feel nothing. He has threatened so much over such a long time, but none of it has come to fruition because he's too busy with his next conquest. I face him. And it's about time.

'Don't use our children as bargaining chips. Don't you dare. They've gone through enough. But all they will see from me now on is stability. But sure. Go for it. Go for full custody. Get your mummy to back you up. Tell all the lies you want. See where it gets you. But don't talk to me about it. Talk to my solicitor.'

He stalks over to his car. Just before he opens the door, he turns dramatically.

'This isn't over, Lauren.'

I watch him jump in and slam his own car door hard. It's

chilly and the leaves are falling from the trees. This place is pretty, but it's time to leave. I suddenly feel a deep sadness. This really is the end. He sits in his car, and I wonder if he thinks I will rush over, banging on the window, arguing with him.

I will never do that again. I won't engage with him. First thing tomorrow, I will contact Sam Smithers and start divorce proceedings. Make sure he sends Daniel a letter setting out not only contact with the kids but also with me. It is over. It is.

I turn around as he drives away. I don't stand and watch him, pining after him. Everything is suddenly more vivid and I wonder if this is what the world always looked like.

Back in the kitchen, Lisa has made more tea. She's got a pinny on now and I think she's really enjoying this. She takes some jammy toast through to Ben and Angel and puts a plate of it in front of me.

'Just like when we were in halls.'

I laugh. 'Bloody hell. That was a long time ago. Things were a lot less complicated then.'

She bites into a huge slice and chews thoughtfully. 'Yeah. But sometimes you just need a reminder that somewhere, underneath all the build-up of life shit and trauma, that person is still there. You were always brave.'

I almost spit my tea out. 'Brave? Bloody hell. Let's not get carried away, mate.'

But she is serious.

'Brave isn't always big, loud statements, is it? You knew what he was up to, but you stayed. You kept it all stable for those two.' We look into the lounge at Ben and Angel, relaxed on the sofa, laughing at the TV. 'And that's paid off right in this moment. After everything that happened with you, then Jem, they just came home and that's what it is. Home.'

I nod. I am starting to see what she means. She continues.

'Your problem is you are too hard on yourself. They're all

saying that this made you strong. Jem. That woman on breakfast TV who doesn't even know you. That what you went through in the last few days made you strong. But you were already strong. It was that strength that got you through. You don't have anything to prove. It's already right there.'

CHAPTER THIRTY-SEVEN

It's Thursday and I am getting ready to meet Jem. She messaged me last night asking me to meet her at The Blue Bear coffee shop in town. The message sat below the message she didn't send asking for help.

Daniel has the children. I spent the first part of the week in welcome normality with Ben and Angel. The school run. Bickering at breakfast and legs over each other's to watch a movie. Then tucking them into bed and telling them how much I love them. I will tell them every day now and that will fill the space in my heart left by the pain that has disappeared.

I feel much better. The hospital gave me some antibiotics and told me the water could be dirty and this was just a precaution. And to make sure my hand healed properly. My arm wasn't broken, but bruised and I have a nasty sprained wrist. Lisa had supervised medicine time, making sure I look after myself. Reminding me to put myself first.

She's gone out into town to do some shopping and, for the first time since I got out of that horrible space, I am alone. I am calm and I sit on the sofa in the sunshine until it is time to leave.

Just before midday, Belinda's red convertible pulls onto the drive. She hasn't been here since Daniel left, and I feel the old familiar dread and brace myself. I watch as she pulls a bag from behind her seat and pushes her sunglasses up onto her head. She walks round the side of the house and I rise to answer the door.

'Belinda! What a surprise. Come in.'

I go for her customary air kisses but she lunges forward and grabs me tightly.

'Darling girl. Darling girl.'

She is crying. She holds me so tightly that I can hardly breathe. Then she lets me go and steps back. There is a silence that could be awkward if it wasn't so laden with meaning. I realise in that space that sometimes what you don't say means more than the agenda-loaded words you can't help but speak. Eventually she shakes her head.

'I'm so sorry. I had it all wrong.' She hands me the bag. It's got some salad which I presume is from her greenhouse, and a bunch of Shasta daisies. She wipes a tear away. 'They're from the ones you planted that day when you brought Baby Ben and... Lauren, I am so sorry.'

I flick on the kettle. I'm not meeting Jem until one so I have time.

'Let's sit down.'

I lead her through to the lounge and she composes herself. I make the tea and bring it through.

'Thank you for the flowers. I missed your garden.'

'I feel like I haven't been fair to you. I've... favoured Daniel. He said some terrible things about you and I believed him. But I heard what you did... Jem. You...'

I hold my hand up. I speak very gently. 'Look, Belinda, Daniel was telling the truth. Probably exaggerated but we all do that sometimes. I did do some terrible things. But you have to understand I was very upset. I thought our marriage was forever. But it wasn't, and here we are.'

I stare at her. She looks at her tea.

'I wanted you and Daniel to be like me and Tony. We've had our issues but we stayed together. But I think that's out of the question now. So I need to tell you that from now on if you need any help with the children I'm here. Or to chat.'

I run some of the more difficult things that are going on in my mind into a conversation with Belinda and almost laugh. But I don't.

'Thank you. That is very kind of you.' I bite the bullet and tell her what has been on my mind. 'I wanted to say thank you to you too. I was going to send you something but as you are here, I might as well say it. Thank you for shielding Ben and Angel from everything that has happened. I can absolutely promise you that from now on everything will be normal. At my end. Obviously I can't speak for Daniel.'

She sighs. 'I fear he will still try to make trouble. Not for you so much. Just in general. He seems very mixed up.'

She's still talking about him like he's a teenager going through puberty. Like she doesn't understand that his first priority is Daniel. Again, I rise above it.

'Yes, he probably is.' After both me and Jem stood up to him, he will be very mixed up. 'I have to ask, Belinda, what made you change your mind about me?'

'Well, you'd think it would be being abducted and saving Jemima from drowning. But it wasn't that. Speaking honestly, I still thought you had something to do with it, because Daniel said you had. It was Ben. He was sitting there watching TV and he suddenly said "I haven't seen my mum for ages. I really miss her".' She wipes away another tear. 'As you know, we don't talk about feelings much in our house. But I am a mother, Lauren. In that moment I knew what you meant to

Ben. You weren't Daniel's insane ex or someone very convenient to disapprove of. You were Ben's mum and he loved you. You had achieved everything I aspired to be even if I didn't agree with your lifestyle. You were loved by your child.'

I feel a lump in my throat and fight back tears. She continues.

'I thought about it and no matter what, you will always be Ben and Angel's mum. I have been unfair. But I hope I can put that right.'

She takes my hand and I nod. 'Yes. New beginnings.'

We chat about her garden and she leaves. I don't tell her I am meeting Jem because I still don't completely trust her. It will be a long time until I trust anyone again.

Twenty minutes later I am standing across the road from The Blue Bear coffee shop. I see Jem sitting at a window table. She looks flawless and nothing like the last time I saw her and suddenly I am afraid. One heart to heart a day is enough and I wonder whether to phone her and tell her something has come up.

But I remind myself that I am brave and I am calm, and I walk across the road and open the café door. She is looking at her phone, scrolling, but when she sees me her face lights up.

'Lauren!'

I feel a surge of relief. She isn't angry or annoyed. She isn't sad or accusatory. Her eyes have regained their light and she looks healthy. I exhale and sit.

'How are you? I've been worried about you.'

She blushes bright red. 'Yeah. Me too. I worried if you were okay. I wondered if I should have rung you?'

I shake my head. 'It's fine. I needed to regroup.'

She fidgets in her chair. 'Anyway. Thanks for keeping your side of things. With Tracey. Or whoever she is. BB told me she was onto her already. And what with the forensics. It looks like she will get the help she needs.'

I wince at her BB reference. Bekah would hate that. I look out of the window. She has been charged and bailed. I told the truth. I told them how she came to my house and about Tim and about how she must have planned to push me through that door. And how she told us she'd covered it up. I told them how I thought she might have done this before, because Tim certainly had. Jem was a little easier on her, but the evidence will tell its own story. Maria won't get help. She'll be lucky if she doesn't go to jail.

Even so, I nod. 'Yeah. So what now. Where do we go from here?'

I don't know what her plans are. All I know is that she is pregnant with Ben and Angel's half sibling. I've thought carefully about it and I want that baby in their lives. I want them to know their baby brother or sister. I see her take a deep breath.

'Well, I have something to tell you.' I think for a moment that she is going to tell me she is reunited with Daniel. Nothing would surprise me. I check my stomach for butterflies, but I am completely calm. She continues. 'I'm telling you because it might affect you. He's moving out of The Rosarium. I'm going to be living there alone. He says he's moving back to Belinda's but I am guessing that won't be for long as it will cramp his style. So he might want you to sell the house.'

I laugh. 'Thanks. I appreciate it. But after what's happened, he can tell me he's going to the bloody moon and it won't bother me.'

She is suddenly serious. 'I didn't know what to say to you. After...'

I take her hand across the table. 'Jem...'

Our eyes meet and I see the depth of her feeling. No words

are needed. Her skin is warm and she's had her nails done and I am glad. Our drinks arrive and we sit in comfortable silence. But I do have something to say to her and now is the time.

'You were right, you know. I know you were having a go, but you were right.'

She pouts and frowns. 'About what?'

'About me. I didn't put myself first. I hate saying this, but you really helped me.' I watch her face carefully to make sure she has caught my half-smile. She has, and her lips curl into a lop-sided grin.

She snaps her fingers in the air. 'See. Right there. I knew it. There's the silver lining!'

I laugh. 'Oh, I thought the silver lining was that we are alive.' I sober. She needs to know I understand. 'It could have been so different. To be honest, it all seems like some kind of bad dream now. Like it never happened. But it did. And I have the bruises to prove it.'

I pull up my sleeve and show her the huge blue-green bruise on my arm. She pulls a face.

'Yeah, me too. And my legs are only just back to normal. But seriously, you saved my life.'

I stare at her. 'You saved mine too. If it hadn't been for what you said to me, what you made me realise, I would have slipped back into the drama. But I won't now. I'll be selfish. Like you.'

We roar with laughter and it feels good. She stirs her mint tea. 'I got Pepe back. Dan is with that Amber now. He told me.'

I feel a small dagger of jealousy. 'Oh. You've seen him?'

'Yeah. I had to get some things. And tell him about...' She averts her eyes. 'I went up to the house unannounced. She was there. Sprawled on the sofa. He tried to get her to leave but she insisted on staying and it was fine by me. Her face when I told her I was moving in and he was moving out.' She sniggers. 'But seriously, that is my house. Bought with my money. Well, my parents' money. He said he would contribute but he never did. And now he's paying for that lie. We're not married, so he gets nothing. Nothing at all.' She points her spoon at me. 'Don't let him get to you. He'll try.'

'He already has. He tried when he dropped the kids off. But I told him to speak to my solicitor.'

She holds her hand up for a high five and I have no choice but to match it. We laugh for a moment. Then she is serious. 'Look. I have to go in a minute. Dentist appointment. And I've got some pretty big decisions to make in the next few weeks. I just wanted to say thanks and let you know the kids won't be at The Rosarium. But I hope we can keep in touch?'

'Of course we can. Drop me a message.'

I say it before I realise the irony. She pulls a face and picks up her bag. All her clothes are new and she is coiffed to within an inch of her life. But I have seen the Jem underneath all that, and she knows it. We stand and she pulls me towards her. She holds up her phone and I suddenly realise that she is taking a selfie. She makes her Instagram face and I smile at us both smiling on the screen as I officially enter her online life.

She puts her phone away. I hold her tightly. In that moment I feel genuine care and I know I have finally separated from Daniel and my marriage.

We walk out of the café into our own lives. Our plans and dreams. House moves and babies that will wash a watercolour filter over this whole episode eventually. There will be lasting marks and it will rise again from time to time as I battle my way through, but there will also be a settling. In time.

CHAPTER THIRTY-EIGHT

SIX MONTHS LATER

I stand outside the house that has been my home for seven years. I'm going to miss it, after all. Lisa is directing the removal men, and I watch as they ship crates from the house to the van. I savour the crunch of the gravel, because this will be the last day I hear it.

Ben and Angel are at Daniel's. He still lives with Belinda and Tony, and the kids told me it isn't the same without Jem and Pepe. Predictably, Amber has now moved in. Angel told me she went round removing all the pictures of Jem. I wanted to ask what Belinda did in response, but I kept quiet.

They seem to have taken it in their stride. Back to school. Back to their routine. Back to their demands of takeaways and *can they have a mobile phone*. They don't know all the details. When they are older, they will inevitably google my name and find out what happened. But for now, the explanation that mummy and Jem were in an accident but are back now has glossed it over. I will talk to them when the time is right. They are my everything and I will never, ever forget how it felt to almost never see them again.

He brings Amber with him to pick up the kids. Just like Jem, she stays in the car and doesn't speak to me unless she absolutely has to. I don't have her number on my phone, despite Daniel's insensitive insistence that I do. For emergencies. No. I don't speak to either of them unless it is about Ben and Angel and something very, very critical.

I spoke to Sam about the divorce, and he sent a letter to Daniel spelling out the fact that if he contacted me on any other matter other than the children, further steps would be taken. That prompted a predictably expensive flurry of letters between our solicitors that resulted in us agreeing that 'family matters' would be settled out of court. The divorce is proceeding, and I do not have a single regret.

I put my half of the equity from the house on a small three-bedroomed semi-detached nearer to the city. More me, and handy for work. It has a small garden and we're going to get a dog. I'll be working from home online most of the time in my job. The surgery holds staff meetings on a Tuesday and I have reduced my surgery time to two mornings so the dog won't be alone much.

I watch as the removal van pulls away with all my belongings. I step back inside and run my hands over the stone worktops and look into the beautiful lounge with the picture windows. It could have all been so different. But it wasn't. I had a decorating company in to remove the graffiti and give the place a makeover, but it sold the first week it was for sale.

Lisa pops her head around the corner. 'Ready?'

I nod. I wonder if the ghosts of the previous occupiers walk through their old homes? I remember the happy times we sat together as a family. We laughed and played, and Daniel and I made love. I push away the memories that made me leave and step outside. I lock the door and put the key in my pocket to drop off at the estate agents. Lisa is waiting in her car. We're going for tea while the removals take place. Then I can step into my new world.

I get in the car. She's touching up her make-up and spraying deodorant under her arms.

'You okay?'

I check. Am I okay? *Am I?*

'Yep. Let's go.'

And I am. I have been going to counselling and working and treating myself better than before. Making decisions. There is a surprisingly big hole where scheming on how to get back at Daniel and Jem used to be, and I am filling it with notes for a course I plan to take to work with victims of severe trauma. Bekah Bradley pointed out to me that if I am serious about giving something back, I need to step up. That woman doesn't have a diplomatic bone in her body, which is probably why she is so good at her job.

She has prosecuted Maria. It's ongoing. Jem has agreed for the details to be made public so it can be a test case in the investigation. I have a feeling it will be the first of many. I asked her if there was a way to erase my name from being on the internet. I don't want to risk my children seeing it. She looked me in the eye and told me it was there forever. There were ways to apply to have it taken down, but all the reporting around this case would remain.

So I own it. I am not blocking it out or pushing it to the back of my mind, behind everything else. I've done too much of that. I am facing it. Along with the Tim situation. After about a month, he sent me a long message saying he only did it because he wanted to be with me. That's he'd moved out of the family home now and had a place above a shop on North Road. Would I like to meet to talk about what had happened?

Even though he completely deceived me and Maria, I missed him. I hadn't realised how much those weekends away had distracted me. Or how much I had fallen for him. I missed the messages and the calls and even the gaps in between when I looked forward to them. But I never responded to his message, and I never will. It could never be right after what happened and he would be a constant reminder. But I am sure that there will be someone else for me. Someone who is available. Someone who feels the same as I do. Rather than prop up my resolve that all men are unfaithful chancers I have come to believe that I just hadn't found the right person. But I will. I just know it. But there is no rush. None at all.

And I no longer go to the void between the end of my relationship with Daniel and the beginning of something else. In the past months there have been times when I felt myself slipping, but I never went there, not even once. Then, one morning I woke up and the void had closed. The bitterness had faded and the weight of my guilt had shifted to a lighter feeling of gratitude that I had managed to pull myself back.

Jem kept her baby. We had a lot of Facebook message in-depth chats where she told me she will have a social life and we should meet up as she will have shared access to her baby with Daniel. I had to stifle a smile at Belinda enduring sleepless nights – Amber didn't seem like the baby kind. Jem invited me round for the baby shower and Lisa and I joined her with her yoga-loving friends. She mentioned that she might have a painkiller-free water delivery and, again, I marvelled at her naivety.

But I am fond of her. Her bruises have gone now, but I can see that she still struggles.

We arrive at the restaurant early. I am jittery with nerves even though this has been planned to precision. Jem is already here. I stand in the doorway and, like everything I do these days, I take a second to make sure it is what I really want to do. No pressure. Lisa stands behind me.

'Okay? Is this what you want?'

I laugh. I could never have imagined this in my wildest dreams six months ago. 'I do. It's a good thing.'

I glance over to where Jem sits. She is wearing trendy dungarees and pumps and she looks absolutely fantastic. My heart warms as I see her laugh with Belinda, who brought Ben and Angel. Jem sees us and waves. Lisa laughs.

'Bloody hell. She's so bloody enthusiastic.'

I laugh too. I am glad. I am glad she is smiling. My anxiety rises slightly. I am a little wary of crowded places, but my mantra gets me to the table. *We hold each other up. We hold each other up.*

She looks lost in thought and suddenly snaps out of it. I hope it will get better for her, but Lisa says it will take time. She told anyone who would listen at the baby shower that she was building a YouTube influencer profile focusing on motherhood and baby clothes. She looked at me as she said it and made a little heart with her hands. It wasn't exactly what I meant when I told her to distract herself, but it would do for now.

She posted the selfie of us on her Instagram account with #sisters. I wouldn't go that far, but it was the start of something and she snaps us again now. On the surface she is back to her 'influencer-cum-guru' identity, but I know deep down she is still processing things. She manoeuvres me into position and pulls a pout. I smile as I feel her warm hand on my shoulder. She takes lots of photos at different angles. Yes, it's the start of something. Something permanent because I have come to realise that only Jem and I will ever fully know what happened in that room. What it felt like.

We are all bruised. It's as if we haven't reached our final destination yet. The pin on the map is Maria's sentencing which isn't for a while yet due to psychiatric reports. They are still looking at whether she has done this before and while Bekah is hopeful they will find some evidence, she is not certain.

Jem air kisses us all despite our protests. The waiter pulls out our chairs and we sit. Ben and Angel sit between me and Jem, and Belinda smiles across the table at them. I order sparkling water. Lisa and Belinda share a bottle of white wine and we all look at the menu.

I am impatient. I want the next step. I join in with the small talk about small plates and listen to Jem's detailed description of holistic childbirth. Finally, the door opens and Jem's parents appear. They have a baby carrier and my eyes follow them across the room. I still feel my shoulders tense after all this time. What will it take to be free, finally?

Jem stands. 'Everyone, meet Dakota Lauren.'

She picks the little girl out of the baby carrier. Ben and Angel's eyes follow her. Angel turns to me.

'Mummy, is she our sister? Really?'

I smile. 'Yes, darling. Yes, she is.'

Jem hands Dakota to Belinda and the children are transfixed. I peer at her. She has Belinda's nose. Daniel's nose. And his dark hair. I suddenly wonder what I was so scared of. She is just a tiny baby and can do me no harm. My shoulders relax and I sip my water. There is nothing bad about this. It's just a lovely, family occasion. I surprise myself by hoping it is one of many.

I look around the table. All smiles now after the chaos of the past year. I silently toast everyone and my gaze drifts to the window and a car parked outside. I know it's Amber's car, a flashy BMW straight out of Daniel's stock. I see her crouched low, looking through the window. I can almost feel her pain.

Jem sees me and we exchange a glance. She nods. I go outside onto the pavement. She doesn't wind the window down so I beckon her. She looks afraid at first, then sits up straight. I smile but she doesn't smile back. I walk towards the car but she starts the engine and drives away. I watch as she screeches down the high street and know there will be another time.

Two hours later I am standing on the drive of my new house. There is no gravel this time, just some herringbone paving that is shiny in the rain. The children run inside and Lisa follows them. I feel the wind on my face and I am completely calm. I have done well. I have moved on. Not just physically, but emotionally. I haven't forgiven, or forgotten. No. But I have understood and moved on. I have done what I said I would do.

And I have put myself first. It's been a challenge, and every act of self-care comes with the guilt of what I did previously. But I will forgive myself for all the things I did to Jem and Daniel. That's over now and I must replace them with the positives. I will never be perfect, but I can be better. And I will be.

I will sleep well tonight.

THE END

ACKNOWLEDGEMENTS

The idea for this book came to me as I thought about an incident in the distant past where a I knew woman in a relationship with someone was due to be a bridesmaid at the wedding of a couple they were close to. They split up, and the man's new girlfriend wore the same bridesmaid dress and literally replaced my friend as the bridesmaid. I could feel her deep visceral hurt, and that hurt was the seed for this story.

I would like thank my lovely agent Judith Murray for all her wise counsel on this story. Also, everyone who read the draft and gave me input. I am so grateful. And to Bloodhound Books who are so responsive and brilliant to work with and have made the whole publishing process so exciting and straightforward. Thank you for loving this book and the opportunity to work with you.

I am also grateful to two officers for Greater Manchester Police who answered the niggly questions I had about surveillance devices, police interviews and what was possible in various scenarios. You went above and beyond, but you always do.

Big thanks to all my writing colleagues – too many to list here but you know who you are – for your support. Especially Anstey Harris for her endless support and Pheadra Patrick for her lunch availability and listening ear.

Thanks to Lindsay Bowes for her enduring friendship and for listening to my rambling plots, more lately over long distance Whatsapp. Thanks to Sue Lees for the discussions in Costa

Coffee and the reminder that good friends can find each other again.

London Writing Salon provided space for me to just write with other writers online with no pressure. It was exactly what I needed to keep going and stay productive and thank goodness it's still going strong. Thank you Matt and Parul for what turned out a writing-life changer.

When I was nearing the end of writing this novel, Adele released the song 'Easy on Me' and, in the middle of a very uncertain period at the end of COVID19 lockdown, I found confidence in creativity again. It also reminded me that we all make mistakes, but those mistakes don't make us. So I am grateful for the magic of the writing process that I pretend I don't believe in but live every day, and the opportunity to do it.

Thanks to my children Michelle, Victoria and Toby for their patience and to my grandchildren Evan, Leah, Lincoln and Phi for just being themselves. And to my brothers for their observations and being proud of me. You all keep me going.

But the biggest thanks goes to my partner Eric. You help me more than you know and make this whole thing a lot easier that I ever imagined it could be. Thanks, love.

A NOTE FROM THE PUBLISHER

Thank you for reading this book. If you enjoyed it please do consider leaving a review on Amazon to help others find it too.

We hate typos. All of our books have been rigorously edited and proofread, but sometimes mistakes do slip through. If you have spotted a typo, please do let us know and we can get it amended within hours.

info@bloodhoundbooks.com

Printed in Great Britain
by Amazon